Praise for the Novels of Jill Eileen Smith

"Smith's stories are always exciting; she puts our imagination into full gear."

Interviews & Reviews

"Smith is a master storyteller and really keeps the reader captivated."

Life Is Story

"Smith excels at writing fiction that brings women in from the margins of biblical history and allows their achievements to shine."

Booklist

"The author does a wonderful job capturing the time and place and helping us understand an ancient culture."

Evangelical Church Library Association

"That's one thing I love about Jill's books: she takes biblical people or stories I think I know and gives them layers that make them even more real."

Christian Fiction Book Reviews

"Jill Eileen Smith's writing is superb."

Urban Lit Magazine

The
ARK and
the DOVE

Books by Jill Eileen Smith

THE WIVES OF KING DAVID

Michal

Abigail

Bathsheba

WIVES OF THE PATRIARCHS

Sarai

Rebekah

Rachel

DAUGHTERS OF THE PROMISED LAND

The Crimson Cord

The Prophetess

Redeeming Grace

A Passionate Hope

The Heart of a King

Star of Persia

Miriam's Song

The Prince and the Prodigal

Daughter of Eden

The Ark and the Dove

When Life Doesn't Match Your Dreams

She Walked Before Us

The ARK *and* *the* DOVE

The Story of Noah's Wife

Jill Eileen Smith

R

Revell

a division of Baker Publishing Group
Grand Rapids, Michigan

© 2024 by Jill Eileen Smith

Published by Revell
a division of Baker Publishing Group
Grand Rapids, Michigan
www.revellbooks.com

Printed in the United States of America

Library of Congress Cataloging-in-Publication Data
Names: Smith, Jill Eileen, 1958– author.
Title: The Ark and the Dove : the story of Noah's wife / Jill Eileen Smith.
Description: Grand Rapids, Michigan : Revell, a division of Baker Publishing Group, 2024.
Identifiers: LCCN 2023022713 | ISBN 9780800737658 (paper) | ISBN 9780800745721 (casebound) | ISBN 9781493444854 (ebook)
Subjects: LCSH: Noah's wife (Biblical figure) | Women in the Bible.
Classification: LCC BS575 .S488 2024 | DDC 220.9/2082—dc23/eng/20230821
LC record available at https://lccn.loc.gov/2023022713

This is a work of historical reconstruction; the appearances of certain historical figures are therefore inevitable. All other characters, however, are products of the author's imagination, and any resemblance to actual persons, living or dead, is coincidental.

Published in association with Books & Such Literary Management, www.booksandsuch.com.

Baker Publishing Group publications use paper produced from sustainable forestry practices and post-consumer waste whenever possible.

24 25 26 27 28 29 30   7 6 5 4 3 2

To our beloved kitty Tiger.

This was the first book you didn't get to "help" me finish. Since the book is filled with so many animals, I think you would have enjoyed knowing that it is dedicated to you. Any cat mentions in this story are for you.

God blessed us with five cats to love in this life, but you were the sweetest, and the only one who was there for every published book until now. You were my muse. My pen-chewing, finger-holding-as-I-tried-to-type, best-snuggling, most loving kitty ever.

Missing you doesn't get easier.
You were deeply loved.
September 5, 2005–August 15, 2022

Part 1

Then the LORD said, "My Spirit shall not abide in man forever, for he is flesh: his days shall be 120 years." . . .

The LORD saw that the wickedness of man was great in the earth, and that every intention of the thoughts of his heart was only evil continually. And the LORD regretted that he had made man on the earth, and it grieved him to his heart. So the LORD said, "I will blot out man whom I have created from the face of the land, man and animals and creeping things and birds of the heavens, for I am sorry that I have made them." But Noah found favor in the eyes of the LORD.

Genesis 6:3, 5–8 ESV

Prelude

I never thought my life would turn out this way, and to be honest, I would never have chosen this path, given the choice. The world is a harsh place now, though when the boys were young, it was harsh in a different way.

I remember the day Shem came home with his lip split and bruises on his face. My middle son was strong-willed and a little rebellious, but he'd never been in any kind of fight. I rushed to his side and pulled him close. He was thirteen, still a child in every respect. I never should have allowed him to go to the market alone.

"What happened?" I held him at arm's length, then hurried to the cooking room to retrieve a rag. After dousing it in water, I returned and placed it over his swollen eye. "Tell me."

"Some boys chased me down the street." He looked beyond me as though embarrassed.

"You didn't get these bruises from being chased. What happened?" I took his face and gently coaxed him to look me in the eye.

"They punched me. I fought back, but they were bigger than me." He hung his head, and a tear slipped onto his sandals. He shook his head. "I'm fine, Ima. Next time I will take a stick. I'll beat them good."

Oh, Elohim, help us!

I didn't know whether to laugh or cry, but there was no possibility that I would allow him to go anywhere without Noah or Japheth. Ham was younger still, and I would protect him, protect them all, as long as I could.

I did not realize that the older they got and the longer we lived, the more hurt they would suffer. The more violence they would encounter. The world was not like it had been when I was young. And I did not like what it had become.

Chapter

1

2275 BC

The cool mist that rose from the ground covered Emzara's feet as she walked through the small plot of ground behind her house in Seth's City. Birds twittered and sang in the trees above her, and she caught a glimpse of a male and female cardinal looking down on her. The male stood tall and proud among the leaves like a bridegroom coming from his chambers. Zara smiled, her heart swelling.

Such a perfect day for Shem's wedding.

She drew in a deep breath, gratitude filling her. In this increasingly unbelieving city, the Creator had seen fit to give her and Noah believing women to marry Shem and Japheth. How foolish her worries seemed now on this beautiful day. How gracious God was, blessed be He. The month before, Japheth had wed Adataneses, a descendant of Zara's grandfather Methuselah, and now Shem would marry Sedeq, the daughter of Vada, one of Zara's closest friends.

She lifted her gaze and raised her arms to the heavens. *Thank You! Praise You, Adonai Elohim, for Your kindness to us.*

She and Noah had prayed all their lives for their family to stay true to the Creator. To realize that He had heard and answered their prayers, to know that God was pleased with them, warmed her heart. Sedeq would be a welcome addition to their home, a daughter-in-law to love who also loved Elohim. As best as one could love the Almighty One.

Memories surfaced as Zara thought back on their long history. She did not know the Creator as Eve and Enoch had, as Noah did, but she did love Him. But oh, to love Him more! Was it possible? She could not see Him as Eve once did, only the things He had made. Perhaps that was enough.

He had made Adataneses and Sedeq to join their family. Now she need only worry about finding an equally kind and loving woman for Ham.

A chipmunk scurried across her path and hid in the tree's undergrowth. Today was Shem and Sedeq's day. And it seemed as though all of creation rejoiced.

The crunch of stones sounded behind her. She turned. Her mother, Abriyah, appeared along the side of the house, walking toward her.

"Ima." Zara hurried toward her, arms open to embrace her. "You're up early."

"As are you, my daughter. I could not sleep. There is too much to do." She linked arms with Zara, and together they walked about the garden. "Where are your baskets? I will help you pick the vegetables for the stew and the sauces." She released Zara's arm and looked about. Spotting a stack of baskets behind the house, she walked toward them.

Zara chuckled. "There is still time, Ima." She had hoped for a moment more alone with the Creator, but apparently that was not to be. She glanced again at the heavens. *Help us today.*

"Are you coming, Zara?" Her mother knelt in the dirt and filled a basket with ripe cucumbers.

Zara joined her and took several baskets from the stack.

14

"I think we will make a cucumber dill sauce to dip the bread in along with the vegetable barley stew. Adataneses should be up soon to begin the baking. I set the starter in separate bowls last night."

"She is not baking all the bread by herself, is she? I'm expecting half of the town to come. I've certainly invited many." Her mother stood, lifted the first basket, and carried it into the house.

Adataneses emerged from her room just then and met Abriyah and Zara as they entered the cooking area. "Good morning," she said, smiling at them. "I'm ready to begin the baking." She took one of the bowls of starter and pulled the sack of ground flour from the shelf.

"Have you broken your fast? You don't want to grow faint from hunger." Zara set a basket of cucumbers on the wooden table.

"I'll eat a few dates and pistachios Japheth and I shelled last night as I work. Don't worry about me." Adataneses poured out some of the flour and mixed it with the starter and water.

Zara returned to the garden to pick some carrots for the stew and took them to the well behind the house to wash. Voices from the rest of the waking household drifted to her, the air of excitement palpable. This would be a good day. She wondered if her mother was right about the crowd she expected.

Since Noah had first heard from the Creator forty-five years ago regarding His judgment of evil, the world had grown more chaotic and violent. Traveling alone was unheard of, especially for women and children, unless they carried a weapon. Even the men rarely walked the city streets by themselves.

All during that time, Noah had preached repentance. His words had not endeared their family to the rest of the city, or even to their own relatives. Another reason why she was grateful to have found believing women who loved her sons.

She finished washing the dirt from the carrots and carried them into the house.

"How much bread should I make, Ima Zara?" Adataneses gave Zara a confused look.

"She needs hundreds of loaves. And I hope you have neighbors and family baking too." Abriyah picked up another bowl of starter and poured flour into it. "I will help her, but my help will not be enough." She leveled Zara with a commanding look as Shem entered the cooking room and snatched a cucumber from the pile. "Those are for the sauce!" Abriyah stopped her kneading and slapped his hand. He put it back.

"I'm hungry." He rubbed his middle and gave Zara a piteous grin.

"Go to the cellar and get some dried fruit and cheese. You are on your own today. But stay away from the food for tonight." Zara shooed him out of the room and faced her mother again. "The neighbors are also baking bread, Ima, so you needn't worry. And Vada has her family bringing food tonight. We will have plenty." She put an arm around her mother's shoulders.

Abriyah continued to knead as Adataneses reached for another bowl of starter. "Good. But you still need to hurry." She set one round of dough to rise and began another. "Start chopping the peppers. Where are your serving bowls?"

Zara hid a smile. Her mother loved taking charge, even in Noah and Zara's home. But Zara didn't mind. This day was for Shem and Sedeq.

She opened a cupboard and set the bowls on the worktable. "I will chop the peppers when I finish gathering." She grabbed another basket and went to pick the radishes.

The sun had risen above the horizon, and suddenly she felt the urgency her mother did. They had much to do and little time to do it.

The house was bursting with relatives and friends, as Zara's mother had expected. Zara looked about, checking the wine, wondering how many had come for the food and drink more than for the celebration. She stood in the room she shared with Noah, wishing they had built a bigger home to accommodate her sons' wives, but there was no place to expand within the city. Perhaps it was time to move. Would they be safe outside the city walls with the Watchers always roaming the forests and fields? They stalked humans as they came and went from the safety of the cities.

She shook the thought aside as she pulled a fresh tunic over her head and tied the belt of her robe. She clasped a string of jewels about her neck, adding earrings and bracelets and rings to enhance her appearance. Glancing into the bronze mirror, she tied up her long, heavy hair beneath a veil. Satisfied, she exited the room and nearly ran into Adataneses emerging from the room she shared with Japheth.

"You look beautiful." She touched Adataneses's shoulder. "Are you happy to welcome a sister to our home?"

Adataneses smiled. She was truly a beautiful girl with an equally beautiful spirit. Sedeq was a little more strong-willed like Shem but still kind and loving. Would the woman they found for Ham be the same?

"I am more than ready, Ima Zara," Adataneses said. "A houseful of mostly men is not easy to handle at times."

They both chuckled. How well Zara understood.

"I am grateful the Creator sent you to us." She turned with Adataneses and walked with her to the cooking room. "The rest of the people should be here soon. Let's set some of the food out and make sure they have something to drink, though perhaps not too much. We will serve the rest when Shem returns with Sedeq."

The noise coming from the sitting room and the courtyard outside carried to them. Zara's mother and the neighboring women entered the house through the back door, and soon their children carried trays of food and drink to the people milling about.

At last Noah called above the crowd, "Let us be going to bring Shem's wife home."

A cheer erupted. The young men surrounded Shem and nearly carried him through the door and out into the street. Zara and the women followed, leaving only her mother behind to watch over the house.

The streetlamps burned, lighting the path, and the crowd sang boisterous songs as they walked. Zara blushed at some of the words coming from the mouths of the younger men and even some of those nearly Noah's age. She should be used to these things by now, for the whole world had set aside proper speech long ago. Weddings were the worst as people lost restraint and sang sexual songs with images better left unsaid.

Though Zara inwardly cringed, she noted that Shem was laughing with the crowd. She knew his heart, so perhaps she was too concerned about these things. He would mellow once he married Sedeq, wouldn't he?

The singing abated as they approached Sedeq's home. Shem was pushed to the front of the crowd, and Noah joined him. Shem knocked on the door and called out, "I have come to claim my bride and place my covering over her."

"He wants to do more than cover you," a voice shouted from the back of the crowd, and the men laughed.

Zara wanted to tell them to be quiet, but Shem did not react, nor did Noah. The door opened, and Sedeq's father, Raiden, stood there smiling. He walked around the side of the house and retrieved a donkey tied to a post. After bringing it to the door, he helped Sedeq to mount and handed the reins to Shem.

"I give my daughter into your care," Raiden said to Shem. He looked on Sedeq with fondness. Though he and Vada no longer believed in the Creator as Sedeq did, Zara was grateful that they were loving, kind parents. "Make sure you treat her well." He brushed moisture from his eyes, and the house emptied of him and Vada and their children as they followed Sedeq to Noah's home. Sedeq's friends surrounded her and tossed flower petals along the path.

Shem led his bride through the streets, and this time the songs were of the bride's beauty, the traditional words Zara had heard all her life.

She sighed, falling into step beside Vada. "I am glad this day has come." She looked at her friend. "Now we are family, not just friends."

Vada looked on her daughter, pride in her gaze. "She is beautiful, isn't she? You will enjoy her as I have." Emotion clogged her voice. "Treat her with kindness, Em. I know you will."

"Of course!" Had she ever treated anyone any other way? She prayed not. "I already love Sedeq as my own. And you are welcome to visit us anytime."

Vada glanced at Zara, her gaze suddenly clouded. "Oh, I won't be doing that. At least not often." She lowered her voice.

Zara frowned. "Why ever not?"

"Raiden forbids us from spending too much time near Noah or his family. He agreed to this marriage because Noah paid a high bride-price and because Sedeq seems to think like her grandmother rather than her parents."

Zara knew Vada's mother believed in the Creator. Sedeq had learned of Him from her. "Surely our faith should not keep us from being friends. We are family now."

Vada shook her head and looked about. Zara followed her gaze to where Raiden walked with Noah as though they were close companions. "Raiden has not liked Noah's influence since he began to preach against all we believe. I'm sorry, Em. This will be our last day to be 'family.' After Sedeq is in Shem's care, she knows she will not be ours. I will try to come if I can. But she is yours now." Vada choked on the last words and turned away.

Zara's eyes widened. How had she not seen this coming? She'd had no idea that Vada or her husband felt this way about Noah. She thought they were friends. Had been for years. Apparently until now.

Sorrow filled her, but as they neared her home, she forced it back. Surely things would not be as bad as Vada suggested. Their children would draw the families together. Sedeq would coax her father to change his thinking or at least change her mother's thinking.

But as she watched Raiden and Sedeq's brother and the rest of the crowd celebrate through the night, she wondered.

Chapter 2

Sedeq left the room she shared with Shem and met her mother-in-law and sister-in-law in the cooking area. The men had left before dawn to travel to their places of work. In the hours before the sun rose, the city was finally quiet and they could move about in relative safety. Sedeq shivered, remembering the fear that came over her when she needed to visit the city square where the shops and government buildings were. There were no safe times to travel alone except at that early hour.

"How are you feeling today?" Ima Zara asked, pulling Sedeq's attention away from her troubled thoughts.

Sedeq tied the belt of her robe a little tighter. "I'm ready to do whatever you have for me." She shared a smile with Adataneses, then looked at Ima Zara. Living here with Shem these last few weeks had been so much quieter and less stressful than living in her father's house. The memory brought a hint of pain.

"You are troubled, my daughter." Ima Zara tilted her head and gave Sedeq a concerned look. "Is anything wrong?"

Sedeq shook her head. "I'm well. I was simply thinking how much more at peace I feel here than I did living with the unbelief of my family. Lagina, Faustina, and Dalton never felt the way I did. They get along well with my parents because they don't believe in the Creator as my savta did. As I do. I wish I could say something to make them see." She looked away. She had never confided her concerns about her family to anyone but her grandmother, may she rest in peace. How strange it felt to trust this new family before she even knew them well.

Her mother-in-law came around the wooden table and placed a hand on her arm. "You love your family, Sedeq, as you should. I have been burdened over your mother's change of heart for years. When we were young, we both believed in the Creator. I fear your father's unbelief caused her to change her thinking. Your father has a wild rebellious streak, and your mother was drawn to that."

Sedeq sat on a stool and rested her arms on the table. "Tell me what she was like before she met my father. I was born after all my siblings already followed the worship of other gods. If not for my savta, I would not have known the Creator existed."

Ima Zara took a stool next to her and handed her some flatbread that they'd baked before Sedeq had risen.

"Thank you." Sedeq broke off a piece.

"Your mother and I grew up together," Ima Zara said. "During those days many people in Seth's City worshiped the Creator. Methuselah's descendants heard him speak of the Creator often, so it was common to know people who believed as we did. For a time, Vada's faith was strong." She looked beyond Sedeq as though the memories took her to another place. "But when she met Raiden and he asked her father to marry her, Vada was only too happy to do so. She was not worried that he had different beliefs and accepted many gods, the gods of Cain's City, and even considered the Watchers good rather than evil. I ached to see her marry him, though I do not despise your father. I only wish he had come to know the Creator and had not taken my friend onto a different path than the one she appeared to love. She has not seemed as happy since, though she would insist she is."

Sedeq nodded. "Ima is not happy, at least as far as I could see. Our household had moments of peace, but those were the times when Ima had too much to drink and slept or fell into a strange state when she worshiped her goddess. My father was often angry." She bit into the bread.

Adataneses moved about the cooking area, pulling food from a cupboard to begin the stew for the evening meal. "My family was not much better," she said, sorrow filling her large dark eyes. "They didn't outwardly worship other gods, but neither of my parents was faithful to the other. Sometimes I wondered if we siblings all had the same mother and father, as often as they would go out and engage other men and women." She paused and looked away. "I feared the same thing would happen to me when I wed, but Japheth is nothing like my father." She looked at Ima Zara. "I think I trusted him immediately. He is a good man."

Sedeq looked between the two. "I wish I didn't, but I understand your feelings. My father is not faithful to my mother either."

Adataneses's look held sympathy. "I have not spoken of this before, though I did tell Japheth, and now you both know. But it is not something one likes to tell. It was my aunt who believed in the Creator and taught me of Him. None of this came from my family."

"It sounds like we both faced the same things." The burden Sedeq had awakened with lifted slightly, though she wondered if she would ever stop feeling sad when she thought of her birth family.

"Well, I am glad you both know the Creator now," Ima Zara said, drawing her thoughts back. She patted Sedeq's hand. "I am happy to have two fine daughters-in-law. And we will do our best to keep our family from being unfaithful or full of strife like you lived with for too long."

"We will create our own strife, I think," Sedeq said, smiling. "But at least we can work things out because we all understand the same things about the Creator. Knowing Him should make a great difference."

"Yes, it should." Ima Zara stood and began helping Adataneses.

Sedeq finished eating, her thoughts still retreating to her family of birth. *Please, Adonai Elohim, bring them to a place where they can know You and believe.*

How often she had prayed that prayer! She could not lose heart. Surely there was still hope.

Noah slung the leather pack carrying his tools over his shoulder and walked toward the setting sun, picking up his pace with every step. The Watchers frequented the woods that flanked the broad path, and he was in no mood to encounter one tonight.

He did not fear them. The Creator had told him Elohim alone was to be feared, for He had the power to rescue from any evil intent. Still, Noah did not attempt to engage the Watchers or even cast his gaze in the direction they often stood or roamed. And despite the increased wickedness in Seth's City, he felt a stronger measure of safety and peace when he passed through its gates and they closed behind him.

He shifted the pack, grateful for the work he had acquired building a house in Jabril's City, but he did not enjoy the journey there. The city had been infiltrated by the Nephilim, though their numbers were few. Their existence troubled him, and he wondered how long God would allow the intermating of these demons and women to continue. How much longer would the people of Seth's City keep them away?

How long, Adonai Elohim? Except for one visit from Him nearly fifty years earlier, God had remained silent on the matter of the judgment to come.

Longing to understand filled Noah's heart. He quickened his pace again as the sun splayed its colorful array of yellows, oranges, pinks, and greens across the expanse above. Every night a different celestial painting guided him home. Every night, including when one of his sons accompanied him, he worshiped the Creator more, thanking Him for such beauty.

He drew in a deep breath, seeing the lights from Seth's City in the distance. Soon he would be home.

Suddenly a brilliant light stopped him. His breath caught, his heart beating faster, and he fell to his knees and prostrated himself before the being. There was no mistaking such a rare appearance of Adonai Elohim, Creator and Judge of the universe.

He waited, unable to speak, yearning to look up and gaze upon the overwhelming love and glory emanating from the light. A touch on his shoulder drew him to his feet, but he kept his gaze downcast, unable to look on the Creator's glory as He spoke.

"I am going to put an end to all people, for the earth is filled with violence because of them. I am surely going to destroy both them and the earth. So make yourself an ark of cypress wood; make rooms in it and coat it with pitch inside and out. This is how you are to build it: The ark is to be three hundred cubits long, fifty cubits wide, and thirty cubits high. Make a roof for it, leaving below the roof an opening one cubit high all around. Put a door in the side of the ark and make lower, middle, and upper decks.

"I am going to bring floodwaters on the earth to destroy all life under the heavens, every creature that has the breath of life in it. Everything on earth will perish. But I will establish My covenant with you, and you will enter the ark—you and your sons and your wife and your sons' wives with you. You are to bring into the ark two of all living creatures, male and female, to keep them alive with you. Two of every kind of bird, of every kind of animal, and of every kind of creature that moves along the ground will come to you to be kept alive. You are to take every kind of food that is to be eaten and store it away as food for you and for them."

I will do as you say.

A moment later Adonai Elohim vanished. Noah's heart pounded as holy fear encompassed him. His breath came fast, and his mind grappled with this news.

All people. Surely not those few who still believed. As he thought on them, he realized that they almost all were the generation of his father and grandfather. They could die before this judgment came.

He squeezed his eyes shut, then opened them again, still aware of the fading glory around him. *You and your sons and your wife and your sons' wives.*

They would need to find a wife for Ham, and soon. One woman shouldn't be hard to find, should she?

He picked up his tools and looked about, then slowly continued toward Seth's City. His eyes struggled to adjust to the dimness of the earth in comparison to the Creator's glory.

Judgment. The whole earth.

Oh God, forgive us.

But would God yet forgive? If Noah continued to preach repentance, would the people listen?

God had not said He would save any besides Noah and his family. Would anyone on earth take the Creator seriously once they saw Noah building the ark?

Sorrow rose within him. The *adams* had greatly grieved the Creator. For Him to regret having even made them and animals caused all manner of confusion in Noah's heart. Couldn't God stop the evil another way? Couldn't He change the hearts of men and women to turn from sin and repent? To offer right sacrifices on His altars? To stop practicing the ways of the devil and his followers? To put aside their idols and worship the Creator as He deserved?

As he neared the gate to the city and heard the clamor of rowdy voices within, he glimpsed one of the Watchers in the shadows near the wall, as if the demon wanted Noah to see him. No doubt the Watchers knew God had spoken with him. They knew the Creator better than the *adams* did and feared Him, even in their hatred of Him.

This was why God grieved and could not abide humanity any longer. The Watchers had destroyed those made in the image of the Creator and intended to corrupt every last soul if they could. They wanted to ruin the Creator and His plan to send a Redeemer to rescue them. And they would succeed unless God stopped them. Apparently, that was exactly what He planned to do.

Chapter
3

"Come, all of you. We must talk." Noah moved to the sitting room, obviously expecting his family to follow.

Zara's heart skipped a beat. She knew what was coming. Had lain awake for hours trying to come up with a suitable wife for Ham. The urgency had not left her the entire day. She followed her sons and daughters-in-law into the room and took her seat beside Noah.

"What's so urgent, Abba?" Japheth leaned forward, his expression eager. "Has something happened?"

Zara looked at Noah, bracing herself for their surprise, their questions. Had God really told Noah to build an ark?

"I have heard from the Creator." Noah paused. "I have often told you of my earlier encounter with Him, before you were born. His news to me then was about His promise to judge the earth. At that time, He gave the *adams* one hundred and twenty years. Time enough to repent and turn from evil, but as you are all well aware, that has not yet happened. Now with about seventy-five years left after that vision, the Creator has given me a new command." He picked up a parchment he'd started working on and spread it out on the table. "He told me that He is going to send a flood to destroy everything that lives and breathes on the earth. But He will save our family and the animals that He will send to us."

"A flood?" Shem put his arm around Sedeq's shoulders, and she scooted closer to him. "Wait. Destroy *everything*?"

Japheth shifted in his seat, frowning. "Surely not, Father. Why would God destroy everything He has created?"

"Especially the people," Adataneses added. "He will save only us?"

"How is He going to save all the animals? Do you have any idea how *many* animals exist on the earth?" Japheth pulled Adataneses close. "He is asking the impossible. We can't possibly save them all."

"We aren't going to save them all, my son," Noah said. "God will send us representatives of each kind of animal. And with the dimensions He gave me to build an ark, I'm sure there will be room for all." He ran a hand over the parchment that held a preliminary sketch he had made the night before. "He told me to build an ark and gave me the dimensions and the wood to choose and how to keep water from getting in. But much of what He didn't say, we are going to have to design and plan and calculate before we can even begin to gather what we need. All of you will have to stop the other work you are doing and pour your energies into helping me build this. Fortunately, God has blessed us with wealth through the years, enough to purchase the materials and complete the work." He took the stylus and ink Zara handed to him.

"The Creator said He would save our family." Zara looked at each of her children. "We must find a wife for Ham."

"Only our family, Abba? Truly?" Japheth asked, repeating Adataneses's unanswered question.

Noah looked up from the parchment, appearing distracted, as if he assumed they would all readily accept God's plan without question. As he had done. "We will continue to preach of the Creator to everyone who will listen," he said, taking in each one of them. "None of us wants to see those we love perish in the flood. If they repent and believe, we will welcome them on the ark."

"And God said they can also come?" Ham spoke, his look troubled.

Noah looked beyond them, not meeting anyone's gaze. Zara's heart quickened. God had said nothing about others, unless Noah forgot to tell her that part.

"The Creator did not say so specifically," he said. "But He is merciful. Surely He wants everyone to believe in Him and trust Him. He will not destroy those who believe and find favor in His sight." Noah rolled the tension from his shoulders.

"But He did not say that?" Shem's brows knit. "I would like to know if there is hope for anyone else."

"There is always hope, my son. We have our lifetime to believe. We need to focus on what the Creator has asked us to do and trust the rest to Him."

"And find a wife for Ham," Zara said again, looking at her youngest son.

"I already know who I want to marry." Ham took a drink from the water cup at his side.

Zara glanced at Noah, then held Ham's gaze. "And who might that be?"

"Her name is Naavah. When I was managing Ima's housing goods shop yesterday, she stopped in. She is visiting Seth's City with her family to celebrate the wedding of a distant cousin."

"Where is she from then?" Noah's brow furrowed into deep lines.

"Cain's City." Ham took another drink, avoiding their gazes.

"Cain's City?" Zara had surely heard wrong.

Silence met her ears, then Ham lifted his head. "Yes. They are from Cain's lineage, but one of her cousins moved here several years ago, which is why they were visiting. We talked at length when the shop had few patrons. She's beautiful, and I want her for my wife."

"Is there no one from Seth's clan you could find, my son? Does she even believe in the Creator?" Zara longed to give in to the desires of her youngest, but Cain's City? She held back the urge to release a deep sigh.

"I didn't ask her what she believes, Ima. I just met her. But shouldn't I be able to choose who I want to marry? I'm the one who will have to live with her." Ham crossed his arms, defiance in his expression.

"On the ark, we will all have to live with her, my son. The woman we pick is going to have to be agreeable to all of us." Zara locked gazes with her son. She could be stubborn too, but her heart told her to tread with compassion.

"How long are we going to have to live on this ark?" Shem interrupted. "And are we going to float above the earth, just us with a lot of animals?" He shook his head. "I can't imagine it, Abba."

"We're talking about my future wife," Ham said, glaring at Shem. He looked again at Noah and Zara. "I want Naavah." How like a child he sounded.

Noah set the parchment aside and rubbed the back of his neck. "You don't know Naavah. You met her once."

"I can tell she likes me, and I like her. She's beautiful, and I want you to talk to her father for me. There is no one in Seth's City that I've ever seen that I want more. And I've spent a lot of time looking." Ham straightened, and Zara knew the battle with him would not end well if she and Noah did not give in. But should they?

Noah cleared his throat. "A few hours is not nearly enough time to know if a person is a suitable match. But I will speak to her father on the condition that you leave the final decision to me. If I find her father is not agreeable or that Naavah worships false gods, then the answer is no."

Ham frowned, but at last he nodded. "They are only here until the end of the week."

"I will go tomorrow." Noah picked up the stylus again and tapped the parchment. "Now . . ." He looked at each of them again. "Are there any objections to obeying the Creator? Because we need to concentrate on making lists of things we are going to need. We must decide how to keep all the animals that will come to us safe within the ark. We must understand how to care for them, how to keep the pens clean, how to keep the air in the ark fresh, how to grow and keep food for us, and a host of other details. Most of this just scratches the surface of what we are going to have to do."

"I am willing to do anything you ask, Abba," Shem said. "But I still have questions. And I'm not sure I can work on this without better understanding why." He glanced at Sedeq.

"I can't bear the thought of my family being left behind." Sedeq directed her words to Zara.

"Nor I." Adataneses leaned closer to Japheth. "What of my brothers and parents? What if they won't believe?"

Japheth pulled her close. "What about our other family members too?" He looked at Noah. "Are Saba and Savta going to be destroyed?"

Zara felt a sudden desire to hold each one of them close, wishing she could comfort them as she had when they were small. To tell them all would be well, there was nothing to fear. But there was plenty to fear. Especially the judgment of God. Might God change His mind?

Please keep all of us in Your care.

"I told you, God will not destroy those who know Him and worship Him." Noah's words broke into her prayer. "We suspect that your grandparents and other ancestors will pass on from this life before the flood comes. But you are still young. And God promised to spare us."

"Why us?" Ham's tone held an edge. "Why not more people? I just don't see why the judgment has to be so harsh. Couldn't the Creator make them believe?"

"The Creator is to be obeyed freely, my son," Noah said, his tone patient as if he suddenly realized that not everyone heard from God directly and obeyed without question. "He doesn't force people to believe."

"Why spare us then? Sometimes I have doubts," Japheth admitted, surprising Zara. "That is, I don't disbelieve in the Creator. I just don't understand Him."

"Doubts are normal, though He wants us to trust Him," Noah said.

"Your father has found favor in the Creator's eyes," Zara said. "He has lived his life believing in and obeying the Creator, and God is pleased with him. The rest of the world has grieved the Creator's heart." She clasped her hands in her lap, leaning forward.

"So we are only spared because the Creator favors Abba? Not because He wants us?"

Zara blinked at Shem's unexpected questions, but before she could respond, Noah spoke again.

"He wants all of us," he insisted. "But some of our people have gone so far that they think only evil all the time. And the Watchers have corrupted our race. I think God has to destroy everything to destroy the way they have corrupted His image bearers." He reached for a leather holder and returned the parchment to it.

"I saw one of the Watchers when I was working in Saba's fields a few days ago," Ham said.

"I hope you did not engage it," Noah said. He and Zara had learned long ago to always keep their distance and refuse to enter into debates with the Watchers.

"No. I did not go near it. I only saw it watching from the shadows among the trees that border Saba's field." Ham leaned back in his chair, but his eyes held a wild gleam, as though he would have enjoyed fighting the creature.

"Good. We will likely see more of them as time goes on, but in the end, they will be defeated."

"I'll be glad for that, but I still don't understand God." Shem lifted his hands in a defenseless gesture. "I mean, I believe in Him, but I don't know why this flood has to be the only way to bring us back to being good."

"None of us are good, my son." Noah leaned forward and held Shem's gaze. "We are born with the nature to sin, and the only way for God to look past that is if we obey Him and believe in Him and His promise of a coming Redeemer. I think the Redeemer is the key to His ability to overlook our sin even now. He looks at us with that promise in His mind."

Shem looked doubtful. Silence fell between them for several moments.

"We will talk more of this later," Noah said. Darkness came through the open window. "I know this is not news you expected to hear. And we are tired from a long workday. Let us get some sleep. We are not going to solve anything in one night, and we are never going to fully understand the One who made everything we see and know. One day He may explain more to us, but for now, let's just accept that He is serious and we must do as He says if we want to live." Noah stood, and the others rose with him.

Zara waited until they had dispersed to their rooms, then turned to Noah. "You fear Him."

"Yes. Which is why I obey Him."

"But you don't understand Him."

Noah shook his head, sorrow in his eyes. "Not at all."

Chapter

4

The next morning Noah walked with Ham to the house of Naavah's cousin, where Naavah was staying with her parents. They stopped at Zara's shop first to open it up for the women who worked there, leaving Vada in charge until Ham returned.

"We're going to have to hire Vada to run this place once we're ready to begin work on the ark." Noah glanced at Ham in the slanted light coming through the clouds.

"You're not going to mention judgment or try to preach to Naavah's father, are you?" Ham stopped in the road by the well Seth had built, where the women who lived near still came to draw water. He faced Noah, arms crossed.

"I should. I need to know what they believe, Ham. We want to find you a wife who believes in the Creator." Noah touched Ham's shoulder, but he flinched, shaking it off. Noah gave him a pointed look. "I can turn around now and forget this mission if you are going to grow demanding."

Ham let his arms fall to his sides. "I'm sorry, Father. I don't mean to demand. She just seems perfect for me, and I would like you to get her for me."

How quickly he acquiesced when he thought it would bring about what he wanted. Noah merely nodded and continued walking. The boy needed to learn to trust the Creator and seek Him, but Ham had never been open about his thoughts of God. He said he believed in Him, but there was a part of him that he kept from the rest of his family, a part that seemed distant from all of them.

They arrived at the home, a large estate in the middle of the city, and Noah knocked on the door. An old woman opened it to them. "Yes?"

"I'm looking for the father of a young woman named Naavah. I'm told they are staying here." Noah glanced into the house but saw no sign of anyone else.

"You mean Faustus, son of Tane. I will get him." She shut the door without inviting them inside.

Noah looked at Ham, who merely shrugged. He faced the door again, waiting. At last it opened, and a haggard-looking man stood before them. "What do you want?"

"Are you Faustus, son of Tane?"

"Yeah. Do I know you?" He squinted as though the light of day bothered him.

"No. My name is Noah ben Lamech, and this is my son Ham. Two days ago your daughter Naavah entered our shop and talked with my son. He is quite taken with her, and we are coming to inquire if she is betrothed. If not, are you willing to make an alliance with us?" The words nearly stuck in his throat, but Noah was determined to at least show Ham he had tried.

The man ran a hand over his face, then opened the door wider. "Come in. Let us drink something. Then we can talk."

Noah and Ham followed the man into a large sitting area where other men were seated at different tables. The place looked more like an eating establishment than a home. Noah and Ham took the seats offered them. Faustus called for beer, which he gulped down. Noah and Ham declined the drink.

"You don't drink beer?" Faustus wiped his beard with the back of his sleeve.

"Not in the morning." Noah folded his hands and rested them on the table between them. "I would rather we discuss your daughter."

Faustus frowned, looking them up and down as if seeing them for the first time. "The daughter you just met and you already want to marry?" He laughed. "That one is a handful, let me tell you. But if you want her, sure. If you can pay the price, she's all yours."

"How much do you want for the bride-price?" Noah searched Faustus's face, but he would not meet Noah's gaze.

"A pound of gold." Faustus grinned and glanced about at the others in the room who, at his loud remark, had turned to listen.

Everything within Noah wanted to turn away from this man, this place, this girl Ham thought he wanted. But he clenched his jaw and drew in a breath instead. "I'd like to meet the girl first. My son has only seen her once. I want to see if she is worth the price you require." To bargain thus for a woman felt wrong, but if he wanted to win, he had to play Faustus's game.

Faustus slapped the table. "Another beer! And someone fetch my daughter."

A servant appeared with a tall clay cup of beer and called to another woman to find Naavah. Moments later the girl appeared in the room, a veil covering her hair, her eyes downcast. She stood silent beside her father and would not look at Noah or Ham.

"Naavah, do you recognize these men? This one"—he pointed to Ham—"wants you to be his wife. But this one"—he pointed to Noah—"wants to see what you look like before he pays for you.

Show them you are worth a pound of gold." His look was brazen, making Noah cringe.

The girl started to open her robe, but Noah held up a hand. "That is not necessary."

The girl closed it and glanced up, looking relieved.

"She is acceptable. I will pay the pound of gold."

Faustus stared at Noah, disbelieving. A moment later he slapped the table again and laughed loudly. "She's yours then. But we will have to sign an agreement and wait a month for you to have her. And I will need to have the gold inspected. How soon can you get it?"

"I will pay you half when we sign the agreement and half when she marries Ham." He looked at Ham, who could not take his gaze from Naavah. The girl glanced at him, obviously shy.

"Let us draw up the contract." Faustus stood on unsteady legs and left the room. A moment later, he returned with a man carrying a clay tablet and stick. The man sat and took down the terms of the marriage as Faustus and Noah spoke.

"We are signing this in good faith that you will give us your daughter, Naavah, in one month's time," Noah said. "I will pay you the rest of the amount you requested then."

"Done!" Faustus said when at last both men had put their imprint to the clay. He looked at Noah and held out his hand. Noah pulled the gold nuggets from a pouch at his side and dropped them into the man's palm. Faustus weighed them. "Come to Cain's City in a month. We will give her to you then. Ask for me at the city gate."

Noah stood and Ham followed. Pity for the girl filled Noah, and he almost wanted to ask her father to give the girl to them now. But such a thing was unheard of, no matter how he thought the girl was treated. He could not ask Naavah about the Creator now, but perhaps in time, in a loving family, she would come to know Him. He'd done the best he could.

Zara, Adataneses, and Sedeq sat together in the outer court-yard of their home. Two looms stood near each other in one corner, and Sedeq worked feverishly on one to make a large curtain for the entry to a new room that Noah, Japheth, Shem, and Ham had quickly built. Three weeks had barely been enough time to put together additional space for Ham and Naavah to live.

"We should have just made Ham's small room work for now. This room is hardly private." Adataneses rarely spoke her mind, and never critically, but she was obviously feeling what they all felt. A month to welcome a new bride and plan a wedding was too rushed. Especially for a bride coming from a life and home they did not know.

"I hope Naavah is kind and easy to be around." Sedeq looked up from her weaving for a brief moment. "Do we know anything about her or her family?"

Zara worked the spindle, coaxing the dyed wool into usable yarn for Sedeq. "Ham has had some contact with her father through the cousin that lives here regarding their plans for the wedding. Everything is still set for next week. I will admit, I've never seen him so excited about anything in his life. Naavah has certainly captured his thinking." Zara let the spindle wind down, removed the orange yarn, and rethreaded the spindle with white.

Adataneses sat at a pottery wheel at the far end of the court near the kiln. Adding another family member meant they needed more bowls and jars, though Zara knew they could make do with what they had for a time. But the knowledge that they were also making these things for the ark spurred her on.

"It is an exciting time." Sedeq stopped her work and turned to face Zara. "We will do our best to welcome her, Ima Zara. In time I'm sure we will learn to love her as I hope she does us."

Zara smiled. How blessed she was to have these two lovely girls living with her and Noah, loving their sons. "It will take time." She looked toward the loom where Sedeq worked. "It looks like you're almost finished."

Sedeq nodded. "I want to add a thread of black to bring out the contrast of the red, yellow, blue, and white." She bent over the loom and attached the new color.

Zara lifted her gaze heavenward toward the canopy of water and clouds above them. Seventy-five years until the waters fell and no longer stood as protection against the sun God had placed in the sky. Surely it would be enough time to gather and build all they would need.

The pounding of running feet met her ears, and she turned to see Ham, chest heaving and out of breath. He stopped near her. "Ima, where is Father? He must come at once!"

Zara set her spinning aside and stood, gripping his arms in an attempt to calm him down. "Tell me what has happened."

"Naavah's father has called off our agreement! He can't do that, Ima. Abba needs to go and talk to him." Ham's voice rose in pitch. He was on the verge of hysteria.

Zara took his arm and turned him toward the front of the house. "Your father is in town. He is about to purchase a piece of land outside the city and went to city hall to file the paperwork and pay for the property."

"I must find him." Ham turned and took off running before Zara could say more.

Her knees weakened as the news sank in. Why would Naavah's father call off the agreement? The covenant of marriage was sacred and not easily broken. Though in recent years, that had not been entirely true. Men broke their promises far too often, and covenants were simply contracts made to be changed by whatever whims passed through the minds of the people involved.

She sensed her daughters-in-law before she heard them
drawing up behind her.

"This doesn't sound good." Adataneses rubbed the wet clay
from her hands into the dirt beside the path.

"Not at all." Sedeq placed her arm about Zara's shoulders.

Zara looked from one woman to the other, grateful once
more for these two women. If only Ham could find as kind a
wife. But if Naavah was truly no longer going to be his wife,
who would they find to marry him quickly? Despite the years
they had ahead of them, Zara was anxious to settle this matter.
Before the city heard of Noah's work on the ark. Before no
one would want anything to do with their family.

Chapter
5

Noah descended the steps of city hall, the deed to the new property tucked in the pouch at his belt. He would take it home and put it in a safe place, then go out to inspect the property again. He glanced around, watching as people milled about the busy city offices, buying and selling and settling disputes and court matters. They had no idea how short life would be for them when God judged the earth.

A young couple, probably no more than one hundred years old, walked arm in arm with three young children following. They might not live to see their children's children. The thought saddened him as it always did when he considered the future. Would it help to go to them and tell them of God's judgment?

Oh Adonai, what would You have me do?

Shouts in the distance caught his attention. He turned, recognizing the voice.

"Father! Father!" Ham rushed up to him and grasped his arm. "Father, you must take me to Cain's City at once. We must talk sense into Naavah's father." He tugged Noah's arm toward the city gate.

Noah stopped him. "Slow down, my son. What are you talking about?"

Ham coughed and drew in long breaths. "Naavah's father has canceled our covenant. He can't do that, can he? We must go to him and convince him to give us Naavah today!" He gripped Noah's arm again and pulled. "Come!"

Noah touched Ham's hand and released his hold. "Control yourself, my son." He waited for Ham to calm. "Tell me, how did you hear this?"

Ham put his hands on his knees, dragging in his breath, then stood and faced Noah. "Faustus's cousin has kept in touch with them. When I went to him today to see if he had heard anything new, he told me that the wedding was canceled. Why would he say that if it wasn't true? We must go and convince Faustus to change his mind. He can't do this."

The sun had risen nearly to its midpoint, and the walk to Cain's City was long. They could take donkeys. That might make the trip faster.

Noah turned toward the home of Faustus's cousin. "Come." He would make sure his son had heard correctly. He had no desire to travel to Cain's City one moment before he had to, and certainly not twice. If they went today, they would bring Naavah home with them.

Ham fell into step beside him. "What are we going to do?"

"First, I'm going to see whether you were told the truth. Then we'll find transportation to Cain's City to see for ourselves. If it is as you say, we will remind Faustus that he cannot simply break a covenant. If we can, we'll bring your bride home with us tomorrow."

"We need to leave now if we are going to get there before nightfall." Ham hurried to keep up with Noah's quick strides.

Noah glanced at his son. "We will go before dawn tomorrow. I will not spend the night in that city. We will go early and return quickly."

They would have done the same on the day of the wedding. Naavah would simply be joining them earlier, if he had anything to say about it.

Noah took the saddlebag from Zara's hands and kissed her. "If all goes well, we should be home by dark with Naavah. If the Creator grants us favor in the eyes of Faustus."

"Are you coming?" Ham stood in the road, tapping his foot. He held the reins of two donkeys rented from a neighbor.

Noah met Zara's gaze. "We will hurry."

"Be careful of the Watchers." Zara took his hand and squeezed it. "Don't let our son talk you into staying even one moment longer than necessary." She whispered the words against his ear, then stood back, releasing him.

"I won't." He turned and joined Ham, taking one of the donkey's reins. They mounted their beasts and rode through the dark city streets toward the gate.

The sun crested the horizon as they passed onto the highway that connected Seth's City to the others scattered over the area east of Eden. Cain's City was the farthest and the most established. The most corrupt. When people went "the way of Cain," everyone knew that they had followed the path of the man who had murdered his brother and led his descendants away from the Creator and all that He offered.

Noah coaxed his beast to a faster trot, wishing he'd had access to some of the horses used in racing. But the donkeys would have to do.

The terrain grew hilly as the sun rose in the sky, and in the distance the outline of the walls of Cain's City came into view.

"We're almost there," Noah said. He glanced at Ham, who kept hurrying his beast and then had to slow down again. His son would have run the whole way if Noah had allowed it.

"Now can you let me ride ahead?" Ham's irritation belied the fear Noah knew resided in his heart.

"We will arrive and leave together. This is not a place you want to enter alone. I'm coming." Noah coaxed the donkey to catch up with Ham.

The gates loomed ahead. Before them stood large stone statues, monuments to Cain and to Lamech his descendant. Both murderers. Noah disliked the fact that his father had the same name as this Lamech, though they were vastly different men from different forefathers.

They passed the statues and stopped at the gates, dismounting their beasts.

"State your name and your business." The gatekeeper stood between the walls behind a latticed window.

"Noah ben Lamech, descendant of Seth. We come to see Faustus, son of Tane. We have business with him." Noah pointed to Ham. "This is my son."

The gatekeeper laughed. "What business does a son of Seth have with a son of Cain?"

"It is our business. But rest assured, we are not here to stay." Noah tightened his grip on the donkey's reins, holding his anxiety in check. "We will need directions to Faustus's house."

"Very well." The man opened the door to them. "No need to act that way. It's my business to ask questions." He pointed to the right. "Follow that road around a bend. You will come to a circle of homes. His is the first home toward the rising sun."

Noah nodded to the man and paid him a nugget of silver, then led Ham through the streets. He quickened his pace as they passed strange men frowning at them. He and Ham stood out here. Probably because they did not have the hardened expressions so many of them did.

Oh Lord, have mercy on these people.

If only He would. If only He could. But the Creator had

given this town and all the others hundreds and hundreds of years to return to Him. To follow His ways instead of their own. To be what He'd created them to be. And few cared.

They rounded the bend and came to Faustus's house. Ham started up the steps to the door, but Noah restrained him. They tied their donkeys to a post, then Noah went ahead of Ham and knocked on the door. Would he find Faustus home? The man was likely working by now.

The door opened, and a woman stood there. Naavah's mother? "Yes?"

"I am Noah ben Lamech. We are here to see Faustus, son of Tane." He glanced beyond her but saw no one else.

"He's at the quarry working. What do you want?" Her eyes were red as though she had been weeping, and her tone had a sharp edge.

"We were told that he canceled our marriage covenant with my son here"—he pointed at Ham—"and your daughter Naavah. We have come to find out why."

The woman's eyes filled with tears, and she held a cloth to her mouth, clearly holding back her emotions. "I am Naavah's mother, and you heard correctly. Your son cannot marry our daughter."

"Why not?" Ham stepped closer. "We paid for her. She belongs to us."

The woman burst into tears. Noah stood still, trying to decide what to do.

"Has something happened?" He took a step back, not wanting to appear brash.

The woman nodded. "She is gone. The Watchers took her. She's not coming back."

Noah's heart sank, and Ham cried out, "What? It can't be!"

"It's true. You can find Faustus and he will tell you himself." She pointed toward the back of the city, deeper into its heart. "The quarries are just outside the wall."

Noah had no desire to travel any farther into the city. "How do you know the Watchers took her?"

The woman sniffed and dabbed her eyes with the cloth. "Faustus looked for her after her friends told him she was taken. He couldn't find her, so he went to the magistrates, and they summoned one of the giants who rule here. They confirmed that Naavah belongs to them now." She lifted her head, her dark eyes desperate, pleading. "If you know how to get her back, please help us. Faustus would not have broken your agreement if he didn't have to."

Ham sank to his knees. Noah stared at the woman for a lengthy breath. "I have no power over the Watchers. If they have her, then our covenant cannot be kept. Please tell Faustus that he can keep our payment. We are sorry for our loss and yours."

The woman nodded. "He didn't plan to give it back. He didn't think you would come."

"Why would he think that? We are men of our word."

The woman shrugged. "Most are not."

Obviously, Faustus was among those who did not keep his word, since he had not bothered to tell them of Naavah's loss. If not for the chance word of his cousin, they would still be expecting a wedding in a week. But Noah had no faith in the man or even in what this woman had told him. Might she be lying in order to keep his gold and give Naavah to another? He would never know.

He turned and took hold of Ham, and together they walked their beasts back through the city.

"Can't we look for her?" Ham's plaintive question hit Noah hard. How he wished he could give his son what he wanted.

"I will ask at the gate. Though if they are lying to us, I have no idea where to look. We know no one here." He stopped at the gate and inquired of the gatekeeper, who led them to a room where people brought complaints. Noah refused to enter, not trusting the man.

A giant emerged, blocking the sun as he stood in the door. "What do you want?" His voice bellowed, nearly pushing them backward.

"We are here to discover what has happened to my son's wife Naavah, daughter of Faustus, son of Tane," Noah said. Ham gripped his shoulder.

The giant stared at them, but Noah did not flinch. At last the giant spoke again. "I know of no human by that name."

Noah backed away. "You are sure?"

"I said so, didn't I?" His voice boomed louder, and Noah took hold of Ham and hurried through the gate.

The weight of the news and the fear the place evoked followed them until they were long past sight of the city.

"She is lost then." Ham looked at Noah as they mounted their beasts.

"Yes." There was nothing else to say.

Chapter
6

Zara sat in the outer courtyard of her home near the hearth, watching the road. Dusk descended before she heard them walking toward her. She stood as they entered the courtyard, Noah looking haggard, Ham utterly downcast.

"What happened?" She opened her arms, and Ham fell into her embrace. She clung to him, letting him weep, as her gaze met Noah's.

He shook his head. Obviously, Naavah was not with them and would not be joining them. She rubbed Ham's back as she'd done when he was a small child, longing to console him but not knowing what to say. At last, his tears spent, he pulled away from her and wiped his eyes.

"I'm so sorry, my son." She touched his arm. "Why don't we sit and you tell me what happened?" She motioned to the seats surrounding the court.

Ham perched on the edge of the stone seat while Noah and Zara sat near him. He opened his mouth to speak, but words would not come. He looked at Noah and nodded.

"The Watchers took her." Noah grasped Zara's hand. "At least that is what her mother told us. Faustus was not at home, and we didn't feel safe or welcome there, so it wasn't feasible to go looking for him. Naavah's mother seemed heartbroken, so we went to the city gate and inquired. But the giant there claimed he knew nothing of anyone named Naavah. I don't know whom to believe, the giant or the woman. Either way, there was no way we were going to find Naavah or bring her with us."

Zara's heart constricted. The treachery of the Watchers was well known throughout the world, but Cain's City had seemed to embrace their teaching, their lies, their rule. She leaned forward and squeezed Ham's hand. "I am sorry, Ham. I wanted to meet her, to welcome her to our family as you did."

Ham swallowed hard. "I don't know what to do." He put his head in his hands.

Zara fought tears. Watching her children hurt had always been the hardest thing she'd ever done. "There is no reason to think about what to do right now." She smoothed his hair. "You are worn out with grief. Let us go inside and get some food and then sleep."

He looked up. "I'm not hungry."

"Come inside and rest then." Zara stood and coaxed him to stand. She linked her arm with his, Noah behind them. Ham followed without speaking.

Her mind whirled as she offered food and drink to Noah. The rest of the family joined them, all of them aware of Ham's distress, saying little. How were they going to find someone to marry Ham now?

The next day, Zara left the house as soon as the men went off to plan and discuss where they would build both the ark and a new home and storehouse for their family. She walked the worn cobbled streets to her mother's house.

Abriyah rose from her seat in the courtyard and kissed Zara's cheeks. "You are troubled, my daughter. I can see it in your eyes. Come." She ushered Zara into her sitting room. "Tell me what happened."

Zara sighed, not realizing until that moment that she'd been holding her breath tightly. "Ham's intended is not going to marry him," she said.

Her mother's eyes widened. She leaned close, elbows on her knees. "Go on."

Zara told her what Noah had said the night before. "Noah is not certain what actually happened to the girl. She could have been taken by the Watchers. Or her father got a better offer for her. We have no way of proving anything."

"Ham is devastated, I'm sure."

"Completely. He retreated to his room soon after they told me the news. He could barely get out of bed today." She twisted her belt, uncertain where to place her hands. "I cannot think of anyone to replace her, Ima. Which is why I've come. Do you know of any young women who might be suitable for Ham?"

Abriyah straightened, assessing her. "Let me get us something to drink." She jumped up and left Zara, then returned with cups of water a moment later.

Zara took the cup and sipped. It was her mother's way to work as she pondered a problem. She herself had inherited a similar trait.

"I know of a family," her mother said. "They have a young daughter. She is younger than Ham but old enough to marry. They live west of here, and Keziah often helps me with the garden." She sat again and took a long drink. "I can make inquiries of her mother. If they are agreeable, Noah can make the arrangements."

Zara set the cup aside. "Tell me more. Does she worship the Creator? Do her parents believe in Him?"

Abriyah slowly shook her head. "I do not know for sure

what Keziah believes. We have talked of the Creator, and she does not disagree with me. But she has told me that her mother and sisters worship the goddess."

Zara's heart sank, though she was not surprised. "Does Keziah worship with them?" Surely her mother had some idea of the girl's thoughts and practices.

Abriyah shrugged. "She has never said she agrees with her family or with me. I think she considers my words, but she also does not ask questions. I don't see her seeking the Creator, but when we are working in the garden, we don't talk much."

Zara tapped the table beside her with one hand. "Introduce me to her." She would meet the girl and try to assess her beliefs before she let her men make any more decisions. This time she would see to it that things worked out for her son.

"Very well. Follow me." Abriyah led her through the back door and across the property, past the nearest neighbor's house to the one beside it. A girl answered when she knocked on the door.

"Welcome, Abriyah!" She smiled, then noticed Zara and gave Abriyah a curious look.

"Keziah, this is my daughter, Emzara, though she goes by Zara. I wanted her to meet you since you have been so helpful to me." Abriyah faced Zara. "Zara, this is Keziah."

"It's nice to meet you, Keziah." Zara silently assessed the girl and followed her mother into the house when Keziah invited them in.

Keziah's mother, Malee, welcomed them and offered them refreshments. While Malee retrieved cups of a spiced fruit drink, Zara glanced about her. There was no obvious shrine set up to the goddess in the living area.

"Thank you," Zara said as she accepted the cup from Malee.

"Yes, thank you," Abriyah said. "I was telling Zara about how much Keziah helps me, and she wanted to meet her. My daughter likes to look out for me. She also has a question for you." She smiled at Zara. The comment was unexpected, but Zara should have known her mother would get straight to the point.

She cleared her throat and looked from Keziah to Malee. "Yes. We are looking for a wife for my youngest son. My mother suggested that Keziah might be willing."

Malee's eyes widened. "Keziah is young." She looked at her daughter. "She just came to be of marriageable age."

Zara studied the girl again. Too young could be problematic. Young and immature or young and wise? She took a sip of the drink, then set it aside. "If she believes in the Creator, she would make a good choice, though of course my husband will need to be consulted." Had she said too much? And yet, most of the city knew of Noah's preaching. Once she told them her husband's name, they would know.

Malee looked at her hands as if the answer resided in the markings on her palms. At last she met Zara's gaze. "We believe in the goddess, though we do not deny that there could be a creator. Keziah has not decided yet what she believes. We present our children with all the differing beliefs and allow them to decide that question for themselves."

Zara nodded, though she wondered at the wisdom of teaching many different things without any guidance as to what was true. "I see." She looked at Keziah. "Do you believe in the Creator, Keziah?"

"I don't know," the girl said softly. "Abriyah talks of Him. I would like to know more about Him."

Perhaps she would come to believe after she married Ham. "I would enjoy telling you about Him," Zara said. She stood. "If you are open to it, I will speak to my husband, and if he is agreeable, he will visit your home." She turned toward Malee. "Do I have your permission to speak for Keziah's hand?"

Malee looked at Keziah. "Are you agreeable?"

Keziah's expression clouded, and Zara didn't miss the

uncertainty in her gaze. "I would like to meet this man you want me to marry."

"We can arrange that," Zara said, smiling.

"You will love him," Abriyah said. "My grandson is a good man."

Keziah shrugged. "I am willing to meet him."

Malee stood. "Have your husband and son come to our home. Then we will decide."

"Very well." Zara walked with her mother back to her house.

Would Ham find Keziah wanting and less than what he'd seen in Naavah? How much should they reveal to Keziah about the coming judgment before securing her hand in marriage? Zara pondered the thought on her walk home, fearful of losing this chance but wondering if they would be wrong to keep the truth from the girl.

Later that evening, Zara waited until her sons and daughters-in-law had retired for the night to approach Noah. "I've found a woman to be Ham's wife." She sat next to him as he leaned over the table, adding to the sketches and lists he had made.

He looked up. "Have you now? Who is it?" He glanced at the parchment again, clearly distracted.

"My mother's neighbor has a young daughter. She is of marriageable age, though younger than Ham. She is beautiful and helpful to my mother. She has not been taught of the Creator, but she shows interest in Him. Her mother worships the goddess, and apparently her parents have exposed their children to all the idols worshiped in the city. They do not guide them in any way."

Noah leaned back, giving her his attention. "I suppose it is not going to be easy to find a woman with the faith we believe. But aren't you acting too soon? It's only been a day, Zara. Ham is not ready."

"Is there a reason to wait other than Ham's feelings? We must secure a bride for him, and I say the sooner the better. Once people know what you are building, life is only going to get harder, and we don't want to be looking for a wife for him while you are in the middle of building our new home and the ark. There will be little time then." Zara shifted, attempting to get more comfortable.

Noah tapped the stylus against his chin. "Ham needs time."

"He doesn't have time, Noah. You must convince him that he needs to wed, and he will grow to love this girl in time. He didn't actually know Naavah, after all. How devastated can he truly be?" She had often wondered how this child could become so instantly enamored of something and then demand to have his way. They should not have given in to him in his childhood. If they hadn't, perhaps now he would be less insistent on having his desires met and focus more on others' needs. But there was no going back.

Noah moved the end of the stylus back and forth between his teeth. He said nothing for a lengthy breath. "I will speak to him. But give me a few days. There is no reason we cannot wait even a week or two." He held her gaze, then returned to his work.

She stood. There would be no convincing him to act sooner than he deemed best. Sometimes Noah could be as stubborn as Ham. Or perhaps Ham was too much like his father.

Chapter
7

Three weeks later, Zara walked to town with Keziah. The woman had married Ham the week before, much to Zara's relief, though she could see no joy in Ham's eyes in the presence of his new bride. The thought saddened her. She tried so hard to help her sons, to give them everything they needed, and Ham had needed a wife. But Keziah was not his choice, and he'd made that abundantly clear once Noah had told him of their decision.

"Are you telling me I do not have the right to choose the woman I want to marry? If I can't have Naavah, I don't want anyone!" Ham had stomped out of the house, his voice echoing off the walls.

Zara wanted to jump up and run after him, talk some sense into him. "What are we going to do?" she asked Noah.

"He will come around. He has to marry, and he knows it."

Noah had seemed so sure then, but now, as Zara glanced at Keziah, she wondered.

"I'm glad you joined our family, Keziah." Zara touched her shoulder, but the woman barely looked at her.

Keziah did not speak for an entire block. At last she met Zara's gaze. "I do not think Ham wants me."

Zara stopped and faced her. "Ham has had many trials lately. He just needs time." What else could she say?

Keziah looked down and shook her head.

Zara cupped her shoulder. "Marriage is not easy for anyone, Keziah. Please give him time." What would she do if Keziah sought her father and asked for an annulment? Breaking of marriage covenants had become a common thing in recent years. Worry gnawed at her. "I will speak to Ham."

Keziah looked up at that. "No!" She glanced beyond Zara as the sound of male voices met their ears.

Zara turned to see a gang of young men sauntering toward them, laughing and whistling.

"Look at what we have here!" The lead man held something smoking in his hand, lifted it to his mouth, and breathed deeply. The smell wafted to them.

"Looks like we're going to have some fun." Another man passed the first, walking fast.

Zara's heart slammed into her chest. She grabbed Keziah's hand, and they turned and ran back the way they had come.

"Where're you going? We just wanted to talk to ya."

Footsteps sounded heavy behind them. Zara kept running, praying.

A side street came into view, another route toward the center of town, and Zara took it, too fearful to look back. They raced through the city, clinging to each other's hands, breath coming fast.

The city square came into view with people milling about, and Zara slowed, then came to a stop when they reached her shop. She bent forward, dragging in air. Keziah clutched the post where merchants tied their pack animals.

Ham emerged from the shop as Zara looked up. His gaze moved between them as though he was not sure which one to go to first. At last he approached Keziah. "What happened?"

She burst into tears, and Ham pulled her close and patted

her back. "It's all right. I'm here." He glanced at Zara. "What happened, Ima?"

Zara straightened, drew in several deep breaths, and spread her hands in a defenseless gesture. "We were on our way here and were approached by a gang of men. We didn't wait to see what they would do."

"Did you run the whole way?" Ham looked down at Keziah. How small she seemed next to his taller frame. But Zara took comfort in the way he held her in a protective embrace.

"Yes. We took another route. I knew things were bad, that the city is not safe, but I did not think they would trouble a woman of my age." She glanced at Keziah. "I am certain it was your bride they were interested in."

Ham tightened his grip on Keziah. Good. Perhaps today's scare would show him that he needed to keep her safe. And care for her.

"I will take you home when you are ready to leave," he said to Keziah. "Do not come here again without one of us." He held her at arm's length. "Never come alone."

She nodded, gazing up at him, a warm expression on her face. Zara released a sigh. There was hope for them if Keziah thought of Ham the way she seemed to. And Zara knew Ham could not bear to lose another woman to evil men or demonic beings. Despite his hurt at Naavah's loss, he was a good son. He would do the right thing.

Noah walked over the parcel of land he had purchased, Shem and Japheth with him. Ham had spent the past few months preparing to sell Zara's shop, something Noah had determined they must do in order to put all their energies into completing the work God had given them. Especially after his wife and daughter-in-law were almost attacked walking to town. He shook himself. The violence had grown worse with every passing year. This was not like a group of boys bullying his sons when they were youths. These were grown men. He did not need to imagine what they would have done if they'd caught Zara and Keziah.

He turned his attention to the task at hand, willing the images to leave his mind. They couldn't stop the violence, but they didn't have to live near it. "We will build the house here," he said to his sons. He stopped at the farthest edge of the property and portioned out the length and breadth of the house with his steps.

"Do you think that will be large enough for all of us?" Shem rubbed his beard. "I know we won't be here forever, but with seventy-five years before the judgment, that's long enough to need our space."

"Especially since we'll be living close together on the ark and we don't know how long we'll be there." Japheth moved beyond Noah and waved his arm over more acreage. "Why don't we increase the size by half again as much? I know Adataneses will be pleased, as will Ima."

"And Sedeq, and probably Keziah too." Shem nodded, and they both looked at Noah, reminding him of how they had come together to get their way as young boys.

"All right, all right. You don't have to tell me twice. I know when I'm outnumbered." He laughed. "Did your mother put you up to this?" Zara had told him to promise to make the house bigger than the one they had. He had no doubt she might have talked to their sons to get them to agree with her.

Japheth and Shem shrugged, but by their expressions, he knew. Chuckling, he jotted down the measurements on a tablet as Japheth and Shem put stakes in the ground where they would begin to build. "Let's mark out the storage unit next, though I must insist that it be bigger than our house," Noah said. "We will be filling it with many things before the time is up."

They moved to an area some distance from the house, allowing for a large garden in between. He looked over the land again. There was room to grow fields of grain, but they could not begin to store it until perhaps twenty years before they boarded the ark. He did not know if grain would keep beyond that, but it would be enough for them to feed themselves without being dependent on others. Perhaps they could even sell anything left over to help fund the expense of the ark.

He measured a large section for the storage area, keeping it close to the property line. "Now let's decide how much room we need for the ark. The rest of the land we will use to grow the food we will need."

"What if it's not enough?" Shem followed him as they walked over the uneven ground. They would need to hire laborers to plow the fields and help with planting and harvesting.

"It will be enough. If it is not, we will ask my father and your uncles to grow some food for us." They would help him, surely.

"Saba will. And Adataneses's family will as well." Japheth seemed so sure, but Noah had not seen faith on that side of Methuselah's family.

"I will ask them." He led them toward the largest section of the property, placed a stake in the ground, and began walking the length God had given him.

"It's so long!" Japheth walked beside him. "Are you sure, Abba? Though I suppose we will need the space if we are to take more people as well as all kinds of animals. So far, I've counted at least five hundred kinds that I've seen or cared for over the years. But I know there are more. Many more." Japheth had always loved the animals, and Noah saw now that God had been preparing him for such a time as this.

"Let us plan for three times as many. We will also be taking a mate for each kind and in some cases several pairs." He raised a hand toward the skies. "The Lord said that the ark is to have three stories." Noah placed the stake for the length in the ground and continued on to mark the width.

"We are going to need men trained in shipbuilding, are we not?" Shem asked. "Saba Rake'el is willing to help." Like Noah had done before he married Zara, Shem worked now and then with Zara's father on the docks, and he had broached the subject with him when they first discussed the ark.

"Yes, I know. Though I'm not sure how much time he will have to be away from his ships. And to build a ship in the middle of a field will make no sense to him." Noah wasn't sure it made much sense to him either, but he had known the Creator long enough to sense when to ask questions and when to simply obey. He stopped, placed another stake in the ground, then recorded the measurements. "Go to the docks tomorrow and see if your grandfather will come to the house for a visit. He rarely leaves the docks even to be with your grandmother, as you know, but perhaps we can persuade him to come and help us plan."

Noah glanced at the heavens as they journeyed back toward the house. How easy was God going to make this for them? Would building each thing come together as some of the houses and ships he'd helped build had in centuries past? Or would they struggle with difficult laborers and, even worse, those who might try to stop them?

He searched the clouds for some sign, but God had said all that He planned to say for now. The rest would come in time.

The house was completed several months later. Now that they were settled, Zara gathered all she could to begin spinning, weaving, making pottery, and planning the gardens and fields for food. She joined her daughters-in-law in the outer court after the men left to secure materials for the ark.

"Let's set up both looms, one for the wool and one for

the linen, in this corner under the canopy," Zara said. "The person spinning can sit nearby. The pottery wheel can go in the far corner away from the house and the looms." She walked toward the area, examining her choice. She looked at Adataneses, who had the most skill at the wheel.

"I can work there. I will set it up right away." Adataneses went into the house to retrieve the wheel while Sedeq took a handful of flax from a basket and sat on a bench to spin it.

Keziah looked at Zara. "What would you have me do? I like gardening best." She offered Zara a slight smile, though it did not quite reach her eyes. How long would it take for her to feel at home with them?

Zara had no way of knowing what went on between Keziah and Ham. Neither one shared much with the others. Zara longed for closeness and kept telling herself that it would come in time. But how much time?

"Why don't you draw up plans for the garden then?" she said. "I will look them over when you're done. I have seeds in jars waiting to be planted. The only thing we can keep for years are the seeds and grains and perhaps the dried fruit, though I think we need to take our time and prepare well before we worry about gathering and storing everything." She smiled at Keziah. "Does that sound good to you?"

Keziah nodded. "I will study how to preserve food so we can perfect that before the flood comes." She glanced toward the area where the men were having logs brought to begin building. "Do you really think the Creator will send such a massive flood?" It was the first she had mentioned what Noah had been telling them since he'd had the vision.

"I do. If Noah says he saw the Creator, then he saw the Creator. We have learned to obey Him without questioning Him. I know that is unpopular today, as most people do not believe in Him. But we have heard the prophecies from our grandfather Methuselah since we were small, and he is still preaching repentance to those who will listen. When he is gone, then the end will come. That has been told of him since his birth. I have no reason to doubt it." Zara gave Keziah a curious look. "I know I've asked this before, but now that you've heard the prophecies, do you believe in the Creator?"

Keziah shrugged. "I am beginning to. I had heard talk of Him, but my parents considered Him a myth—stories of long ago that were made up by our ancestors and no longer needed. I had no reason to doubt them." She turned away to retrieve a scrap of parchment and a stylus. "I will get to work on the garden."

Zara watched her go. So her parents *had* given an opinion to their children of the Creator, and not a positive one. The realization helped, though it saddened her.

She looked at her girls as they busied themselves, quietly thankful for each one. *May they all be blessed and a blessing to our sons.*

Zara picked up the basket of wool she had received from Noah's father. She would join Sedeq in spinning. They would need many curtains to act as walls in the ark, and who knew how many blankets and rugs and other garments?

She only hoped that the four of them were capable of taking care of all that would be needed. She didn't want to hire help as Noah was doing unless she had to.

THE FRIDAY WITH

Chapter
8

2270 BC

The cool mist of early dawn greeted Zara as she walked along the edge of the garden Keziah had planted and maintained each year. The girl had grown into an even more beautiful woman, but Zara noticed an edge in her attitude toward all of them. She had mastered a subtle ability to get her way, especially with Ham, and Zara struggled to understand why she felt the need to do so.

The sound of voices came from the house into the back courtyard, and Zara turned to see Adataneses and Sedeq walking toward her. The two of them got along fairly well with each other, but not as well with Keziah. Why were they up so early? Perhaps something troubled them, though she prayed not.

"Greetings, my daughters. You have found my quiet place."

"May we speak with you candidly, Ima Zara?" Sedeq tucked a strand of her flowing black hair beneath a headband holding most of it away from her face.

"Of course. Don't you always?" Zara looked from one woman to the other. "What is it?"

"Keziah." Adataneses crossed her arms over her chest. "She told us last night after you had retired that you are putting her in charge of deciding all our meals, and that since she planted the garden, she is the one to decide what we do with the food. She even said that since we have so much, she was going to let her mother and sisters come and work with her and keep whatever they wanted. Did you tell her this?"

"What Adataneses means is that while we are in agreement to help the poor as we've always done, her family is not in need. She isn't in control of our entire food supply, is she?" Sedeq's brows knit in a worried frown.

Zara blinked, trying to make sense of what they had just told her. "I never said anything like that to Keziah. She plants our gardens and tends them, but I help her with the weeding. She makes decisions, but I never—" She paused. Had she given Keziah the impression that she was in control of this part of their lives? They all had so many responsibilities, and each woman handled her own area of expertise. "I can see why she might think she is head of the gardens, because she is. Just as you both are in charge of the pottery and the weaving."

"I don't mind that she is in charge of planting and harvesting," Adataneses said. "But she twists things to make them sound like we are not allowed to pick our own food for our husbands. And if her family is going to come here to reap the benefits of her work, then my family should help me, and Sedeq's should help her." Adataneses glanced back at the house as though afraid Keziah would suddenly appear.

"Are you sure she meant those things?" Zara had seen the struggles between her daughters-in-law, particularly as the years had passed and they'd had less interaction with those living in the city. Perhaps they should invite the families of her daughters-in-law to visit, or at least their mothers. If they would come.

"She said the words. We can only surmise that she meant

them." Sedeq sighed. "We try to get along with her, Ima Zara, but it's like she is always rephrasing our words. If I tell her something, when Adataneses hears of it from her, it's not what I said at all! I know the gardens are her domain, and I don't even mind her longing for her mother and sisters, but it was her tone. She's acting like she looks down on us. And I don't know why."

Zara nodded. Hadn't she seen it over and over? "I don't know why either. I will speak to her again."

"No, please don't." Adataneses held up her hand. "She will know we complained to you. We just wanted to make sure of what you had actually said and not just believe her words."

"You don't want me to say anything?" How was she to fix the rifts in her family if she couldn't talk to them?

"Please, no, Ima Zara." Sedeq stepped closer and touched her arm. "We trust you. We want to like Keziah, especially for Ham's sake, but perhaps that is the problem. I think she tries to control us because she can't control him."

"Why would she want to control him?" Adataneses raised a brow. "I hadn't thought of that, but I can see it now."

"He doesn't give her what she wants from him," Zara said. She had fretted over their relationship more than once since Keziah joined them five years before. For a time it seemed as though she and Ham were a perfect match. Why couldn't things stay that way? Then again, she and Noah had had their share of ups and downs over the many years of their marriage. Ham and Keziah would weather this difficult time as well.

"Sedeq, what would you say about paying a visit to your mother?" Zara said. "I haven't seen Vada in so long. Adataneses, we can do the same with your mother. Bedelia and I used to be close. Perhaps a few hours away to visit each one would help. It would give us a break from each other here and the monotony of the work."

They both nodded and smiled. "I do miss my mother, though

I will be surprised if she will see us after what she said of visiting us years ago." Sedeq glanced beyond Zara, her expression melancholy. "But I will be happy to see her."

"Good," Zara said. "Adataneses, we will go to your mother's house after we meet Vada. Then I will take Keziah. Perhaps a change of pace will do us all a lot of good."

The women agreed and returned to the house, seemingly less downcast. Keziah might be the one who needed her family the most. She had been the youngest when she married and the most insecure. But something must be done about her manipulating the others. If she and Ham could just get along better, perhaps everything would work out.

The following morning after the men left and chores were completed, Zara left Adataneses and Keziah and took Sedeq with her to the outskirts of the city, where Sedeq's family lived. They each carried a stout walking stick, which they had learned to wield in the passing years. They could not pull the men away from work on the ark to travel if they needed wool from Noah's father or help from Zara's mother, so they had learned to defend themselves.

"She may not be home." Sedeq gripped the staff, her knuckles white, though they had encountered no trouble as they passed the other houses. "I heard she has taken up with a new group of women. I'm not sure what they do each day, but they like to meet in different homes."

Zara glanced up ahead. Vada's house was around the next bend. "How did you hear this? Did Shem hear it?"

Sedeq nodded and slowed her pace. "He saw my brother Dalton when he was speaking to one of the merchants to purchase the thousands of wooden pegs he would need. They spoke briefly, and Shem asked after my parents. Dalton didn't say much, as he's not one to gossip. I need to speak to Lagina for that."

"Your sister Lagina is off living with her husband's family, yes?" Zara had heard that Sedeq's brother and two sisters had married, though Sedeq, Shem, and their family had not been invited to celebrate with them.

Sedeq stopped within sight of the house. Sadness filled her expression. "As far as I know, yes. This visit today"—she glanced at the sprawling house—"may simply reaffirm all that I fear. I am not welcome here, so I'm wary of knocking on the door."

Zara reached for Sedeq's hand and gently squeezed. "We will trust the Creator to grant us favor with your mother. And if He does not, then we'll know we're not welcome. Perhaps at a later time. But if we don't try, we won't know."

"You're right, of course." She offered Zara a weak smile. "I suppose we had better try."

They came to the house, entered the courtyard, and knocked on the door. There was no sound from within, so Zara knocked harder and waited. At last they heard footsteps approaching.

Vada opened the door, looking dazed. She held a hand to her eyes as if warding off the glare of the sun, though the sun was not at that angle. "Sedeq? Zara? What are you doing here?"

"We wanted to see you, Ima. It's been a long time. I miss you." Sedeq released a breath and stood straight, holding her mother's gaze.

"It was my idea. The women miss their families, so I suggested we visit." Zara searched Vada's face. "May we come in?"

Vada glanced beyond them, seeming uncomfortable. "I don't know. Raiden does not want us to visit you. He is even more convinced Noah has lost his mind since you all moved out of the city to build that ship. You actually make for the basis of some good laughter." She chuckled, then stopped when she met her daughter's gaze. "But you did come to me, after all." She opened the door and allowed them to enter. "I can show you my new object of worship. Come to the outer court."

Wary, Zara followed behind Sedeq as they passed through the house to the backyard. In the center of the large courtyard stood a statue of a woman, arms raised and holding a round orb.

Vada approached it and bowed low, said some words Zara could not understand, and stood. "This is where I worship."

Zara's heart sank, and she wanted nothing more than to take Sedeq and leave this place.

"What is the circle she is holding, Ima?" Sedeq's question caught her attention.

"Why, the sun, of course. I realize I could have made the image better. The next time we will make it out of pure gold." Vada beamed like she was bathed in sunlight. "We bow before it, repeat certain phrases, and empty our mind of everything that could distract us. As we empty ourselves, the sun fills us with its light until our whole body warms to it, and we carry the feelings of joy and beauty the rest of the day. It is wonderful, Sedeq, Zara. You should join me." Vada looked from one to the other, then focused on her daughter. "You could learn much from our worship. The sun is brilliant, and not just its light."

Zara stood dumbfounded, searching for words. She glanced at Sedeq, who seemed to ponder what her mother had said.

"What happened to you, Vada?" Zara spoke, wanting to draw Sedeq's attention more than she wanted to hear Vada's explanation. She knew her childhood friend and coworker had long ago left her faith in the Creator. But to take it to the level of making her own images, her own god? "Does Raiden worship your god as well?"

Vada frowned, then shook her head and laughed. "Of course not! This is a woman's god. He has his own." She pointed to another shrine beneath the trees. "Sometimes the men gather with him and do things . . . . Sometimes strange women join them, but I do not." Her voice trailed off, and she wore a pinched expression as though what Raiden did was distasteful to her. Was that why she worshiped as she did? To distract herself from her husband's waywardness and possible unfaithfulness?

Zara looked at Sedeq, saw the worry in her eyes. Vada was not going to give Sedeq the comfort or the support she needed. Asking her to help Sedeq with dyeing the wool and spinning it into thread had crossed Zara's mind, but if she welcomed her under their roof, could she keep her from talking of this new god?

"I think we should go." She touched Sedeq's arm. "Thank you, Vada. It was good to see you again."

"You're not going to stay? I was about to offer you some of my new spiced wine from Raiden's vineyards." Vada did not seem to notice that it was still early morn.

"Thank you, but no. We have much to do back home and only had a short time to come. I do hope you will visit us one day soon." Zara walked around the side of the house, avoiding entering it again. Now that she had seen Vada's and Raiden's objects of worship, she understood why the house seemed dark, almost oppressive. Why hadn't she noticed it when they first arrived? But such things could be subtle. And she'd wanted to believe Vada had changed, was returning to the faith she'd had as a younger woman, before Raiden began to follow the ways of the whole world.

"Thank you for having us." Sedeq looked back at her mother as they neared the street. Suddenly she rushed to Vada and pulled her close, hugging her tight. "I love you, Ima."

She turned about before Vada could accept or reject her and joined Zara. They walked home in silence.

Chapter
9

Noah stood beneath a tent canopy, bending over the plans he had drawn up for the construction of the outer structure of the ark. Beyond him and to his left, a growing pile of logs filled the land, waiting to be used. In front of him, the base of the ark took shape under the skilled hands of Rake'el and his craftsmen. Japheth and Shem worked with another group of hired men to cut and saw the logs into usable planks for the ark. Noah glanced at the wood. They would need to have more trees felled and brought to them before they were finished.

Ham approached, carrying another scroll. "I've finished calculating the number of cages we will need for the larger kinds of animals. If this seems good to you, I'll work up the dimensions and drawings for them. When Japheth finishes calculating the number of smaller animals and birds, I'll draw up those plans as well. Some of the birds and animals will be with us on the top level, with the larger animals on the two other floors. Does that sound good, Father?"

Noah looked at the number and the sketch Ham had drawn

of where the animals would fit on the lower level of the ark. "We need to add to this sketch a way to feed them and give them water. It must be something that will be easy to use and not cause us to have to open any of the cages. We do not want to have to contend with the animals every day."

Ham chewed on the end of his stylus, thinking. He glanced at Noah, then quickly drew a rough addition to the sketch. "We could build a walkway above the cages and add chutes to carry the food into feed troughs. We can do the same separately with the water." He drew for several moments, then showed his idea to Noah. "Like this."

Noah took the parchment and studied it, then set it on the table and took his own stylus to adjust the design in a few places. "I think this will work. Draw it to exact specifications for the size of the ark. We can reinforce the walkway by attaching it to the tops of the cages and secure one cage to another so they do not shift when the boat moves with the waves."

Ham nodded, took the scroll from Noah, then paused. "Father, do you ever wonder what it will all be like? You've been on a ship as it sailed on the Euphrates, but will that be anything like this? We won't be able to look out on the water unless we are on the roof. How are we going to circulate the air or rid the ark of the animal and human waste? I can't imagine being inside for I don't know how long and having no glimpse of the sun." He looked up at the sun splaying its golden rays through thick white clouds.

Noah also glanced at it, pondering Ham's question. Would living on the ark be like sailing on the open river? He shook his head. "I don't think our time on the ark will be anything like life on the earth. We have not walked this path before, and we cannot know what to expect. But we can imagine and plan in the best way possible." He patted Ham's back. "Draw up the plans. They are good ones. I think we will follow the same pattern on both lower and middle levels. The top level will be our living quarters, and we can care for the birds there."

Ham moved to the back of the canopied area and sat before a table to draw the plans to scale. Noah returned to his work, then noticed Adataneses and Sedeq walking toward him, carrying skins of water and a basket of food. The women took turns each day to offer them refreshment.

He set aside his work and greeted them. "Thank you, my daughters." He took the skins, and they set the basket on the table beside his work. Shem and Japheth emerged from the group of contractors and joined them.

"Just in time. I finished all the almonds I brought with me." Japheth smiled at his wife, then peeked into the basket.

Adataneses lifted the linen napkin, pulled small loaves of bread out, and handed them to each man. Japheth took a bite, and Shem pulled Sedeq close, thanking her. Noah broke his loaf and had lifted it to his mouth when voices called to him from the area of the woodpile.

"Noah ben Lamech!"

Noah recognized Adataneses's brothers, Payam, Theron, and Caz. They walked toward the tent, shouting as they came.

"Our men are concerned at all the trees you are killing in order to build your ship," Payam said. "They fear there will be none left of the cypress kind. Why should we continue to supply you with wood when you're harming the earth?"

Shem stepped forward, but Noah restrained him. Japheth placed his arm around Adataneses's shoulders.

"You've poisoned our sister with your crazy plans, old man." Payam stood just outside the tent and glared at Noah. Theron and Caz flanked him. "The world goes on as it always has and always will. There has never been a flood and never will be. No one has ever even seen a flood. You are wasting the earth's resources and filling the people's minds with lies."

Noah crossed his arms over his chest and leveled Payam

with a stern look. "Why have you come, Payam?" He glanced at Theron and Caz. "Was this your idea or did your father suggest it? I am paying you and your men a fair wage to gather the wood for us, and you know very well that there are plenty of forests left on the earth to keep these kinds of trees alive. You have no reason to be angry." He glanced at Adataneses, whose lips were pinched tight, probably in an effort to keep from yelling at them. "Go home, all of you. If you do not want the work, I will find someone else. We don't need your accusations." They had put up with opposition over nearly every aspect of building the ark thus far, from trouble getting the wood they needed for the planks and pegs to the challenges of getting iron screws and anchors and more.

"You have no business preaching against us." Theron stepped forward and gripped the pole holding up the canopy. "All your work is going to end up showing you to be a fool. If you think you're actually going to live on this thing, whatever it is, to save you from some kind of disaster, you'd be better off climbing a mountain and living away from the rest of us. We don't need you here. Just give us our sister and we'll be on our way."

"What?" Adataneses stepped out of Japheth's hold and moved closer to Payam. She pushed against his chest. "What do you think you're going to accomplish by coming here and criticizing my family? I belong to Japheth's family now. You are worthless, the whole lot of you!" Her cheeks reddened, and she looked like she was about to punch Payam.

He took a step back and held up his hands. "You don't have to be so nasty, Neses. You know we just want to save you from this crazy man." Payam pointed at Noah. "And his family." He looked at Japheth and spat in the dust. "Our father should never have agreed to this marriage. If he had known what would become of you, what you were all going to do, he would never have said yes."

"Then it's a good thing that you didn't know, because I am happy here, Payam. I don't want to return to your unbelief." She turned about and marched off, Sedeq quickly following.

"Go home, Payam. If you don't want my silver or gold, I will find another who does." Noah crossed his arms, his sons doing the same and coming alongside him.

Adataneses's brothers stood still a moment, then looked at one another. "We will get you your wood," Payam said. They left, not waiting for a response from Noah.

The men of the city criticized him and maligned his character, but none of them looked twice at accepting his gold.

Zara ground grain in the front courtyard of the house while her daughters-in-law worked in the back. Trees bordered the land on three sides, with a path coming from Seth's City. But the city walls were distant, and Zara relished the peace from its chaos and clamor.

She spotted a lone figure coming toward her and squinted against the sun's angled rays. *Ima.* That her mother walked alone outside the city troubled Zara given her age, but Abriyah never worried. She'd learned to take care of her household while Zara's father was off riding the waves across the rivers, and even now she could defend herself, though Zara worried how well.

She brushed the flour from her hands and covered the bowl, then stood and walked toward her mother. "What are you doing here, Ima?"

"Is that the way you greet your mother?" Abriyah opened her arms to embrace her.

Zara held tight to her, wondering how many more years she would have the comfort of her arms. "You're right. I'm glad you came. Please, come and sit."

"Surely you have something for me to do. I came to help

you, not to sit." They walked toward the courtyard, and Zara motioned toward the stone bench.

"I will find something, but first, let us talk."

"Better to work and talk, my daughter." Abriyah picked up the sieve and dumped the grain into it.

Zara took the hint and sat again before the grindstone. "It is hard to hear above the noise." She waited to turn the wheel, and finally her mother gave Zara her attention.

"Tell me what troubles you, my daughter." She held the sieve still.

Zara sighed. "The girls." She lowered her voice and cast a glance behind her. "They are in the back working, and normally I enjoy their company, but ever since Adataneses returned from hearing her brothers jeer at Noah, she's grown quiet. Sedeq speaks, but she has been morose ever since she found out that her mother has created her own gods, even different than what Sedeq knew growing up. Keziah continues to complain and criticize them both, and sometimes she criticizes me as well in an attempt to get her way. I feel as though I am going mad, Ima. How will we ever survive the ark?"

Abriyah studied her, and Zara was grateful that her look held compassion. Anyone else might have laughed at her concerns. But her mother knew her better than anyone except Noah, and she had a listening ear.

"I share your concerns, Zara. You are being asked by the Creator to do a very difficult thing. One day you will be the only ones left on the earth, and you will have no one else to talk to." She touched Zara's arm. "You must find a way to keep them talking to you and to each other and forgive any grievances quickly, lest they fester and you have angry silence. Or worse, you end up with a son or daughter like Cain."

"I have tried, Ima. I can't force them to talk to me. I hear them talking to each other, particularly Adataneses and Sedeq, but they do not confide in me often." Did they confide in her sons? Or were her sons oblivious to what was going on when they were off working on the ark every day?

"You say Adataneses is quiet. Have you asked her why? What did her brothers say to upset her? Perhaps she is thinking things she fears you will not like. Tell her she can tell you anything, and always be certain you do not judge any of them. They need your comfort as you need mine." Her mother smiled. "I appreciate that you confide in me, Daughter. A mother wants her children, no matter how old they become, to share their lives with her. To come to her for advice now and then. To allow her to share what she has learned in life."

"I think I can get Adataneses and Sedeq to talk to me. Keziah, I'm not as sure about. Though she has lived here over five years, she is difficult to understand. I never know if she is telling me the truth, yet I tend to believe her until I find out otherwise. What makes her want to control the world?"

Zara had puzzled over Keziah since she'd married Ham. By now she had hoped to be close to all the women, but despite living with them, she had to admit she did not understand them.

"If they know you love them, they will come around. Help them to see how much you value them. They are young and have much life ahead of them. They are going to need you when the judgment comes." Her mother looked at her with fondness, and Zara felt her heart constrict. They both knew that Abriyah would not live to join her and Noah on the ark. None of their parents would. How would *she* survive the flood without her ima?

"I will try, Ima. I am closest to Sedeq. Perhaps she will share her grief for her family with me."

"She will need you, yes. But Keziah may need you even more after what I heard in town yesterday." Her mother leaned close and lowered her voice. "Keziah's brother married this past week. They invited nearly the whole town. It was quite an elaborate affair."

Zara sat back, trying to sort through so many emotions. They were family, and yet they heard of the wedding from her mother after it was past? How could Keziah's family shut all of them out like that? And their own daughter and sister? Keziah would be hurt and feel more rejected than she already did.

"I have trouble enough with Keziah. I never thought her family would shut us out, especially since their daughter has been close to you." Zara shook her head. A heaviness filled her. "I will tell Keziah when Ham gets home. She will need him when she finds out her family did not want her there."

"Perhaps it was an oversight. Though . . . I doubt it." Her mother lifted the sieve and began to sift the grain Zara would need next.

Zara turned the grindstone on the grain, wanting to drown out her thoughts. She wasn't sure what Keziah would think or do, but she knew if she felt rejected herself, Keziah's response could only be worse.

Chapter

10

It should not have surprised Zara that Ham and Keziah would respond in anger against Keziah's family for shunning them. Hadn't they known? Keziah had seen little of her mother and sisters, despite her desire to spend time with them. If only Zara could help Keziah carry the grief.

She searched the grounds for some sign of her daughter-in-law but could not find her. Normally she was working in the gardens at this hour, but she was not there, or in the fields, the house, or the storage building. Had she gone to watch the men work on the ark?

Zara returned to the house, where she found Sedeq and Adataneses, one spinning wool and the other painting a vase she had created. "Have you seen Keziah?" She sank onto a bench beneath the canopy as both women looked up from their tasks.

"I saw her walk off across the field. She was too far away to call to her, so I just let her go." Sedeq's eyes grew wide. "Do you think she wandered off our property? She's been pretty upset the past few days."

"I hope not." Zara did not want to consider that thought. The Watchers frequented the woods, and she had no doubt they watched Noah and the rest of them. They would sabotage the work any way they could and harass them as they spread their evil throughout humanity.

"She was upset. She would not talk to us about it. Perhaps she just wants to be alone. We all need that sometimes." Adataneses focused again on the vase, avoiding eye contact with Zara.

Clearly Zara needed to do something to ensure that these women had a place of their own, especially on the ark, where they could express themselves, write down their emotions, do something creative to keep hope alive. They wouldn't be able to just walk off the ark, though it would be easy to walk among the animals and avoid human contact if the need arose.

Zara placed her hands on her knees and pushed herself up. "I will keep looking. I'll be back soon."

The women nodded as she walked off. These two had been closer in the early years. She had to hope that would continue. They only had about seventy years until the ark was complete, and then the flood would come. While that seemed like a long time, with all they still had to build and create and preserve and gather, the time would go much too quickly. Not to mention the continued efforts they would make to convince their family and friends to join them. The thought that they might never get through to them troubled her.

She headed back toward the farthest fields where the grain grew. The heads of wheat were half as tall as they would be when they were fully grown. Zara touched the tender shoots, thankful that the weeds were few. She glanced about as she neared the tree line but still saw no sign of Keziah. She searched as far as she could into the forest but saw no movement other than squirrels running up the trees and birds flitting from branch to branch.

Reluctantly, she turned and headed across the property toward the area where the men were working. She hated to interrupt Noah or her sons, so she would just look and see. She wouldn't tell Noah her concerns yet. Keziah was just seeking peace. She would not have gone into the city, would she?

Fear pricked her heart with every step that showed no sign of Keziah. She reached the outer edges of the space Noah had portioned out for the ark. A quick search revealed nothing, but as she neared the canopy under which Noah worked, she glimpsed Keziah sitting among the grasses, out of their line of vision.

Thank You! Relief filled Zara. She approached and sat beside her daughter-in-law. "Keziah."

Keziah lifted her gaze to meet Zara's. "I'm sorry I'm not working, Ima Zara. I will return soon."

Zara brushed the idea away like a bothersome insect. "I'm not concerned about the work. I'm worried about you." She rested her hand on Keziah's shoulder. "I'm sorry you've had to endure so much rejection from your family, and more so since you married Ham. I hope you know how much we love and value you. We are so glad you're part of our family."

Keziah's eyes filmed, and tears shone on her lashes. "I know." Her voice cracked, a mere whisper. "I was once close to my sisters. The rest of them were so much older that I didn't interact with them as much. But Talitha and Chantal were near my age, and we did everything together as children. Even with our differences, I never ever expected either one of them to shut me out. To not invite me to such a big event." Her voice rose with emotion. "To act like I do not exist."

Zara knelt beside her and patted her shoulder. "I am so sorry, dear girl."

Keziah nodded. She gripped Zara's hand. "I am grateful for you too, Ima Zara. And I love Ham. I'm just grieving and missing my family of birth. I long for them to believe in the Creator. But if they will not even speak to me, how can I tell them about Him? It feels so hopeless. To think we will be spared the flood but they will not? I can't bear it." Tears slipped down her cheeks and she frantically tried to brush them away, but they would not stop.

It was the most Keziah had ever spoken to Zara about her love for Ham and faith in the Creator. Zara had wanted so often to ask her, especially given how often Keziah tried to get her own way and criticized those who didn't agree with her. Was her control merely her attempt to deal with the rejection she felt from her family?

Zara pulled her into her arms and let her weep. She had not experienced the loss of a parent to unbelief. And most of her siblings still walked in the ways of Methuselah. They were older than Zara, and she wondered whether they would be on the ark or pass into the next life before judgment came.

"What can I do to help, Keziah? I was thinking that perhaps we should make our garments and jars beautiful. Capture the beauty of the Creator in our work. Make musical instruments and take time for a day of rejoicing and worship. We can't work every day." They had to do something to bring joy. The world was too harsh a place without it.

"We do rest on the seventh day." Keziah pulled away from Zara's embrace, wiping her tearstained cheeks.

"I know that. But I think we also need times to rejoice in how God has blessed us and celebrate His goodness by using the gifts He gave us in more creative rather than just useful ways." The thought had been gaining strength in her mind, and she felt a sense of joy in pursuing it.

Keziah smiled, though it was guarded. "I think we would all like that." She pushed up from the ground. "I'm ready to return to work now."

Zara rose with her. "Perhaps you can give me some suggestions on what things we can make to give our living quarters beauty on the ark, and in our home while we're waiting."

Keziah fell into step with her. "I think we should begin with a sacrifice. I need to remember the Creator in that way first. I know I have not always been kind to all of you. I think I've lost sight of Him in all the pain."

Zara smiled and linked arms with her. "What a wonderful idea! I will speak with Noah about it this very night."

Relief and joy filled her as they walked back to the house. A sudden kinship with this daughter-in-law rose within her, and she silently thanked God that she had at last found her girls willing to talk with her. Perhaps they *would* survive living so close together for only God knew how long.

The next evening the family gathered in the sitting area to go over the day's events. Zara listened as Shem recounted his attempt to speak with Sedeq's brother Dalton to help provide them with steel.

"I did as you asked, Father. I sought Dalton at the smithy today. I had to tamp down my anger with him for the way he and his entire family have treated Sedeq, but he's one of the best smiths in the city. I knew we needed the best, so I asked him why his work has not met his high standards and is often late. We need those brackets and screws to connect the inner posts and cages and beams. He had no good excuse for the delay, though he did admit he had given the work to some of his men. He promised to make sure future orders are fulfilled correctly." Shem tented his hands beneath his chin. "He knows we pay him better than most would."

Noah nodded, his expression grim. "I'm glad to hear it, though I'm sorry it has come to this." He glanced at Sedeq. "I know your father trained him to be the best, and for your sake, he should be. Let us hope he does as he says. I will continue to speak of the Creator to your family when God gives me the opportunity."

Sedeq nodded. "Thank you."

"Have my brothers been civil to you of late?" Adataneses lifted her gaze to Noah, then glanced at Zara. Zara dearly wished that this daughter-in-law could have some sort of reconciliation with her family, especially since they were descended from Methuselah as she and Noah were. But not every son or daughter of Methuselah believed in the Creator. And no one could tell them they were wrong. They would not hear it. Sadness crept close at the thought.

"They have not taunted us since that day you were there." Noah took a handful of almonds from a tray on the low table. "I think you sufficiently silenced them." He smiled. "Thank you for defending us."

Adataneses looked at her hands, her face troubled. She visibly swallowed, and Zara knew she had something she wanted to say but could not seem to form the words.

Conversation broke out among her sons regarding the latest problem on the construction of the ark, and then Adataneses spoke up. "What if my brothers are not wrong?"

The room fell silent.

"That is, things have gone on as they always have since the beginning. No one has ever seen a flood. How is it even to come about? What if we are wrong?" She leaned back and released a breath.

Zara gave her a curious look. She'd wondered why Adataneses had been so quiet in recent weeks but had not realized she had been entertaining such doubts.

"They are wrong, Adataneses." Noah's deep voice dropped in pitch, carrying a soothing quality. "To think that the Creator is not able to do something different than what has always been done is arrogant because it puts us above Him. Though it does not seem as though anything has changed, if we look around us, we know it has. Violence has increased. People no longer keep their covenants of marriage. Immorality surrounds us, and the Watchers have infiltrated nearly every city on earth, corrupting the human race."

"And just because we have never seen a flood does not mean that one will never come," Zara said. "Can not the One who made all things do whatever He wills to do? Even if that means destruction of all He has made?" She reached out and grasped Adataneses's hand. "Sin has infected us since the garden, and the Watchers have made things worse. Our God has to judge evil."

"Why can't He just send the Redeemer as He promised?" Adataneses pulled away from Zara and leaned against Japheth, whose arm came around her.

Zara looked at Noah, as the whole family did, waiting for what he would say.

Noah cleared his throat and wiped the dust of the almonds from his hands. "God alone knows when He will send the Redeemer." His gaze swept the group and then stopped to look directly at each one. "The Redeemer will come, and He will come through one of you. But that time is not now. One day in the future, yes."

Zara watched the reactions of her sons and daughters-in-law. If only the Redeemer would come instead of judgment, which was approaching faster every day. Why did time speed up the older she got?

"I think we should offer a sacrifice to the Creator. Perhaps He will forestall judgment or have mercy on more people if we worship Him like we used to," Keziah said, glancing at Ham.

"I think that is a good idea." Noah stood, grabbed a clay tablet and tool, and began to write. "I will make several of these notices. Tomorrow, you"—he looked at his sons—"can post the notice of a sacrifice at the center of town and take it to the homes of Methuselah's children. I will speak to my father for lambs for the sacrifice. We will hold it at the end of the week."

The mood suddenly changed to one of hope.

"Perhaps my brothers will come." Adataneses's smile was tentative.

"Make sure my parents hear of it." Sedeq took Shem's arm and looked with affection into his eyes.

"And mine. I will visit my mother and ask her. Perhaps Abriyah will help me." Keziah, whose rejection and hurt had been so recent, surprised Zara with her words. But she had remained close to Zara's mother, one of the only people she did not criticize.

"I will help," Zara said to Noah. "We will hold the sacrifice at the altar just outside of town, won't we?"

"I will rebuild the altar Seth built that has fallen into disrepair. Let us pray that many people come." He took another tablet and began writing while the rest of the family talked at once.

Zara sat back, listening. This was how she imagined life on the ark. Sitting together, talking, laughing, and caring for one another and for those outside their family.

But would there be others to care for? It was her greatest hope.

Chapter
11

At the end of the week, Noah led his family outside the city to where Seth had built an altar to replace the one Adam had built years earlier. Noah had repaired the crumbling stones and secured the animals from his father's flock.

"Do you think anyone else will come?" Japheth walked beside Noah, leading two of the lambs. His brothers followed behind with the others.

"Your grandparents will come. I don't know about the rest." Noah glanced behind him but saw no one along the well-worn, overgrown path. They should have done this long ago. He chastised himself. He'd been so faithful to follow the Creator before he had been given word to build the ark, but in the many years since, he had failed to make this a yearly priority. How quickly things fell into disrepair.

They approached the altar. Ham and Shem, who had carried the wood, placed it atop the stone structure. Noah held the torch high, then turned and waited. They were early to the sacrifice. Surely some would join them.

Zara walked closer, holding a basket of unleavened bread to offer the Creator. Sedeq held a flask of olive oil, while Adataneses and Keziah each held a rope leading a lamb.

"I think I see them." Zara pointed to the dust kicking up in the distance.

Noah stepped forward, squinting. Zara had keener eyesight than he did, but a few moments later, he spotted his and Zara's parents walking toward them. "Good. I had hoped they would not change their minds."

"Is that Saba Methuselah with them?" Shem joined them, pointing.

"Yes." Noah started down the path, and then he noticed the rest of Methuselah's children and their children following, filling the path. He glanced heavenward. *Adonai?* Was God about to change the hearts of their family so they would join them on the ark? Would they repent of their sins as the sacrifice intended? Hope flickered, but he did not let it flare. He'd watched them for too long to believe his aunts and uncles and cousins and nephews and nieces would return to the Creator just because he'd invited them to a sacrifice.

"Saba. Welcome!" He gently embraced Methuselah, who leaned heavily on his walking stick. "I see you have brought the entire family with you."

Methuselah offered him a wide grin. "They may not like my preaching, but they listen when I tell them they have to come or they won't get their inheritance." He chuckled and leaned forward. "They won't get it anyway, so I'm hoping this moment changes their thinking."

"I hope so too, Saba." He patted Methuselah's shoulder as Zara approached, taking their grandfather's arm.

Noah turned back to greet his family, welcoming them. No one had brought a lamb for sacrifice except his parents and Methuselah. So they were here to spectate, not to participate.

He walked to the front of the altar, motioning for their attention. "Normally, I would have each family bring a lamb to offer to our God. But as we are short of animals for all of you, I will ask those of you who so desire to come to the front and place your hands on the head of the lamb closest to you. We will seek the Creator's forgiveness for all of us."

He waited as his children and parents and Saba Methuselah did as he asked, grateful to see Adataneses's brothers approach along with their wives. The others did not join them.

He prayed over the animals and told his family to confess their sins privately to the Creator. When the prayers ceased, Noah slit the lambs' throats and one by one placed the animals on the altar. He lit the wood, praying God would be pleased despite those who came for all the wrong reasons. God alone knew the heart of each person.

Be pleased with me, Adonai. And with my family. He silently included his extended family, but the hope that had flickered waned with the last lamb offered in sacrifice.

Zara linked arms with Noah as the sun began its descent. The sacrifice had ended long ago, and their sons and daughters-in-law had gone off in different directions. "We're alone." She looked up at this man who had walked beside her for more years than she could adequately remember. "We don't get this opportunity often these days."

He smiled at her and pulled her closer. "Let's walk." He led them past the altar, where they paused one more time. "I hope He was pleased with us."

"Do you doubt it?" She had never known him to doubt the Creator, but if she was honest, she doubted sometimes. Doubted her ability to do and say what she should. Wondered if God favored her for Noah's sake or for her own.

"I don't doubt Him." Noah moved past the altar and took the path to the city. "I just did not see sincerity in the faces of those who came with Saba today. They came because he threatened them, not because they believe. And I wonder if that tainted our sacrifice. I did not hear the Creator speak to the group or to my heart."

Zara walked around a boulder in their path and batted a honeybee away from her face. "If I understand anything about the Creator, I think He looks at each person individually, doesn't He? He would not reject you because of the behaviors or attitudes of others. He knows our hearts." She leaned her head against his shoulder. "I have no doubt He favors you, my husband." That she felt the need to reassure him surprised her. It was usually he who reassured her of the Creator's favor.

He patted her hand. "You're right, of course. I think the work is beginning to overwhelm me at times. I grow weary of those who mock us and malign us, and when we don't hear from the Creator, their doubts make me wonder. Did I hear Him wrong? Are we building this ark based on my foolish imagination?"

The breeze rustled the leaves in the trees overhead. Birds twittered and chirped their indignance at Zara and Noah's presence in their domain.

She glanced up at them, spotting a pure white dove among the greenery. She leaned close to Noah's ear and pointed. "Look."

He lifted his head. The dove seemed to be watching them. Noah raised his hand, and the dove, reluctant at first, floated down and rested on his fingers. Zara held her breath, not wanting to scare it off. Noah gently stroked its head, and Zara watched, mesmerized. She'd heard tales of a time before the fall of humans into sin when the animals were friendly and Adam and Eve could touch them, even speak to them. But she had never seen such a thing with animals that were not domesticated. Was this what the Creator would allow them to do when they cared for the animals on the ark? Would they be able to touch them all and speak to them as Adam and Eve had in Eden?

The bird suddenly flew off, and Noah took Zara's hand as they watched it fly upward. "I should not doubt. The Creator may not speak to us in an audible voice or fill our dreams with visions, but He speaks in His creation. He speaks to our conscience what is true and good and what is a lie and evil. If we seek Him, we will not be easily deceived."

She gazed at him, new affection rising within her. "You are an amazing man, my husband. So gentle and kind, yet unafraid to speak the truth to anyone who listens. I will put my doubts and fears aside. We have much to do in the time we have left."

He nodded, and they continued their journey toward home.

"I'm glad we finally have this time together," she said. Their land came into view in the distance. "We must make time for each other without our family. I need just you sometimes."

He smiled, that half smile with the twinkle in his eye that she had grown to love long ago. "We will make a way, both on this earth and on the ark." He kissed her cheek. "I'm glad we will begin again with each other. I could not survive the new world without you."

"Nor I you." Her heart sang all the way home.

Interlude

I had such hope in the early days of building the ark. People laughed at the very thought of a flood, and it is true that some mocked us and held us in contempt. But most of the men who provided the materials for this great endeavor did so gladly for the gold and silver Noah paid them. They even took pride in their craft, for Noah demanded nothing less.

Over time, the relationship I had with each daughter-in-law continued to improve, though spats still broke out between us. It is the human condition to grow irritable at times. I think they seek each other's company more now as they see less and less of their families of birth.

I suppose that is what saddens me the most. How can a mother forget her children, even one? Yet Vada seems to do just that with Sedeq. I know it bothers Sedeq to never see or hear from her mother. It troubles me as well. I miss our childhood friendship. I fear the time will come and she will not repent.

Adataneses never sees her brothers anymore. They stopped providing wood for Noah when he finally had all he needed, and they lost interest in the "crazy man" building a boat in a field. What can I say to that? To the world, nothing we do makes sense.

Keziah has softened toward our family as she and Ham have grown to care for one another. She has accepted our family as hers since her birth family continues to reject her. She still likes things her way, but I've come to realize that she never got to choose what she wanted in the home of her father. She had sought refuge in the gardens with my mother, which she does now in ours.

Though I have seen better changes in the relationships we have with each other, our standing in the community continues to slide with each passing year. The ark has taken shape and is now three stories high. The men built scaffolding around it to continue adding to it. Ham designed a moon pool to relieve the stress on the hull and allow fresh air in and stale air out. Shem and my father have both insisted that this will not flood the ark but make it work better. I believe them, but I do not fully understand it.

It is hard to believe that judgment will come in twenty years. We continue to fill the storehouse with containers to hold the food and water and with cages to be assembled and added to the first and second floors of the ark. We've designed our living quarters, and each month we add new furnishings for the rooms.

I wonder often if anyone else is going to join us. Should we make living quarters for those who might come at the last? How much food should we store, especially if there are more than eight of us?

These things trouble me and, I'll admit, sometimes keep me up at night. But Noah is certain everything will fall into place as the Creator intends. I know he is right.

Yet sometimes I still worry.

Chapter
12

2220 BC

Zara set a plate of hot bread on the table along with dates and fresh cheese, a gift from Noah's mother. One by one her sons and daughters-in-law emerged from their rooms, took bowls, and filled them with food.

Noah stood at the back door, watching as the sun rose, tapping one foot.

"He'll come, husband. Do not fret so." It was normally she who did enough worrying for all of them.

"He should be back by now." Noah turned and took a round of bread in his hand, broke it, and offered a silent thanks. "Shem is strong, but he is not strong enough to battle the Watchers or those who have sabotaged our work over the years. He was simply to keep watch. He should be home by now."

The door creaked open at that moment.

"See?" Zara said.

Sedeq hurried to Shem. "All is well?" She handed him her plate.

Shem's breath came fast, as though he had run part of the

way. "All is well, though I was not sure it would be. I saw two Watchers in the woods behind the ark. They showed themselves to me and drew close to the ark, but they didn't touch it while I watched them. I don't know whether they will do harm to the ark now that I am here and no one is there to witness their actions." He bit into the bread as Sedeq filled another plate for herself.

"I will go now." Japheth set his plate aside. "The rest of you come as you can." He stuffed two pieces of flatbread into his pockets, and Zara handed him a sack of almonds. He kissed Adataneses and hurried out the door.

Zara watched him go, her knees weakening. She sank onto a stool and sighed. "We are going to be worn out with keeping watch. We have twenty more years of this?" She met Noah's gaze. "Let us help you so you all do not grow overly weary."

Her daughters-in-law nodded their agreement.

"Yes, let us help." Keziah's eyes lit in eagerness.

"I'm not sure I want to stay in the fields alone all night," Adataneses admitted, her brow furrowing. "What if we built a shelter near the house with a view of the ark? Close enough for us to call for help. Then we could all take turns without fear of harm."

Noah rubbed the back of his neck. Zara knew that look. His mind was turning with possible ways to allow all of them to help. "It is quite safe to stay on the ark up on the roof. No one can reach us there, and we can easily see anyone who approaches. I just need to set up an alarm to sound loudly, like a trumpet, at the sight of a problem. We could hear it from the house and the rest of us could come running."

Zara shivered at the thought of being alone on the ark all night long. But they needed to help the men. Keeping watch meant they had one less man in the day to help with all the projects they still had to do. Perhaps she could find a way to make use of the time besides just watching the fields and forests.

"I'm willing to try." Sedeq took her empty plate to the table and stacked it with the others to wash at the pump outside. "I can begin tonight."

Shem touched her shoulder. "I'm not sure I like you being there by yourself."

"Wait until I can make an alarm," Noah said.

Sedeq nodded. "Don't take too long." She looked at Shem. "Go get some sleep. I will wake you in a few hours."

Shem obeyed without having to be told twice. Zara noted the dark circles beneath his eyes. The work and the watching were taking a toll on her men. And now it would burden her girls as well.

Oh Adonai, this waiting is so hard. And yet we know that it's Your patience that can lead people to repentance. Thank You for waiting. Give us the strength to finish the work You have asked us to do.

She put the food in the cellar and walked outside to join her daughters-in-law in the spinning and weaving and weeding. Soon they would need to gather and preserve. But for now, they just kept creating all they would need, and every day they seemed to think of something more. She prayed they did not forget anything essential, for once the flood came it would be lost forever.

"We're going to need material for pipes to carry the water to the storage area above each animal's pen." Noah looked up from his drawing for what felt like the hundredth time. He smoothed it over the table in the sitting room, where his sons sat in a circle around him.

"Bamboo should work well for that, Father." Japheth tapped the area where Noah had drawn the pipe. "It's hollow and can easily be strapped together with twine. We'll just have to make sure to reinforce the joints."

"And seal them with resin to make them waterproof." Shem

glanced toward the window that faced the ark. He would not rest until Sedeq came home safely on the morrow. She was at the ark now that Noah had created a system for her to call for help should she spot trouble. And Shem had made sure she had locked the ark's only door behind her.

"Check with Adataneses's brothers and see whether they can secure bamboo for us." Noah looked at Japheth. "I know we have not needed them in some time, but hopefully they will accept another job."

"I will seek them out tomorrow." Japheth sipped warm tea from one of the mugs Zara had brought to them.

"Good. And find someone who can supply us with a lot of flax in addition to what we've grown to make twine. Perhaps we can find someone to make the twine and save us the trouble." He rubbed his bearded chin. "We may need to go to another city to gather all that we need. We're going to need a lot of piping, not to mention resin. Ham, can you seek out suppliers of pitch or resin?"

Noah saw the eagerness on his sons' faces. They were making great progress now that the outer structure of the ark was complete, and the cages were waiting in the storehouse to be added to the ark. But so many smaller things still had to be constructed and put into place.

"Wasn't there a supplier of resin nearby when we worked on the house in Jabril's City?" Shem crossed his ankles and leaned back on the cushion. "I seem to recall a shop there that carried different types."

Noah looked up from the drawing that had pulled him back to studying it. "Yes, I do recall such a shop. Why don't you travel there and purchase as much as you can. Take a donkey with a cart to carry the load back with you."

"I will go tomorrow," Shem said.

Morning dawned. Zara greeted Sedeq, sending her off to sleep after she'd eaten, and saddled Shem with food for his journey to Jabril's City. Why Noah had sent him to travel alone, she could not understand, though she had asked him repeatedly the night before. He simply assured her that Shem would not be harmed. Zara did not share his confidence.

She watched Shem lead the donkey toward the path that led to Jabril's City, praying for his safety. Then she moved to the back courtyard to work on an indoor gardening system she'd designed after seeing the way light and rain might come through the long window of the ark. The rain would not reach the lower floors, but it could be collected into cisterns and used to meet many of their needs, including watering the plants.

She sat on the stone bench and picked up a clay planter Adataneses had created with holes for water to run out. They could use some of the leftover cypress wood to build an indented table to hold the planters and keep the water from soaking the floor of the roof, giving the plants enough moisture to thrive.

Adataneses sat beside her, examining her design. "I hope I didn't make the holes too big."

Zara shook her head. "I think they're just right. Get me some of the seeds from the cellar and some beans. I'll fill this with earth and then we'll see how well they grow. I can take this to the ark tonight when I stand watch. You can begin making more. I'll count how many will be needed before I'm done."

Adataneses left to gather the seeds, and Zara filled the container with dirt. The day was bright, filled with promise, but after they'd worked the morning away, an unsettled feeling came over her. Was something wrong?

She walked to the door where she had watched Shem leave that morning but saw nothing. She paced to the back of the house, but the women still worked at their jobs. Even Sedeq was awake now and weaving again. Why did she feel so out of sorts all of a sudden?

She had turned away from watching the road and returned to the court when Keziah hurried from the gardens.

"What is it?" Zara stood at the urgency in Keziah's eyes.

"It's Abriyah. One of her servants met me in the fields just now. You must come." Keziah's breath came fast, and she accepted a skin of water Sedeq handed to her. "Thank you." She kept the skin and tied it to her belt.

Zara's heart pounded as she took another skin from Sedeq and left to follow Keziah. *Ima. What's happened?* Her mother had been healthy for so long, but of late she had not been to visit as often as she had in the past.

They crossed the fields and entered the town where her mother lived. Zara picked up her robe and ran ahead of Keziah, not stopping to knock on the door of her mother's house. She opened it and was met by a woman who helped her mother now and then.

"What's happened? Where is she?" Zara took a frantic glimpse of the room and headed to the area where her mother slept.

"She is not well, Mistress Zara." The woman touched her shoulder, causing her to stop and face her. "She suffered a malady in the night and has not awakened. Her breathing is shallow."

"But she is still breathing?"

"Barely." The woman's look was sympathetic. "She is dying, Mistress Zara."

Zara stared at her, disbelieving. Not yet. Surely not yet. She sensed Keziah behind her but did not look her way. She moved forward into her mother's room and knelt at her side. Taking her mother's hand in hers, she found it cold.

Fear coursed through her. She leaned close. Was her mother truly still breathing? Relief filled her at the slight rise and fall of her chest.

"Ima?" She spoke softly, next to her mother's ear. There was no response. She pulled up a chair and sat beside her mother, taking her hand again between both of hers. "Is it truly your time to return to the Creator, Ima?" She fought tears. She knew this day would come, but was anyone of any age ever ready to see their mother pass into eternity?

Keziah and the other woman entered the room. Zara looked up. "Has someone told my father? He is working on the docks of the Euphrates, unless he is helping Noah at the ark site. I cannot remember."

Keziah stepped forward and cupped Zara's shoulder. "I will find someone to go to him. Don't worry, Ima Zara."

Zara nodded, too overcome with emotion to speak. She had not expected this kindness from Keziah but gladly welcomed it.

She looked at her mother's helper after Keziah left. "I'm afraid I've forgotten your name."

"I'm Nahia. I don't usually stay with your mother all day, just to help with things she cannot do. But if you need me . . ." Her voice trailed off.

"I need you to stay until more of my family can come." Shouldn't her need have been obvious? "I can pay you."

Nahia brightened at that, and Zara held back a sigh. Whatever had happened to helping a neighbor out of kindness, not just for payment? "I do not have the payment with me, but I will get it once my father arrives."

Nahia nodded. "It is no worry. Tell me how I can help you."

Zara sent her for clean water and rags to place over her mother's forehead. Time stilled as she watched her mother breathe, silently praying.

Adonai, could You give her a little more time? I'm not ready to lose her. I have no one to talk to about You, about my struggles with the family or the people who mock us. Ima understands . . .

She let the prayer fade at the sound of voices. Footsteps grew louder, and she released her mother's hand, placed it on her chest, and stood. She met her father at the door of the room and embraced him. "Abba."

He held her close, and she rested her head on his chest, wondering when the last time was that she'd done that. Her father was not a demonstrative man.

"How is she?" He held her at arm's length.

"Her breathing has grown more shallow since I arrived. I don't think she has long."

The realization came with a peace she had not expected. Her prayers for her mother's healing would not be answered as she'd hoped, but she believed she would see her again. The Creator had made them to be eternal beings, and she knew that one day they would be with Him in a different place.

Her father released her and moved to his wife's side. Zara stood beside him, and soon Noah, Japheth, and Keziah joined them. The others remained behind to keep watch on the ark and the house.

"I should have been with you more." Her father's choked words filled the crowded room. "I spent too much time on the water."

Zara touched his arm, but he broke down and wept despite her attempt at comfort. A moment later, Abriyah breathed her last.

Zara's tears came unhindered then, and grief filled her as she forced herself to send the men from the room and then worked with Keziah and Nahia to prepare her mother for burial. The men left to build a bier to carry to a cave outside the city.

Twenty years were left until God judged the earth, and her mother was the first of her generation to pass on. Zara knew more grief was coming.

Chapter
13

They buried Zara's mother that evening, before Shem returned from Jabril's City. Noah invited Rake'el and the others who had gone to the cave to return to their house to eat. Neighbors brought food, and families who had stayed away, including those of his daughters-in-law, showed their support. The thought should have comforted him, but he doubted their concern would last.

He watched the women, particularly Vada, surround Zara, as Rake'el wandered outside to the courtyard. The man did not enjoy the confines of a house. He would have no need to return to his own house now except to possibly sell it.

Noah followed his father-in-law and joined him before a fire that burned in a hearth. They sat in silence for a lengthy moment. Rake'el cleared his throat and spoke in a hushed voice. Noah strained to hear him.

"I should not have left her for so long. In the end we barely knew each other anymore." Rake'el drew a hand through his hair, setting it askew. "Did she even know I loved her?"

Noah had often wondered that very thing. "I'm sure she

knew you cared. She was a strong woman. She did well on her own." He hoped it was the truth.

"Don't flatter me, Noah. We both know I'm a stubborn old man and too selfish for anyone's good." Rake'el leaned forward, elbows on his knees, staring at the fire.

"We are all selfish from time to time. Some of us struggle with it more than others." Did Zara see him the way she saw her father? She *had* complained to him a time or two that Rake'el could spend more time visiting and staying with her ima.

Rake'el nodded. "You speak truth." He looked at Noah. "Do you think this is why the Creator will judge the earth? I don't want to be swept away in a flood. I've seen the damage the rivers can do when a wind kicks up. I hope you're making a place for me on that ark of yours."

Noah met his gaze, surprised at the request. "I am sure we can make room for you. You've seen the size of the ark."

"I still wonder why the Creator asked you to build it in the middle of a field. But yes, it is large enough for one more person, I think. But what of your parents and Methuselah? And aren't there others in the family who still believe?"

Noah shrugged. "No one has said so except my parents and Methuselah. But we know that the judgment will come when Methuselah dies."

Rake'el leaned back, his look thoughtful. "Perhaps we will all die before that time." He glanced into the deepening darkness. "I hear footsteps, like the clomping of a donkey."

Noah stood. "Shem must finally be home." He hurried through the gate, Rake'el on his heels, and met Shem as he appeared beneath the torchlight.

Shem pulled the turban from his head and shook it out.

"You're back." Noah looked at the empty cart and the donkey but saw no bags hanging from its sides. "Without the resin you went to secure?"

Shem patted the donkey's head. "It's been a long journey.

We were first stopped by the Watchers who blocked our path, then questioned by the Nephilim before we could enter Jabril's City, then the owner of the shop refused to sell to me despite my gold. We were clearly not welcome there, and he questioned me thoroughly about my reasons for purchasing resin. I wanted to lie, but I just couldn't." He gave Noah a sheepish glance. "I told him the truth, and he told me to leave."

"But you were gone all day. If they sent you away so soon, where did you go?" Noah studied him, fearing that it was going to get harder to acquire the supplies they needed.

"I went to another city and met with more trouble on the way. Large rocks we couldn't get around in the path, fallen trees. I had to take longer paths. In the end, I gave up and turned around. I will take the donkey to Saba Lamech in the morning." Shem looked from Noah to Rake'el. "Wait. Why are you here?" He glanced beyond them to the house glowing with light and filled with the sounds of many voices. "Did something happen that we have so many visitors?"

"Savta Abriyah left the earth to be with the Creator today. We have just come from burying her. I invited the family and friends who came to join us here." Noah took the donkey's reins. "Saba Lamech is here. We can let him take the animal home with him."

Shem followed Noah around the house, where they tied the donkey. He turned to Rake'el. "I'm sorry about Savta. I know you loved her." He placed his hand on his grandfather's arm.

"Thank you, my son."

Noah led them back to the front courtyard, where it was quieter. "We are still going to need resin for the ark," he said to Rake'el. "Do you think you can get it for us?"

"Of course. I will sail across the river to a city that will not have heard much of you. I won't tell them why I need it. They will think it's for my ships." Rake'el's face brightened, as though this purpose gave him something to do besides grieve.

"Do you need me to go with you?" Shem asked.

"I need you here, my son." Noah met Rake'el's gaze. "That is, if your grandfather can manage without you."

Rake'el nodded. "I have many men to help me. Don't worry. You will have your resin as soon as I can set sail."

Noah thanked him as Shem went into the house to greet the others. They were meeting a lot of opposition, but he was not surprised. If God wanted this ark to be built, He would make a way.

Zara walked from one end of the ark's roof to the other, trying to see where she might place planter boxes to grow food beneath the canopied window. With only a single oil lamp and the light from the moon, she watched the area surrounding the ark for any trouble.

It would have been nice to light the entire area with torches, but the Watchers or saboteurs could use them to try to set the ark ablaze. They could also bring their own fire, of course, but Noah did not want to give them any help should they consider it.

Zara stopped to peer into the deep darkness, then moved to another section of roof and did the same. When she had completed a round of checking, she focused again on the planters Adataneses had built. The beans had begun to sprout, so she lifted the skin of water at her side and liberally watered them. She would wait to see if the sun came through well enough to make them grow.

The roof was large enough to hold many planters. She was counting out the space, measuring with her feet, when she heard a strange sound in the distance. Hurrying to the opening beneath the roof covering, she looked in the direction of the sound. Light came from the city. Many lights. Torchlights.

Her heart pounded as they moved closer, encroaching on their land. She counted ten torches. Enough to do significant

damage to the ark if they were able to catch it on fire. She
rushed to the signal and blew hard into the ram's horn. A loud
blast sounded. She blew again. And again. Her breath came
fast, but she did not stop until she had sounded the alarm ten
times. One for every torch, though she was not sure Noah
would realize her reason. The whole city could be awakened
by the noise, something she didn't want, but perhaps some of
her family would come to help.

She watched the approaching crowd and glanced toward
the house, praying, *Please protect this ark You commissioned
Noah to build. Don't let them be able to set it on fire. Send Your
angels to help us.*

She wasn't sure where the idea to pray for the angels' protection came from, but if the Watchers could fight against them,
perhaps God's holy angels could fight for them.

The torches drew closer, nearly upon her now. In the distance, she could see torches also coming from the house. The
men were coming. Would they make it in time?

She suddenly wished she had a pile of rocks to throw down,
something to stop the people from coming closer. Why hadn't
they thought of that? Was she safe to stay here, or would it be
better to leave to help the men?

But she would never make it to the door in time. She paced
from one edge of the roof to the other, straining for a better
glimpse of those coming toward her. Shouts sounded, and she
thought she recognized Noah's voice, but it was hard to tell
from this distance.

The men from town advanced, and as she'd feared, they
tossed their torches at the ark, aiming for the scaffolding. If
she didn't leave and the scaffolding burned, how would she
ever get off the ark? The door was too high off the ground to
jump down from.

Fear filled her. She gripped the ledge beneath the roof, silently praying.

Noah and her sons arrived, and the other men fled, leaving their torches behind to burn.

"Run to the creek for water. Send the women to help." Noah battled the flames with his tunic, and Shem did the same as Ham and Japheth ran off for water.

Zara left her post and raced down the ramps to the levels below. She reached the door, out of breath, and opened it. Flames shot up from below her, the smoke choking her. She shut the door behind her and raced through the smoke down the scaffolding to reach the earth below.

Once she touched the ground, she removed her robe and began beating back the flames with Noah, coughing and covering her face with her headscarf. Her sons and daughters-in-law soon returned with water and rags, and together they battled the flames, returning to the creek several times for more water.

Hours later, the last smoldering spark died out. Noah sank to the earth, and Zara joined him. They looked up at the damage, though it was hard to see in the moonlight.

"They damaged much of the scaffolding." Noah brushed soot from his face. "But the ark looks intact. I am very glad of that."

"We can look around it now, Father, or wait until morning." Shem leaned forward, hands on his knees.

"We can wait. Dawn is almost here. Let us go to the creek and wash. Then we will try to sleep." Noah pushed up from the earth and offered Zara his hand. "Come home. No one can climb into the ark now. Not until we rebuild the scaffolding."

She nodded, too weary to speak. The angels had not come to help them, and every bone in her body screamed to rest. Her rooftop gardening experiment would have to be started over another day.

Chapter
14

The following morning, Zara walked with Noah and the rest of the family to inspect the ark. Her heart skipped a beat at the memory of the trauma of the night before. "The scaffolding is definitely too damaged to reach the door," Noah said. He had led them around the entire structure and found it still intact. But the work on the inside would be impossible until they rebuilt the scaffolding. "I'm surprised you were able to make it out before the flames reached the door." He looked at her and took her hand, cradling it between both of his. "You could have been seriously hurt."

She warmed to the concern in his gaze. "I did fear I wouldn't get out. I think that spurred me on." She leaned against him as they both surveyed the damage. "Why didn't God protect the work? It is His project, after all."

Noah's arm came around her as their sons and sons' wives surrounded them. He looked from one to another. "God did protect the ark. We can thank Him for that. We are just delayed in finishing the inside, but the Creator is not surprised by the delay. He won't send the flood until we're finished. And He spared all of us. We can be grateful for that as well."

"It's not going to be a quick job to rebuild this." Ham pointed to the lower portion, which was totally destroyed. "Is there a way to rebuild it so that it won't burn if they try again? Perhaps we could pile rocks high enough to reach the door and lay planking on top."

Noah ran a hand over his beard. Zara leaned away from him and walked over to the charred logs. She bent low and lifted ash from the earth. Only a few of the upper logs that had fallen were still usable. They would have to have more wood brought in again. A tedious process.

"It would take longer to find enough large rocks and have them moved here than it would to have logs felled and brought to us," Noah said. "The scaffolding is simply too tall for rocks, as we have no way to mount them high enough. We might as well use brick and mortar and make it a walled-in structure." He shook his head. "I suppose either way, it is simply going to take time." He stepped closer to the ark and knelt beside Zara. "It's a loss I didn't expect, but we have suffered loss before. We must deal with it."

"I wish we had thought to make the scaffolding out of sturdier wood from the start." Ham joined them along with his brothers.

"We can get started clearing this away now," Japheth said. "I will contact Adataneses's brothers to get more wood. Unless you're serious about building a brick-and-mortar wall?" He looked at Noah as he stepped over the charred ruins. Shem helped him lift a log from the ash and carry it away from the ark.

Noah stood, Zara with him. "We will build a trough around the ark and fill it with water. It will make a barrier to slow them down next time, and we will be able to put out any future fires more quickly. We already have the plans to use wood. I do not want to take more time to create plans and find supplies to brick this in."

"It would help to keep a pile of rocks on the roof." Zara picked up a rock in the dirt. "Like this. I could have thrown them down on those approaching. It might have helped."

Noah nodded. "Yes. We should have planned for weapons to defend the ark. I didn't think it would come to this, but I should have realized. People are growing more hostile toward us."

Voices sounded in the distance, coming toward them. They turned as one to see who approached. Zara clutched the stone, ready to defend them if need be. But a moment later, she dropped it. Noah's father Lamech led Noah's and Zara's brothers and their sons.

"We heard talk in the markets today that some men had set the ark on fire." Lamech stopped and surveyed the damage. "What happened?"

Noah filled him in on the events of the night before. "No one was hurt and the ark itself is fine. Just this." He pointed to the rubble.

"We came to help you." Lamech glanced behind him. "We will help you clear the area. Tell me what you need and we'll make sure you get it."

Zara's emotions rose, and tears stung her eyes. This was not something she'd expected. Despite the knowledge that Noah's father believed, she was never sure what their brothers and sons thought of the Creator. No one talked about Him much, in spite of Noah's and Methuselah's preaching.

"I thank you, Father. I thought we would be on our own since we have been facing so much opposition." Noah embraced his father and kissed his cheeks.

"We know you are doing the work the Creator gave you to do," Lamech said. "Your mother and I have always known that you were born to bring us comfort in our labor, and to see you fulfilling your purpose is reason enough to help you." He signaled to the others to get started. They joined Noah and Zara's sons and began clearing the damaged area.

"Japheth, go ahead and find Adataneses's brothers. It looks like we will need that wood sooner than we thought." Noah turned to the women. "Do you think we could find enough food to offer our family for helping?"

"Definitely." Zara walked toward the house, their daughters-in-law following. "We can quickly make flatbread and some sauces to go with it. Let us offer them a feast that will make them glad they came." It was not nearly enough to repay the kindness.

Kindness. Such a rare quality these past many years. Could the people they'd prayed for at last be rethinking their actions and unbelief?

Please, Adonai. Let this be the start of a new dawn of faith.

Much to Noah's surprise and relief, the rebuilding project advanced quickly, and within the month they had returned to working inside the ark. The cages they had kept in the store-house were brought to the ark, while others were constructed on-site. They fitted one wooden cage with iron mesh sides to another, then connected a walking bridge above them with chutes to carry food and water through tubes to the troughs below.

Noah called his sons together. "We need to build the waste removal system next. Ham and I have drawn up the plans for it. Follow me." He led them to the rear of the boat, where they had put in a moon pool that would let water in and circulate the air throughout the ark. "Another pool can be added to dump waste out of the ark into the waters, which will carry them away. We can add bamboo pipes from each of the cages to carry the liquid waste directly to a collection tank. The pressure from the waves and a suction device will force the waste through a shaft here"—he pointed to an area next to the moon pool—"and into the sea. Then if we put slatted floors in the bottoms of the cages, the animals' waste will either fall or be pushed below. We can more easily collect it and use a conveyor system to force it into a different shaft and into the sea." Noah walked to the other side of the moon pool to show them where the shafts would be added.

"We will also need to build storage tanks on the roof to collect the rainwater so that we can keep a steady supply of fresh water for all on board." Noah pointed above them. "I think your mother can still have her garden there. The area is wide enough."

"How many storage tanks will we need?" Ham pulled his tablet from the pocket of his robe, ready to record.

"We will build them side by side the length of the roof. Calculate the roof's length and width and leave room on one side for the plants your mother wants, then build the tanks on the opposite side." Noah wasn't sure Zara's plants would actually grow there, but they could try. She had already designed an entire food storage, growing, and preparation area for the living area on the ark. It wouldn't hurt to try one more idea, assuming they could make everything fit.

"Adataneses's brothers said they should be able to get the bamboo for us for the pipes," Japheth said. "It is not the normal type of plant they supply, but since we will pay them well, they will gather whatever they can find. Fortunately for us, bamboo grows quickly, so if they can't find enough now, in less than a year they will have more." He took a stylus from behind his ear and jotted measurements on his small clay tablet.

"While we are waiting for that, why don't you make a list of the types of food each kind of animal eats? Some have become carnivores since the fall and others haven't. We cannot bring extra animals on board just to feed them to those that eat meat." Noah straightened the kink in his back and began walking to the floor above them.

"I can do that." Japheth quickened his pace to keep up with Noah. Shem and Ham followed behind.

"I think we should also gather herbs and recipes for healing the animals in case any of them grows ill." Shem's comment caused Noah to stop and face them.

"Yes, Shem, why don't you have Sedeq do that for us. She has a knack for healing, and we could use her skills."

"I will ask her." Shem glanced at Ham. "But doesn't Keziah prefer working with the plants?"

"Keziah doesn't know the medicinal properties of the herbs like Sedeq does. At least that is what your mother tells me." Noah looked at Ham. "Keziah will not feel slighted in this, will she?"

Ham scratched his chin. "I will talk to her. She does not understand the animals as well as the plants."

"Sedeq will be helping the animals, just using the plants." Noah waved a dismissive hand. "Everyone is going to have to learn to accept the help of others. We will take turns doing everything once we are all living here." He looked about them. "We are going to need a special room to nurse any sick animals and treat injuries. They will need to be kept from their mates while they heal."

"I can design that," Ham said. "Keziah can give me suggestions. She will like that." He looked uncertain, but Noah nodded.

"Good."

Completing these projects would take much time, and there were still other rooms to build. He must write down each thing they had yet to do, lest in his distraction with one he forgot another. He didn't want to leave anything of importance undone.

Chapter
15

Zara stood in the back courtyard, watching Sedeq sew yet another linen shroud to bury another family member. This time her father. Something she'd not expected, especially the manner in which he died. Shem's news still rocked her, and she could not shake the memory or the shock.

"Ima!" Shem's frantic voice had come from the road leading to the house. "Ima!"

Zara set the spindle aside and hurried through the house to the front courtyard. Shem reached her, out of breath.

"What happened? Is your father all right? Your brothers?"

Shem nodded, then shook his head. "Yes. No. I mean, they're all at the ark working. They're fine." He sank onto one of the stones and urged her to do the same. "It's Saba Rake'el."

Her pulse quickened, and she felt as though she'd been struck. "Tell me."

"He was coming off the docks and heading back to his house when a group of men attacked him." Shem placed a hand on her knee, holding her gaze. "They stabbed him. He didn't have a chance against them. Ima, he's dead."

Zara had sucked in a breath and leaned back, feeling the weight of a blow. Dead? Her strong father? How was this possible?

The questions still whirled in her mind as she looked from Sedeq to the distant fields, staring at nothing and everything. She had heard of murder happening in distant cities. Cain, of course, had killed his brother soon after the fall. And murder had become commonplace in certain towns, certain unsafe places. But not on the walk from the Euphrates to her father's house. The Watchers sometimes moved about those areas, but they didn't kill the humans. Humans took the lives of their own. But her father?

Why, Adonai? I knew he would die one day, but why this way?

She looked at the canopy above them, but no answer came to her from the heavens. Would any of their parents' generation join them on the ark? Other than a few aunts and uncles, Noah's father Lamech and grandfather Methuselah were the only ones left who believed. Noah's mother had gone on to live with the Creator years ago, as had most of the older generation.

"Ima Zara." Adataneses touched her shoulder, jolting her out of her grief-stricken stupor. "Can I get you anything?"

Zara faced her. "No. No. I'm fine." *Just grieving.*

Adataneses looked her up and down. "You don't look fine. Perhaps a cool drink in the shade would refresh you." She coaxed her toward the house. Zara followed, her heart empty.

"We will have to provide food for those who come to the burial." Zara looked about the cooking area but had no energy to do anything.

"We don't have to. But if you think we should, Keziah, Sedeq, and I can handle it." Adataneses handed a cup of cool water to Zara. "Just rest a moment."

Zara accepted the water and nodded. "Something small

would be nice. Or Noah can just send them home. I'm not sure I'm in the mood to accept guests this time."

It had been different with her mother. She wasn't sure that comfort from family she'd had little contact with in recent years would help. She needed time alone with the Creator. Time to think or not think.

"I will talk to Noah to see what he wants us to do." Adataneses paused. "Will you be all right while I go to see him?"

"Yes." She waved a hand toward the door. "I will be better in a moment. I don't honestly know why I'm so troubled by this. We know the violence has worsened with time. But this is the first time it has come so close to us."

They'd been threatened and sabotaged, but no one had been killed. How did one get past this? The fact that her father believed in the Creator helped. Surely she would see him again one day.

"I'll go then." Adataneses glanced at her one more time, then headed out to find Noah.

Zara sat in silence a moment longer. She must force herself out of this stupor. More people would likely die before the flood, and the rest would die in the flood if they did not come to the Creator and believe. She must do more to convince those who were left in her family. In the families of her daughters-in-law. She wasn't sure she could bear the loss of everyone except her husband and children. Despite all their planning and preparation for that very thing, the thought was unfathomable.

Several months passed after Rake'el's murder with no closure, no justice. The violence only intensified, and none of the magistrates or leaders of Seth's City seemed capable of holding it in check. The realization troubled Noah, but the work must continue. Time did not stop to allow him to consider what he could not change. He could not allow himself to grieve, as Zara did.

He finished pounding the last brace into the final cage for the animals and tied the cages together in rows. The walkways to feed and send water down the troughs to each cage were finally completed, and the systems for waste, air filtration, and water collection were all in place. They had to finish the extra rooms and fill them with the tools, writings, food, and supplies they would need, but the major components to care for the animals were done.

He straightened, admiring the work, then walked the length of the second level. He found his sons waiting for him.

"We finished our work." Japheth smiled. "The ark is complete, Father. Just as God commanded you to build it."

"Yes, and now we can concentrate on purchasing or making the items we will need to keep things repaired, if need be, and to begin a new life in a new world." Shem ran a hand through his dark hair. "I, for one, am glad this part is finished. I think the rest will be easier."

"I've got the drawings for the other rooms sketched out." Ham patted the tablet sticking out of the pocket in his robe. "How soon do you want to start on them? I don't suppose we can take time to rest now that the harder work is done?"

Noah motioned for them to walk with him toward the door. "We can take a few days. But work is good to keep us from falling behind and from dwelling on our losses."

They followed him out of the ark and closed the door.

"It's my turn to keep watch tonight." Shem stopped at the landing outside the door.

Noah turned the key in the lock and walked down the planking toward the ground. "You can come back when it's dark. No one is going to be able to get inside, and I think we can enjoy a meal tonight without fear. At least, I hope so."

Shem hesitated a moment, then followed. "Ima still grieves

Saba Rake'el. I wish we could find the person responsible and hold him accountable."

"There is no one who would judge him. The judges in this city are as corrupt as the rest of the leaders. What good would it do?" Noah glanced behind him at Shem.

"It would give Ima and all of us closure, I think." Japheth fell into step with Shem while Ham walked with Noah toward the house.

"We will have to accept closure from the Creator. God is going to judge the earth, and Saba Rake'el is no longer here to suffer at the hands of evil men." Noah glanced at the sky. Five years remained to reach the one hundred and twenty years God had initially given. "We have little time left to preach to those who will listen and to complete the work to make the ark our home. We don't know how long we will be living on it."

"Has God told you how long the waters will flood the earth?" Shem stepped closer to Noah. "Sedeq asked me the other day, and I was not sure how to answer her. I don't think you ever told us."

"That's because God has not told me. He will send a flood to cover the entire earth, even the mountains. That will take time. I suspect it will take even longer for the waters to recede once the rain stops." Noah reached the edge of the fields bordering their house and stopped. He faced his sons. "I think we need to be prepared for the possibility that we could spend at least a year aboard the ark. And remember, everything will be destroyed. I doubt we will be able to recover things like tools or books or gems or anything that is now built. Cities will be destroyed. We must be sure to preserve the technology and the writings for making things we don't know much about, for future generations and for help in rebuilding the earth."

"The thought is daunting." Concern filled Shem's gaze. "There is so much information in the libraries in the various cities. We can't just go in and take the writings. And it would take years to copy it all."

"I've begun to copy it," Noah said. "I started when God told me we had one hundred and twenty years. It is daunting, but not as bad as you think. I just want us to be sure I've not missed anything."

"I will visit the library in Seth's City tomorrow." Ham lifted the stylus from behind his ear. "I can bring home anything new once I look over what you already have."

"And I will make a list of what is needed for the metallurgy room, the woodworking room, and the pottery room. Adataneses can help me with that one." Japheth glanced at Shem. "You can set up the blacksmith shop and the area where the women can continue to weave and spin."

"I'm sure Sedeq would like to keep that near our living area." Shem nodded at Noah, who turned again toward home.

His sons continued to discuss how they would arrange each needed area, while Noah's mind whirled with thoughts of reaching the rest of their family who did not believe. He'd tried to persuade people whenever they had come to scoff, and he'd gone into the cities to preach in the squares. Methuselah had grown so old that walking to the square was no longer an easy task. Did his grandfather count the days until he could at last rest with his fathers?

If Noah could show even a few of the people something the Creator had done and convince them that the lies of the Watchers should be abandoned and the Creator again embraced, he would be grateful. How hard could it possibly be to believe? All one had to do was look at the heavens or creation and see that they were not here by accident. Humans did not just suddenly appear without purpose.

But most of the people suppressed the truth because to accept the Creator meant they were accountable to Him. And that meant they could not continue to live as they pleased but must live to please Him. To love Him. To serve Him.

Instead, they'd exchanged the truth of the Creator for lies,

JILL EILEEN SMITH

and they worshiped things their own hands had made or worshiped the creation instead of the Creator. It made no sense.
How had they fallen so far?

Noah most definitely must continue to preach the truth. He
must plead with them to reconsider and come to their senses.
He must do something before time ran out and he could do
no more.

Interlude

I had no idea what life would be like living on the ark, though as the years passed, we found ourselves isolated from much of the world. No one wanted to associate with us, and whenever Noah preached of righteousness and judgment to come, no one listened. People continued to live however they pleased. Young families sacrificed their children to a god they had created. Men and women came together in unions outside of the Creator's bond of marriage, and violence increased in every city, even the one that once belonged to Seth, the son of Adam.

I missed the family who had gone on before me, most recently Lamech. Had he truly been gone five years? Time seemed to move faster the closer we got to the end.

I also missed the friends of my youth. It saddened me to think that what God had said was true. People had turned away from Him to think evil all the time. It appeared there would be no turning back.

Was there truly no hope for the world?

Chapter
16

2200 BC

Zara walked among the trees bordering their fields in the early moments before the break of dawn. Sedeq had joined her, each one enjoying the quiet before the birds chirped their greetings and the sun rose to kiss the horizon.

"I love this time of day." Sedeq pointed to the canopy above them, newly visible in the growing light. "I feel closer to the Creator when the day is fresh and new."

Zara smiled. "Now you know why I so often seek time alone here." She patted Sedeq's arm. "Though I am very grateful to have you join me."

They continued along the path leading toward the ark, and at last it came into view. "I rarely see it in the early light, but I must say the size is impressive from any angle and any light." Zara stopped, spotting Noah and Shem at the base of the scaffolding. Japheth and Ham were already at the door, entering the ark.

"They got an early start today. I suppose we all did." Sedeq linked arms with Zara. "I hope my mother comes today to hear Noah preach. I haven't seen her in so long."

"I know you miss her. I hope you can see her again before we have to board the ark." Zara missed Vada too, though she rarely admitted it even to herself. Time had changed Vada, and nothing had moved her from the idols she had created.

"Shem has seen Dalton on occasion in the city, but my sisters do not attempt to contact me. I've heard their husbands forbid it." Sedeq released Zara's arm and continued walking toward the ark.

Zara followed, her heart burdened for Sedeq. The families of the girls had caused each one of them so much pain, forsaking even the normal familial ties that should have been. All because they considered Noah crazy for building a giant ship in the middle of a field. When she thought about it that way, though, Zara had to admit the attitudes of the people made sense. Sometimes even she wondered if they were doing the right thing. In those quiet moments before sleep claimed her, she pondered it all and questioned whether Noah had truly heard from the Creator.

But of course he had. She had known Noah all her life, and nothing in his character told her that he was one to hear strange voices or attribute a visit from the Watchers to the Creator. Noah knew the difference.

The men and women of the world did not, though. All they could see was what they looked at with their physical eyes.

She looked up from the path to see Shem waving them closer. Sedeq rushed into Shem's open arms, and he lifted her and swung her about, laughing. He kissed her nose, and Zara smiled. How good it was to see her children loving their spouses. They would need that love and much grace once they were confined to the ark.

She reached Noah, who stood examining the ark.

"It's ready." He faced her. "There is nothing left to do but carry the belongings we're still using into the ark and wait for God to send the animals to us. This is the year of judgment, and it will be here soon."

Zara's heart skipped a beat as the reality of his words sank in. Soon. How soon? "Will you preach again today?"

Noah nodded. "I have heard that a crowd is coming to see the ark now that we've announced it is finished. They'll come to mock us, no doubt. Or marvel at the monstrosity we have spent so many years building for no obviously good reason."

"People have said so for years. This is nothing new." Zara turned at the sound of distant voices. "I think they're already coming."

Noah faced the path leading to the city. A handful of people were walking toward them. Noah stepped onto the scaffolding and walked higher, Zara joining him. Shem and Sedeq followed. The higher platform would allow Noah's voice to carry.

Soon a group of about fifty people stood at the base of the ark, laughing.

"So when are you going to go ahead and live on that thing, Noah?"

"Yeah, your waterless ship is finally done with no place to go."

"Think of all the resources you've wasted, old man. You should be charged for the harm you've done to the earth."

The shouts continued. Zara glanced at Noah, who stood in silence. At last, when the voices calmed, he held up his hand. The crowd quieted.

"I know you think this ark is a foolish undertaking. You also do not believe me when I tell you that a flood is coming to destroy the whole earth."

Laughter erupted again, with more mocking.

"Sing a different tune, Noah. We're tired of this one."

"He doesn't know anything else. For as long as he's lived, you would think he'd know better by now."

Noah leaned closer to Zara. "Perhaps you and Sedeq should go home. Or inside the ark."

Zara shook her head. "I'm not leaving you."

He nodded and raised his voice. "The time is very short now." To Zara's surprise, the crowd quieted once more. "I urge you to consider the Creator's warning. Turn from your evil ways. Embrace the truth that there is a Creator and He has the right to do as He pleases with His creation. We are important to Him. He does not want anyone to perish in this flood. You have the chance to join us on the ark when God calls us to enter. Simply believe Him and obey His words."

The crowd waved dismissively, turned about, and walked away.

Zara spotted Vada hanging back as the crowd thinned, holding a child in her arms.

"Sedeq!" Zara called up to her daughter-in-law as she hurried down the planking toward the ground. "Vada." She came alongside her friend. "You came."

Sedeq quickly joined them. "Ima." She offered Vada an awkward embrace, enclosing the child between them. "Who is this?"

"Lagina's son." Vada bounced him on her hip. "I thought by now you would have given me grandchildren."

Zara winced at the accusatory tone, feeling the hurt for Sedeq. For whatever reason, God had kept her sons and daughters-in-law from bearing children, much as He had for her in the days she'd waited to bear her sons. Why, she did not understand, but she knew that one day they would bear children. Perhaps the Creator did not wish to give them the added challenge of raising infants and children on the ark.

"I will have them one day, Ima. The time is just not yet." Sedeq smiled and kissed the boy's cheek. "He is beautiful. Tell Lagina I said so."

"You could tell her yourself if you gave up this foolishness." Vada looked away, unable or unwilling to hold Sedeq's gaze.

"You could come with us, Vada." Zara stepped closer and placed a hand on her friend's shoulder. "It's not too late."

Vada looked up, and for the first time Zara saw a spark of longing in her eyes. Vada looked beyond her toward the ark, then focused on her grandson. "I am needed at home. Not on a boat with no place to go." She looked at Sedeq. "I came to see you one last time. You know you will be the laughingstock of the city and the whole world once the truth is evident and no flood comes. You will never outlive the shame of what you've done. Noah might even be arrested for all the wasted resources that have ruined forests and taken good crops to store for one family."

Zara stared at her friend. She shouldn't be surprised at the comments, but she couldn't stop deep sadness from filling her. *Please, Adonai, bring her to the realization of the truth, even if she finds it once the flood begins. Surely You can still have mercy then. Won't You?*

"I'm sorry you feel that way, Vada. We would welcome you and all your family to join us." Zara glanced at Sedeq, whose expression had stilled. She was holding back her emotion, but Zara knew it was there, just below the surface. How could her mother treat her with such coldness?

Then again, Vada had grown cold from the day Shem and Sedeq had wed. Why did Zara expect change? In all the years of waiting, Vada had made no attempt to include her daughter in her life.

"Raiden would scoff at the mere suggestion of joining you." Vada looked again at her grandson and smoothed the hair from his face. "Lagina needs me to help her with the children." She paused as if thinking of saying something more.

Zara waited, almost ready to turn away and go home, when at last Vada spoke again. She stepped closer to Sedeq and touched her arm. "I have missed you. If you get on that ark and the flood does come, don't forget me. Tell your children of

Chapter
17

Noah walked the length of the plot of land he had purchased seventy-five years earlier, searching the fields for any remnants of food. The grains, legumes, root vegetables, and nuts had been gathered and harvested the month before, the olives beaten from the trees, and the fruit plucked from the trees and the vines. Zara and their daughters-in-law had spent the past six months pressing the olives into oil, preserving and drying fruit, packing seeds into containers for future use, and creating a place on the ark to grow fresh vegetables beneath the window. Potted seedlings for trees and shrubs already lined a short section of wall near their living quarters, and every available space held food for the animals and containers of water to use until they gathered enough from the rainfall.

They were ready.

Noah released a deep sigh, glancing at the canopy of water suspended above him. Would those waters be part of the rain that would flood the earth?

He breathed in the air, grateful for this moment. How long

would he have left to walk on dry ground? A week had passed since the crowd had been there, and since then no one had bothered to come, despite the many people who had never seen the ark. Noah had taken a day to walk through Seth's City with Shem and Japheth while Ham kept watch at the ark, but no one spoke to them. Everyone they passed turned away.

He'd stopped to visit Methuselah, knowing it could be his last time, and found him lying abed, unable to rise.

"How long has he been like this?" Noah looked at his grandfather's caregiver, a distant cousin named Reatha, hiding the frustration he felt that no one had told him of his grandfather's condition.

"A few days. Not long." Reatha walked to a bowl of water, dipped a rag in it, and replaced the one on Methuselah's forehead.

Shem and Japheth surrounded the bed and knelt by Methuselah's side while Noah stood at the foot of his bed. "Saba?" He spoke loudly, and to his surprise, Methuselah stirred.

His eyes opened, and recognition filled his gaze. "Noah." His voice had grown raspier, his skin parchment thin. "The time is soon."

When he is dead, it shall be sent. It was the meaning of Methuselah's name—when he died, judgment would come.

"Yes, it is, Saba. Soon you will meet the Creator."

A smile formed wide over Methuselah's wrinkled face. "I have waited long for this day."

"Yes, you have." Noah pushed down his sudden emotion. If Methuselah was this frail, they would soon board the ark.

"We will miss you, Saba." Shem touched Methuselah's arm.

"You will join me soon enough." Methuselah closed his eyes for a brief moment, then met Noah's gaze once more. "I have done what I could to warn them. They did not listen."

"You did well, Saba. They did not listen to any of us." Noah walked closer and took Methuselah's hand.

132

"I want you to take the cylinder." Methuselah angled his head toward a chest in the corner of his room. He had inherited the cone of writings from his ancestors, passed down from Enoch. Noah had nearly forgotten it.

He motioned to Shem, who lifted the chest in his arms. "We will keep it safe for those who come after us, Saba."

Methuselah had closed his eyes, his mouth forming a slight smile.

Noah swallowed, saddened again by the memory. He shook the thoughts aside and continued walking, then stopped short as a brilliant light enveloped him. He fell to his knees, face to the ground. *Adonai.*

"Go into the ark, you and your whole family, because I have found you righteous in this generation. Take with you seven pairs of every kind of clean animal, a male and its mate, and one pair of every kind of unclean animal, a male and its mate, and also seven pairs of every kind of bird, male and female, to keep their various kinds alive throughout the earth. Seven days from now I will send rain on the earth for forty days and forty nights, and I will wipe from the face of the earth every living creature I have made."

Noah lifted his head for a brief moment, overcome with the sorrow he felt coming from the being who hovered just above the ground. *I will do as You say.*

A sudden burst of love filled everything around him, and a moment later the light vanished. Noah rose slowly, shaken, trying to regain his balance as he stood and readjusted to the earth's lesser light.

Seven days. Methuselah would live seven more days. They would board the ark and the flood would come.

Noah turned to head toward home. Forty days and nights of rain. What would that be like? He had no way of knowing, for the earth's mists had watered the ground every day of his life. Water had rarely fallen from the sky.

He quickened his pace. The animals would come to them soon. They still had much left to do.

Noah burst into the house and called out to all who were inside. "Is everyone here?" He looked about, spotting the women in the cooking area.

"The men are going through the building out back." Zara stepped forward and gripped his arms. "What is it? Have you seen the Creator?"

"Yes. We have seven days. The animals are already coming. As I hurried home, I saw the birds flying toward the ark in pairs, and the land animals will not be far behind." He moved to the back of the house. "Shem, Ham, Japheth! Come!"

They emerged one by one from the storage building, carrying a few containers that had yet to be taken to the ark.

Shem hurried closer. "What is it, Father?"

"The animals are moving toward the ark. Come with me at once. We must settle them in their cages. The birds are already waiting." Noah's heart pounded. He turned toward the women, who had gathered behind him. "Hurry! Gather everything left in the house. We will sleep on the ark tonight."

"So soon? I thought you said we had seven days." Keziah's eyes widened, and Noah saw fear in her gaze. "Wouldn't it be wiser to sleep here until we *have* to live there?"

"Why would we want to stay here another night?" Sedeq asked. She looked about the courtyard and snatched up a remaining water urn.

"I can't believe it's actually happening!" Adataneses looked from Noah to Japheth. "But I'm . . . I'm . . ."

"Afraid?" Zara asked, touching her arm.

Adataneses nodded. "I can't imagine living there. To not feel the earth beneath our feet . . ."

"The Creator said to go into the ark," Noah said. "We must

not keep the animals waiting. If we are there, we can better settle them as they come. This house has nothing for us any longer." Noah looked from one woman to the next. Were they having second thoughts? He offered them a comforting smile, though his own heart was racing. "Don't be afraid. Come!"

"You heard your father. Toss your concerns aside. It's time!" Zara whirled about and rushed into the house, the women following.

"Let's gather the last of the food. The sacks are in the storage building," Japheth said, running back to the building.

Noah ran after his sons, picked up a sack of grain, and tossed it over his shoulder. They would do the rest of their baking in the wood oven on the ark.

The ark. Everything God had told him was at last becoming a reality. His faith would finally be made sight.

Zara carried the last of the cooking utensils to the third floor, where they had built individual rooms for each person and a large cooking and food preparation area adjacent to them. Cages for the smaller birds lined a wall near the area where plants already grew, and a ladder reached to the window that would allow them glimpses of what was happening. The roof held a row of windows that spanned the length and breadth of the ark to ventilate it and collect water. She set the pots and ladles on the large table, then found room for them in one of the drawers and on a shelf below the table. She straightened, surveying the area.

Sedeq approached after adding the last of her personal items to her room. "I can't believe we're really going to sleep here tonight. Once people realize we are now on the ark, will they come again and taunt us until the rain comes?"

Zara placed an arm around her shoulders, and together they joined Adataneses and Keziah. "I think if anyone comes, they will be shocked to see that line of animals walking up the planks toward the door."

"I think you're right," Adataneses said. "Should we help the men settle the animals or prepare the food for ourselves?" She glanced behind them at the food area.

"I want to see the animals coming. There will be time to prepare the food later." Zara led them down the winding slanted wooden path to the floor below. They stopped near the door, where Noah stood. Japheth and Ham waited beyond him.

"Where is Shem?" Sedeq moved ahead of Zara, and as they looked down the passage into the distance, they saw Shem returning.

Noah stepped back as two young bears, male and female, slowly waddled through the door. Ham touched their heads and walked in front of them. They followed as though they knew exactly what to do. Two sloths came next, followed by young elephants and young wildcats.

Zara watched, entranced, as her sons simply touched the animals' heads and led them toward their cages. All were young, some barely old enough to be away from their mothers, and even the tyrannosaurs were small in comparison to how large the full-grown kinds could be. All walked slowly and peacefully, following her sons without turning to the right or the left.

"They are so quiet." She came alongside Noah, who continued to usher the animals through the door. "And so many are still coming."

"We've estimated fourteen hundred kinds and seven thousand individual animals, including the birds. We've loaded five hundred so far. We will keep working even through the night until all are on board." Noah glanced at her as two of the cattle kind moved past them. "If you don't mind, perhaps you can bring food to us so we can eat as we work. We won't have time to gather around the table tonight."

"I suspected as much." She focused on the long line of animals stretched beyond their property, all intent on climbing the scaffolding to the ark's door. "God is directing them." Her breath hitched. "I'm so glad He did not ask us to try to find them all. It would have taken us years."

"He knew we didn't have that ability. Some of these live in remote places or near the water but are land animals. They would have been impossible to locate, especially the kind that fly." Noah looked toward the interior of the ark, where Japheth had returned with Ham behind him.

"We can help," Adataneses said. She, Keziah, and Sedeq gathered near them. "Let us help settle the animals. We can finish sooner."

Noah looked at Zara.

"I don't need their help with the food." She faced the women. "Go ahead and do what the men are doing. We're all going to have to take turns caring for them. They might as well get used to us right from the start."

Noah touched her arm. "If you're sure."

"I'm sure." Zara looked out the doorway once more as the women fell in line to lead each kind to its cage. She searched the horizon and the distant area toward Seth's City, but no one came to watch this amazing spectacle.

They truly were alone now. They and the animals. After today they had six days to wait. If she'd ever had doubts that God was in this, the sight of these creatures silenced them.

Chapter

18

The men and women worked in shifts through the night, and yet the animals still stretched beyond the boundary of their land. Zara rose early to grind the grain to make flatbread for those who still worked.

"Let me help." Keziah yawned and tied her belt as she walked to the cooking area. "Ham said the animals are going to need to be fed and watered today, while we continue to settle those not yet on the ark."

"That's true." Zara handed the sack of grain to Keziah, who poured some into a second mill and began to grind. "Shem and Sedeq left early to tend to those on board, while Japheth and Adataneses are helping Ham and Noah continue to guide the new animals and birds to their places. I'm amazed that more birds and other flying mammals are still coming. It will take at least one more day to settle them all."

Keziah took the ground flour and mixed it with oil, then kneaded it into dough. "Some dried fruit and nuts would be welcome, I think." She lifted her gaze to Zara's, her expression more at peace than Zara had seen it of late.

Zara filled a bowl with raisins and almonds and set it aside. She bent to place the first loaves of bread into the cone-shaped oven. She had used it for the first time last night, relieved when she found that Noah and her sons had vented it well toward the roof, where the smoke would dissipate into the air.

"I will be glad when everyone is on board and we can shut the door and rest." Keziah brushed the flour from her hands and swept the rest from the table.

"I wonder how much rest we will get. With so many animals to feed and tend, I think we will have to make time to rest." Zara tucked a loose strand of hair behind her ear. "I want to see how many animals are still coming. I'm going to look out the window." She walked the short distance to the birds' cages, where the ladder stood affixed to the floor and upper railing.

Keziah followed close behind. "I would like to take a look as well."

Zara climbed up the ladder and leaned toward the window. "The view is not as good from here as it is from the roof or at the door." She looked at Keziah, then strained again to see. In the distance, she could make out the line of animals still coming, and as she turned toward the road to Seth's City, she saw a line of people coming their way as well.

She hurried down the ladder. "People are coming." She took Keziah's arm, and together they ran back to gather the bread and bowl of fruit and nuts.

"Do you think any of them will want to come with us?" Keziah sounded so hopeful. Did she still think her mother and sisters would change their minds? But of course she did. All the women wanted their families to join them.

"I don't know. Let us go and see." Zara did not expect anyone to change their mind at this late hour, but it would do no good to dash Keziah's hopes.

They walked quickly down the ramp to the level below and joined Noah at the door. Zara set the food on a shelf so the others could come and take some as they worked. She peered past Noah toward the line of people drawing closer.

"Have they said anything?" She met his somber gaze as he guided a pair of the horse kind toward Ham. Keziah took a quick look outside, then followed Ham down the long passageway. "She is hoping her family is among them."

Noah nodded. "It is the hope of us all. I have not heard them shouting their taunts yet. I think they came to see the animals."

Zara watched, still mesmerized by the sight of so many creatures walking toward them, drawn by God's unseen hand. The people drew closer but kept their distance from the wild beasts. They stood in silence, about fifty men and thirty women, if her count was correct.

"Should you say something to them?" Zara's gaze moved from the men to the women, then back to the planking where the animals came two by two.

"There is nothing left to say. I have preached my last to them, Zara. They know the truth. If they want to speak to me, let them. I will not silence them. But I cannot change their minds." Noah patted the hindquarters of a male hippopotamus kind as it passed by. The animal did not flinch or stop, the line moving in such rhythm that Zara shook her head in wonder.

"Do you think the animals will remain this docile once they are in their cages? Will we be safe to open the cages of the carnivores and those known to kill? Surely God will protect us and them."

Noah took a loaf of the flatbread she offered him. "I wish I knew. It would make our time with them easier, but the Creator has not told me."

Zara touched his hand. "Eat, my husband. You have been here nearly all night."

He nodded and ate a bite. "Thank you. I am weary, to be sure, but we will sleep once the door is shut and none are left behind."

"I'm glad we can lock the door." She hadn't worried about this before, but now, watching the faces of the people below, she wondered what would happen if some of them tried to enter and harm them before the flood came. "I still worry about the violent ones and the Watchers."

Noah placed a hand on her arm. "God will protect us better than any lock. When the time is right, He will shut the door and no one will enter."

"He told you this?"

"No. But I sense it. We will wait and see."

She stepped closer to the door, keeping her distance from the entering animals, and focused on the people below. She recognized Adataneses's brothers, but there was no sign of Keziah's sisters. Vada had not returned, nor had any others in Sedeq's family. "I do not see any of our cousins. I had hoped . . ." She let the words hang in the air between them.

He kissed her cheek. "Perhaps it is better to not watch them. They are curious, but they will not try to harm us now. I think they fear what the animals would do if they tried to throw rocks or set the scaffolding on fire again. You can help guide the animals if you like."

"I am not a child that I cannot handle watching our family and neighbors without worry and grief. You don't need to send me away."

Noah glanced at her. "I know. But I admit, I grieve to see them there and not here with us. I simply thought you would too." He placed an arm about her shoulders for a brief moment. "I don't mean to upset you, dear wife."

Zara's irritation fled at his admission. "No, you're right. I did not realize how hard it is for you. You have told them the truth for so long. I have told few people, and I wish I had said more."

"They had their lifetime, Zara. Perhaps God will still grant them the ability to believe during the flood. We cannot know."

He had said so before, and she had often prayed thus. But he was right. It did no good to fret now.

"I will go and see what needs to be done for the animals that are settled, then come and help guide the newcomers," she said. "And the birds need feeding. Unless Sedeq did so before she went off to help Shem." They must make a schedule to rotate the tasks, something Noah had only begun to do before God told him to board the ark.

Zara left him then to continue the work, with one last glance toward the people who had begun to drift back toward town. They had come to see what they'd wanted to see. She determined to be satisfied with knowing she and Noah had done their best for them. The choice to believe was still up to them.

Noah woke early. Four days remained until the flood came. He had slept fitfully, relieved that the last land animal and bird had found their way to the ark but anxious to see what God had for them in the days to come. Why did the future trouble him?

He rose, donned his day clothing, and headed to the roof, where he could look out over the land and see in all directions. He told himself that he was checking on the water troughs and the small garden Zara had built there. But a part of him waited for news about Methuselah. Would he live up until the very day the flood came, or would God take him in the next few days? When Methuselah died, should he attend the burial?

Conflicting emotions filled him as he watched the dawn awaken the earth. He searched the forests that bordered the land but saw no sign of humans or Watchers. He glanced at the heavens, yearning for another glimpse of the Creator.

Adonai? Should I leave the ark to bury my grandfather?

No voice spoke to him, nor did the Creator appear as he'd hoped, but a check in his spirit told him he should not leave.

No matter what happened. God had told them to enter the ark, and they were to stay there until God bid them to leave.

I will stay.

He would miss being there for his grandfather, but he had already said his goodbyes. He'd had six hundred years with Methuselah, who had been three hundred and sixty-nine years old when Noah was born.

He looked again toward the various cities. Seth's was just south of them, Jabril's to the west, Cain's to the east, and others to the north and farther south, though Noah could not see them all even from this height. How much would he be able to see once the ark rose with the water?

The anxious beating of his heart continued to trouble him, and he told himself to calm. Four more days. That time would help them to get their schedules in order and become better acquainted with the many animal kinds to best meet their needs. The days would pass before he knew it.

He took one last tour of the roof, searching the grounds. Satisfied that nothing would be left behind, he descended to the third floor, where Ham met him.

"Someone is coming up the planks to the door. Did you see him from the roof?" Ham walked with Noah as they quickened their pace to the door.

"No. I don't know how I missed him." Had this person come to join them? Had he waited all night for it to be light enough to climb the planks?

They reached the door and opened it as Payam, one of Adataneses's brothers, reached them. "I should have known you would see me coming."

"Why are you here?" Ham's tone did not sound welcoming, and Noah gave him a look of censure.

"I'm sure Payam has good reason." Noah crossed his arms. "Why have you come?"

"Methuselah has died. I came as a courtesy to let you know

143

since he was also my sister's ancestor. Will you come to the burial?" Payam glanced beyond Noah as if trying to look inside the ark, but there was nothing to see at the door.

"No. We will not attend, but thank you for telling me." Noah watched the man. "You do know what his death means."

Payam shrugged. "I know what you say it means. What he said it means. I guess we will see if this judgment of yours happens now."

"It's not too late to join us." Noah extended a hand and waved it toward the ark's interior. "You and your family are welcome. We can find room for any who want to come."

Payam shook his head, then laughed. "I'm not crazy, old man."

Ham stepped forward, but Noah restrained him.

"I can see I'm already unwelcome," Payam said. "I just came to deliver this news because for some strange reason I still care about my sister. But she's yours now. I wish all of you well when the whole world sees what fools you've been." He turned and marched down the planks without a backward glance.

Noah turned, pulled Ham inside, and shut the door. There was no sense in watching him go. The end would come now, and no one could stop it.

Chapter

19

Zara climbed with Noah to the roof of the ark to check on her plants, though her true reason was to look out at the land to see if anything had changed. If anyone had come. Three days had passed since Methuselah's death, and each dawn her heart beat fast in anticipation and a certain sense of dread.

"No one has come since Payam's announcement. I'm not sure why we keep looking." Zara glanced at Noah and came to stand beside him as he gazed out over the land.

"We have one more day. We must be willing to accept any who might yet change their minds." He took her arm and linked it through his, patting her hand. "One more day."

She released a pent-up sigh, searching the distance. Movement near the edge of the land caught her eye. "Do you see that?" She pointed toward the area.

Noah leaned closer to the window ledge and shaded his eyes against the angle of the sun. "I see men coming this way."

They watched in silence as the men, accompanied now by many women, approached the ark.

"Are those Nephilim?" She pointed again, though it was hard to miss the giants who towered above the others.

"And Watchers." Noah squeezed her hand. "They are with the humans. Toward the back."

"Should we call the others? They will want to see this." Zara slipped her hand from his and backed away. "I'll call down to them."

"They may not be here long."

"I'll hurry." She rushed to the stairs and took the steps down. "Everyone, come!" Footsteps soon followed her calls. "Join us on the roof. You'll want to witness this."

She returned to the roof with the others following behind. They spread out along the side of it, facing the growing crowd.

Zara joined Noah again. "Did I miss anything?"

He shook his head. "They just keep coming."

"Do they have fire with them? Are we in danger?" Japheth leaned close to Noah, worry lines along his brow.

"No. God will protect us from them."

The Watchers moved to the front of the crowd. They raised their dazzling arms high above them, and all at once the entire crowd bowed low before them, even the Nephilim.

"What are they doing?" Zara spoke softly, though no one could hear them from this distance.

"Worshiping the evil one and his cohorts rather than the Creator. They are making a statement to us, showing us whom they have chosen to believe. There is no doubt, at least among these people, whom they serve." Noah's solemn words were met with silence as all of them watched the spectacle below.

The voice of one of the Watchers bellowed loud enough for Zara to hear clearly. "Worship the created one, the ruler of this world, for he will deliver you from the lies of these people. In three days, you will know without a doubt that this man Noah has preached against you claiming judgment and doom, but it is he who will be judged and condemned once the time he has set for judgment has passed. We will storm the door of this ark and drag each one of them out. Then we will kill them all."

Zara's heart beat double time, and her sons clung to their wives.

Noah put his arm about her shoulders. "Do not listen to this being. He speaks of what he doesn't know. He is of his master, the father of lies. He speaks falsehood, and tomorrow all the earth will know the truth."

His words calmed her racing heart, but none of them seemed able to pull away from gazing at the crowd. When the Watcher finished his speech, a shout erupted from the people.

"Stone them all!"

"Burn it to the ground."

"No, let the animals go first."

"Let's drag them out now!"

Shem pulled Sedeq closer to Noah and Zara. "Is the door locked?" he asked. His voice held the fear Zara felt.

"The door is locked. They will not come up here." Noah did not sound as convincing as before, and Zara wanted to rush to the door and bar it.

But a moment later, the sky darkened and a bolt of lightning flashed from the canopy above them. The people below screamed and ran in all directions. The Watchers disappeared, but the darkness remained, blocking the sun.

"Is it beginning?" Ham pulled Keziah closer. "I thought we had one more day."

"We do. But God is giving them a warning." Noah turned away from the window.

"The sky is so dark!" Sedeq clung to Shem's arm, her voice barely above a whisper.

Keziah began to whimper, burying her face against Ham's chest. Ham gave Noah a helpless look.

Japheth moved to the edge of the roof and looked down.

"What are you doing?" Adataneses ran after him and grabbed his cloak. "Get away from the edge!"

Japheth stepped back, and she clung to him. He patted her back, exchanging looks with his parents. "Should we go below?"

"I want to make sure that door is locked. What if someone is climbing the scaffolding even now?" Shem kissed Sedeq's forehead, disengaged himself from her hold, and headed for the stairs.

"I'm coming with you." Japheth held Adataneses another moment. "Don't be afraid," he said to her.

"There is nothing to fear," Noah said, turning to join his sons. "Ham, Keziah, all of you, let's go below. We can check the door and be assured that God is with us. The warning has begun, but the rain will not start until tomorrow. Let us enjoy this last night of quiet before the rains pour down and the thunder fills our ears."

Zara looked at the women. "Noah is right. We have one more night to rest in quiet. Let's think about our God and trust Him."

Noah grabbed the latch and pulled, but the door would not budge. "I cannot open the door."

"Let me try." Shem took his turn, and each of his brothers did the same, but no one could open the door.

"God has shut us in. We won't be able to leave the ark until He opens it again." Noah sighed, peace settling over him. They were safe. He had obeyed the Creator, and now the Creator would keep His word to him. "Let us tend to the animals and make sure they're secure for the night. Tomorrow everything will change."

They separated then, two by two. Shem joined Noah as they climbed to the second floor to the bridge walkway above each cage.

"I'll take the animals on this side." Noah moved to the bridge on the left while Shem moved to the right. He poured food through the pipes into the holder that would automatically feed the animals for several days. He did the same with the water. Japheth and Ham had remained on the first level to handle the larger animals there.

It took several hours to feed each kind, then they took turns emptying the pipes through the hole that would eventually send the waste into the waters of the flood. For now, the waste landed on the earth beneath the ark.

Noah climbed the ramps to the top floor as dusk came through the window above them. The sky showed a brilliant blue and pink pattern in swirling beauty. Would they continue to see sunrises and sunsets through the window once the rains began?

"Your thoughts are far off, my husband." Zara touched his arm and coaxed him to the general sitting area, where the family had gathered for the evening meal. "Watching the sunset?"

"I wonder how the sky will change once the rains come. Will there be light or only darkness during that time? I was enjoying this bit of color in case we don't see it again for a while."

Zara watched with him for a lengthy moment, then took his hand. "The family is waiting to eat. Come."

Noah followed her toward the area where they had made a circle of cushions with a low table. He took the bread and broke it, bowed his head, and lifted the bread high. "Blessed are You, Adonai, Creator of heaven and earth, for protecting us from Your coming judgment. We are Your people and we worship You. Blessed are You for sustaining us with food to eat while we serve You on this ark. Keep us in Your care."

He opened his eyes and handed the loaf to Japheth, then another to Shem and Ham to share with their wives. At last he took one for himself to share with Zara.

"I am anxious to see how the Creator sends the waters in

the morning." Shem spoke around a bite of food. "I'm not sure I will be able to sleep tonight."

"Nor I." Japheth looked at Adataneses and smiled. "We may be up playing music on the flute and harp for a while."

"The rest of us might prefer you not do so too late." Noah chuckled. "Though I suspect we will all be restless until dawn." He was glad Japheth loved music and had thought to bring every type of instrument onto the ark. Future generations would need to know how to play them and be taught some of the good songs they had sung when the world praised the Creator.

"Should we be singing and making music on the last night before the whole world is judged?" Sedeq crossed her arms over her chest as though warding off a chill. "I understand wanting to forget what is coming, but all I can think of is my family, especially Ima." She swiped away a tear.

Adataneses leaned closer to Sedeq and reached for her hand. "You're right. We can also play dirges and songs of lament. They may help us . . . to grieve."

"What if Payam and the others are right, though?" Ham asked, frowning. "What if we discover there really will be no judgment? They will destroy us."

Noah held up both hands. "Did you not just hear the thunder and see the lightning scare off our accusers? Let us not give in to doubt or fear. Tomorrow God will show us just how serious He is." He looked at Sedeq. "But I share your sorrow, my daughter. And there will be time to grieve. I understand."

"It just seems so wrong," Keziah whispered.

Noah glanced at her, but she'd turned to face Ham, leaning close to him. Apparently, she did not intend to explain her statement. Was she questioning the judgment of God? He didn't want to know.

The conversation turned a corner and continued long into the night, each of them speculating on how God was going to bring the waters and what it would be like, until at last they returned to their quarters and attempted sleep. But Noah struggled to relax. He'd waited one hundred and twenty years for this day. Dawn could not come soon enough.

A boom shattered the silence of the predawn, jarring Zara from a fitful sleep. She bolted upright to find Noah already donning his robe.

"It's begun." She hurriedly dressed as boom after boom startled her. Lightning flashed through the high window, leaving darkness in its wake. Rumbling rocked the ark. Zara grabbed a protrusion in the wall and clung to it as the quaking continued.

Noah moved from the room, holding the walls as he walked. "The fountains of the deep are rupturing. We may experience the quaking until the waters rise."

Shem emerged from his room as Zara made her way to the hall between them. "Won't we continue to feel the swaying of the waters beneath the ark?" he asked. "The ships Saba Rake'el sailed moved with every wave."

"We built this to minimize the waves. We shouldn't face too much rocking once we rise above the earth." Noah glanced at Zara as the sound of rushing waters pounded the roof.

"It's going to be hard to hear above the noise." She raised her voice, feeling as though her own thoughts were marred by the rush of rain, water, thunder, and wind. What was happening to those she loved right now? Those who had refused to join them? Would God give them the chance to yet repent as she'd prayed? Emotion rose within her, and sadness over all who were lost filled her soul with an overpowering weight. She stood still for a moment to catch her breath. Below them the sounds of braying, baaing, trumpeting, neighing, and a cacophony of animals' voices drifted to them.

Noah motioned for all of them to gather in the eating area.

151

Zara managed to hold her desire to weep in check as she made her way to the food preparation room, pulled a bowl of nuts and dried fruit from a drawer, and placed them on the table.

"Let us eat a simple meal and see to the animals right away," Noah said. "They are obviously terrified, and it will take all of us to comfort them."

The boat tilted, then righted itself. Zara clung to the preparation table, thankful that they had planned ahead for this and fastened things down so they couldn't shift easily. If only she could keep her body from swaying.

They ate quickly as Noah pointed out the work and place each of them should take. The men left before they had finished eating, each one taking a sack of nuts as needed. Who knew how long it would take to calm the animals?

"I will feed the birds while you three go ahead and take the assignments Noah gave you," Zara said to the women. "Be sure to take a sack of fruit or nuts for yourselves as well. I have a feeling we will not be back here until the evening meal." She nodded to each one, then turned to retrieve the feed for the birds and fill each trough with food and water.

The roar of the wind and the continued bursting of the springs of the deep pummeled the ark. Zara finished feeding the last of the birds and glanced at the ladder leading to the window. No light could be seen from where she stood, but a longing to look at what was going on below drew her up the steps.

She reached the top and looked out. The once bright blue skies were black as night. Water came in a thick stream from the heavens, and she could see nothing but darkness in the distance. But the churning of the ground told her it was covered now with water. Even if someone had tried to reach them to come aboard, they could not have gotten through the waters.

A loud crash jolted her further, and she held onto the railing until her knuckles whitened. She'd seen enough. She made her way down the ladder, took her sack of food, and moved to the next floor to find Noah. Something had caused that crash, and she needed to make sure it was not something inside the ark. What would they do if their fastenings didn't hold?

She found Noah on the lower level, helping Japheth empty animal waste into the moon pool. "What was that crash I heard a few moments ago? Did something break?"

Noah finished dumping his barrel into the hole, set it aside, and straightened. "The scaffolding fell away from the ark. Can you not feel that we've lifted off the ground?"

Zara looked about her, grateful to see that nothing inside the ark had changed. Of course it was the scaffolding. Why hadn't she thought of that? She released a breath and drew in another long, steadying one. "I'm too shaken by the noises outside, and when I tried to look out, I could see nothing."

"You looked out the window?" Noah stepped closer and put an arm about her. "What did you see?"

"Nothing. Darkness. Water. I wondered if anyone would try to reach us once the rain started, but everything happened so swiftly that even if they'd wanted to, they could not have done so."

He looked sad, an expression she'd seen from him often during the years of building. "It was too late by morning. Perhaps some will call on the Creator even now. It is my constant prayer."

"I have been doing the same."

The Creator might yet have mercy as people tried to escape the flood. If they did not worship the Watchers and were uncertain, as Vada had seemed, perhaps though they died, they would not forever perish.

The thought lifted Zara's spirits as she left to help Adataneses check on the smaller animals. There was much to do, and perhaps some of the tame animals would allow her to give them comfort until they got used to this uncertain future.

Chapter
20

Rain pummeled the ark on all sides, waking Zara with the sound. She rose from her mat, though the level of darkness told her it was still night. Snoring came from Noah's room next to hers, but most of the animals were quiet below. Even the owls and other creatures that came alive in the night seemed focused on their new surroundings and the rising of the ark on the waters.

Zara moved to her sitting area, guided by a small lamp, and curled her feet beneath her on a large cushion. It was too dark to work on a project, but she pulled a scroll from a basket beside the chair and opened it to the place she had been reading. Some of the poets of old had recorded their words, and Ham had taken time to copy them from the library in Seth's City. This was one of the many books Noah had kept in the vast library he'd acquired during the building years. The words spoke of life on the Euphrates River aboard a ship, reminding her of the life her father used to live.

"Come along, Zara. The sun is nearly up." Her father had coaxed her from a pleasant dream. "If you're going with me, we must go now."

Zara scrambled to her feet, donned her clothes, and half ran to keep up with her father's long strides. They reached the dock as the sun was cresting the horizon. He met the other sailors who were already there, and Zara climbed aboard his ship and settled near the bow, waiting for them to push away from the shore.

Before long, the spray of the river dampened her face, and her father stood at the helm, controlling the ship. She'd begged for weeks to come with him, and he'd finally consented.

Looking back now, Zara wished she'd gone with him more often, to know him better. But she'd preferred her mother's gardens and helping her older siblings care for their children.

The gentle swaying of the ark and the memories made her long for one more chance to ride with her father on the river. He would not have enjoyed the enclosed nature of the ark. It was the open water he'd loved.

After the flood, would people ride on ships on open rivers and seas like they used to? Noah had taken care to preserve the technology for building everything from the smallest container to the tallest building to small ferries and large ships, and for anything else he thought they would need in the new world. But they could only take so much with them on the ark, and though they had purchased as many tools as they could, it would take time to find the metals and set up the ability to mine and smelt and forge all that they had taken for granted until now.

Did we bring enough? Did we leave something behind that we will miss?

It was too late now to go back. Noah had made extensive lists during the years of waiting, and they'd made or gathered all they could. They would have to trust the Lord to guide them on how to rebuild the earth. If they forgot anything, perhaps it was better left forgotten.

A week passed, and the rain still came and the ark continued to rise upon the waters. Zara lifted a skin of water and watched it dampen the earth beneath her potted plants. Behind her, Sedeq and Adataneses chopped onions and carrots and squash for soup. Zara clipped basil and rosemary from the plants and carried them to the large clay pot they had hung over a stone pit, which Noah had built to vent to the roof. She moved to the block and chopped the herbs into small bits, looking up as Keziah joined them.

"Are you feeling better?" Adataneses set her knife down and walked over to Keziah.

She shrugged but did not smile, something Zara had noticed for several days. Keziah had taken often to her bed, forcing the others to take up the work assigned to her. Zara had bit back her frustration on more than one occasion over this daughter-in-law's seemingly selfish attitude. Why was she acting this way?

"The swaying of the ark upsets my stomach." Keziah pressed her hand against her middle. "I never feel good, and the smell of the animals makes things worse. I want to go back." Her eyes filled, and Zara feared she would weep.

"We can't go back." Sedeq continued chopping. "Are you with child? Your symptoms sound like what my sisters described to me."

Keziah shook her head. "No. My cycle began again yesterday. I'm just weary and sad, and nothing is right." She turned as though she would go back to her bed.

"Don't go." Zara left the chopping block and came alongside Keziah. "Come and help us prepare the food. I'll go with you to do your tasks when we're finished. It's understandable that you would feel lonely. We all do. We are stuck here with the constant rain and no place to go except the three floors of the ark. We're all going to feel sad sometimes. We can't let that control us." Was she getting through to the girl?

Keziah stared into the distance as though Zara's words meant nothing. "I want *my* ima. My family should be here. We should have done something to make them come." She met Zara's gaze. "I shouldn't be here when they are not."

"Keziah, you know we couldn't *make* anyone join us," Sedeq said. "Even if they didn't believe us, they could have come just in case." She looked at Zara. "Couldn't they?"

Zara shrugged. "We couldn't make anyone do what they didn't want to do. Keziah, it is not your fault that your family did not join us. You mustn't blame yourself."

"I'm not blaming myself." Keziah's eyes flashed. "I blame Noah. I blame all of you!"

Zara stared at her, stunned. She glanced at Adataneses and Sedeq.

"You know we need your help, Keziah, and we can't change what's past," Adataneses said. "We can't survive on this ark without you. It takes all of us to care for each other and the animals each day." She touched Keziah's arm.

Keziah shook off her hold. "None of you are helping. Don't you understand? I don't want to be here! I hate the animals. They smell. I can't stand this swaying ark. I want to walk on the earth, not float on the water. I want to jump through the opening on the roof and drown with the rest of the people I care about most."

The shock on the faces of the other women was matched by Zara's pounding heart. Would Keziah actually do what she had said? How could she act like she'd wanted this life for years and now suddenly wish she had never left her parents' home? Or did she wish she had married another? Did she really think life here was so bad that she would rather drown?

Sedeq cleared her throat and grabbed another squash from the basket on the floor. "We are all going to feel helpless and want to escape this place from time to time. And all of us grieve our families. But Keziah, it's only been a week. We could be living here for a year! You really need to stop acting so selfish and step up and do your part. You can't get through the opening and jump into the water, and you know you really don't want to. So stop making us do your work for you and help us."

Zara's heart skipped a beat at Sedeq's sharp tone. She looked from one woman to another, partly grateful that Sedeq had the strength to speak up and say what they were all surely thinking, and partly afraid that Keziah, with her unpredictable moods, would grow angrier and more depressed. They couldn't force her to do her part, could they? Yet their survival depended on each one helping the others. The animals were completely dependent on them too.

Keziah frowned, glaring at Sedeq. "You have no right to speak to me that way. You have a husband who does anything you ask, who *cares* about you!" She swiveled her gaze to include them all. "None of you has to live with Ham or knows the things he tells me in private. He is not happy here either. He wishes we had never listened to Noah and joined you all!" She stomped off toward the lower level.

Zara felt as though someone had punched her in the gut. *Did* Ham truly feel that way? Was their youngest son sorry he had helped with the ark? Would he have preferred to remain behind with the rest of those who perished? The very thought made no sense. Ham had never revealed such opinions to her or to Noah. Wouldn't they have sensed it?

In the years since Ham had lost his first choice of wife, he appeared to have come to care for Keziah. He treated her well, at least when they were watching. Did Keziah speak the truth? Or had she spoken the words to anger and manipulate them all? To make Zara think somehow she had failed her son?

Did I fail him, Adonai?

She loved Ham as much as she loved his brothers. He was a good, helpful son. Keziah could not have spoken the truth. She was simply unhappy with living on the ark. And their life here had just begun. How were they ever going to survive a year or more—if that was what it came to—if Keziah didn't change?

Ham lifted the latch to allow grain to flow through the bamboo pipes to the cage of the hippopotamus kind, then shut it again when the holder was full. He walked to the jars of water they had stored, lifted one onto his shoulder, and carried it to replace the previous one. The start and stop valves had been a great design, something he looked on with pride and gratitude to the Creator for giving him the ability to think up such things. The technology was proving to do exactly what they had intended.

He released the water through the pipes to fill the trough, then opened another valve to allow the water and grain to enter the alligator kind's cage. He should finish in a few hours and have time to sketch one of the models for some of the buildings and vehicles they would need once they walked upon the earth again.

The sound of rushing footsteps below the bridge met his ear. He looked down. Keziah? He waited for the last of the feed to enter the trough, shut off the valve, and hurried down the steps to meet her.

"What's wrong?" He gripped her shoulders. "Why are you crying?"

Tears stained her cheeks, and she hiccupped on a sob, covering her mouth as she did so. "Your mother and sisters-in-law are treating me horribly! They don't like me, and Sedeq yelled at me. You must do something!"

Ham stared at her, dumbfounded. "What are you talking about? My mother loves you, as do Sedeq and Adataneses. Why would Sedeq yell at you?" He rubbed her arms and pulled her close as his words brought on more tears. "There, there. It's all right. Tell me what she said."

Keziah gulped on several more sobs but finally calmed enough to speak. "Sedeq told me I don't help out enough, that I'm not doing my part. But I work night and day, Ham. You know this! I do more work than any of them, but they act as if I'm lazy."

Ham's mind spun. Why would Sedeq say such a thing? He held Keziah at arm's length. "I will speak to them, and we will straighten this out. I won't allow them to mistreat you. Don't worry."

His anger flared, but with it came a hint of confusion. Keziah's words didn't fit with what he had seen among the four women, and he couldn't imagine his mother mistreating his wife. Would she?

"Go back and do your work. I will come when I can." He would talk to his mother first. Or should he confront Sedeq? Or perhaps Shem?

"No! I don't want to see them again. Can I work with you today? I don't want to work alone, and I don't want to help them." Keziah wiped her damp lashes, and he could not stop his intense desire to protect her from anyone who would cause her tears.

He nodded. "You can go on down the row. Start with the bear kind. I will continue where I left off."

She smiled, her eyes suddenly bright. He had the slightest feeling that she had gotten what she'd wanted of him all along. Was she really having trouble with the other women? Or was she just tired of following the chores his father had set up and wanted things her way, as she had so many times during the building years?

A sigh escaped as he watched her climb the steps ahead of him and nearly skip along the walking bridge. What was going on?

Chapter
21

Zara joined Noah in his quarters after the others had gone to their rooms to relax and rest. She sat beside him on one of the larger cushions and leaned close. "I need to speak with you about what happened today."

Noah gave her a curious look. "Tell me."

At that moment, Ham appeared at the entrance to Noah's room. Zara sat up.

"May I speak with you, Ima?" His expression held concern and a hint of anger.

"Alone?" Zara began to rise, but Ham stayed her with his hand.

"Father can listen. I think this will concern all of us." He stepped into the room and sat on the floor at their feet. "Keziah came to me today, crying. She said that Sedeq yelled at her and that you don't like her. She said you've all accused her of not doing her part, when she does more than anyone else. I can't have my wife treated this way, Ima. We've only been on the ark for a week. The rain never stops and the work is tedious, but it's going to go on for a long time. If she is already feeling this way, it will only get worse unless you all apologize to her and make her feel accepted, as I always thought you did."

Zara sat back, stunned, though she knew she should not have been. Ham would, of course, defend his wife, as he should. But Keziah had not spoken the truth to him. How could Zara make him see what had really happened?

"Well? Are you going to say anything?" Ham crossed his arms, his mouth set in a grim line.

"I am trying to figure out how to explain to you what happened from our point of view, my son," Zara said. "What Keziah described to you . . . she is seeing it one way. What we witnessed was not the same."

"Are you saying my wife is lying to me? I had better not be hearing that." Ham's glare could have cut stone.

Zara drew in a sharp breath. "My son. Have you not noticed that sometimes Keziah does things to make the situation turn the way she desires? Please tell me I'm not the only one who has seen this."

Ham shifted, then slowly lowered his arms. "Sometimes. I guess so. What are you saying, Ima?"

Zara leaned close and lowered her voice. "Keziah has been sad for days. She rises later than the rest of us and complains of not feeling well. Today she told us that she wanted her family. She talked about jumping into the water to drown."

Ham gasped and Noah sat up straighter. Zara looked from one to the other. "Sedeq was firm with her to try to get her to realize we all need each other to make this work. Keziah grew angry and ran off—to you, obviously."

Ham sat in silence for many breaths. "She wanted to die with the others?"

"She said you did too, that you never agreed with your father's plans." Zara searched his face. She needed to hear him say that Keziah was wrong. *Please, Adonai, don't let him think the way Keziah does.*

"That's not true." Ham clasped his hands in his lap and studied them as if seeking answers from the lines along his palms. "I have been grateful that the Creator chose to spare us. I don't know where Keziah got these ideas, but they aren't from me." He glanced behind him, and they all looked toward the door, but Keziah did not appear. "She knows I'm talking to you about what happened." He paused for another breath. "I don't know what to do, Ima. If she is ill . . . Why would she want to die with the others?"

"We are all going to struggle with this judgment even though we were spared," Noah said. "She may feel guilt for living when her family did not. And there are few places to go here to truly be alone. It's a hard adjustment for all of us." He touched Ham's knee. "Would you like me to speak with her?"

Ham shook his head. "No. She will feel as though we're all against her. She needs to hear Sedeq apologize to her. Treat her gently for now. Give her work she enjoys doing. Make her feel as though she is truly contributing something important." He ran a hand through his unruly hair.

No doubt Keziah was using Ham to get her way, but he couldn't see it.

Zara's heart skipped a beat as she envisioned the conflict with Sedeq and Adataneses if she suggested Sedeq apologize for not doing anything wrong. "I think you're asking too much of Sedeq, my son. You were not there. She merely spoke sternly to try to draw Keziah out of her destructive thoughts. We can't have one person deciding each day what they feel like doing while the others end up taking up the slack." She looked at Noah, who nodded his agreement.

"Your mother is right. Keziah must follow the plans we have made for all of us. We rotate our work each week to not burden any single person. If she has a problem with her work, tell her to come to me, and I will see what can be done." Noah stood and retrieved a clay tablet and stylus from where he kept the rotating list of tasks each person did.

Ham rose slowly, frowning. "You are making this harder for me. I am the one who listens to her complaints." His voice was barely above a whisper. Zara knew that he was trusting them with feelings he rarely shared.

"I will speak to Sedeq and Adataneses," she said. "We will try harder to make Keziah feel accepted. But please know that she has struggled with her emotions toward us since you married her. I had hoped in time she would grow and change, and I thought she had. But being here, shut up on the ark with the constant rain . . . I don't think it's what she imagined or expected. None of us knew what was truly coming." She stood and pulled him to her, holding him close.

Ham returned her hug and released her. "Please continue to work with her. Perhaps after we've become used to the ark and the rain stops, we will feel less closed in." He turned and left.

Zara faced Noah. "We've been inside for a week, my husband. We have to find a way to make life more bearable or we will not survive inside the ark any better than those outside it did, for I fear we'll destroy each other!"

Sedeq met Zara on the first level, near where they kept the moths to feed some of the reptiles. "You wanted to see me, Ima Zara? Why here?"

Zara placed an arm around Sedeq's shoulders and walked with her. "I wanted to speak with you about Keziah. Ham wants you to apologize to her for your stern words."

Sedeq pulled away, crossing her arms in a protective gesture. "I did nothing wrong. Why should I apologize? Can you not see that she's trying to control us, as she has over and over again in past years? She's making life nearly unbearable."

Zara stifled the urge to sigh. "I understand your feelings.

And you're not wrong. She's not telling us what she's telling Ham, and that is putting him in an awkward situation. He's asking us to treat her gently for a while."

"So she can disdain us behind our backs and laugh that she's gotten her way?" Sedeq turned as though she would walk away. "I won't do it."

Zara waited a moment, silently praying. *What should I do, Adonai?* Did God care about their personal spats with one another? He'd saved them to repopulate a world where evil ran rampant. But they could not run from the sin in their own hearts.

"Perhaps you don't have to." She came alongside Sedeq. "What if you just talk to her like a friend? Don't mention what happened. Just overlook it and engage her in helping you with something. She enjoys the plants and creating new sauces for the flatbreads. Ask her advice, even if you have to pretend that you don't know something you do."

"You want me to lie to her?" Sedeq faced her, eyes wide. "Ima Zara, if we lie to her and she lies to us, we will never trust each other."

"I don't want you to lie to her. I just want you to overlook what she said and move on. Is that so hard to do?" She checked herself. Was she becoming impatient with this daughter-in-law she felt closest to? "I just want us to try to get along with her, but at the same time not allow her to continue her controlling ways. If you have a better suggestion, I'm listening."

Sedeq's shoulders slumped. "I don't know what to do, Ima Zara. I've tried to be kind to her. I'm not sure I can ever recall seeing her truly smile. And I don't know why. When I ask her questions, she acts superior. When I show interest in her work, she goes on about it but shows no interest in mine. She wants attention but never gives it. I think her outburst was just another attempt to get attention from Ham. Does he not give her enough?"

Zara rested her chin in her hand, her thoughts turning. Did Ham give Keziah the love and attention she craved? Or did he feel used by her as well but refused to discuss it with any of them? She was his wife, after all. He and his brothers were not in the habit of bringing their marital problems to their parents.

"I don't know how things are between them. We only know what we can see. All I know to do is to treat Keziah as kindly as we can and hope things work out."

"That's going to make for a long, tense time in this ark with few places to escape." Sedeq frowned and glanced at the ramp leading to the next level. "We should get back. I'll never catch up with the chores I have, especially if I end up having to do some of hers."

Zara fell into step with Sedeq. "I will try to think of some way to handle this. Don't worry about apologizing to her. I'm not sure she would accept it anyway. We may have to take care in what we say around her, and I know that won't be easy. But once the rain stops and the ark settles, we might all feel better. Perhaps the sun will shine again and the light will come through the roof opening, which will help our moods."

Surely that was the real problem. Keziah was simply suffering from feeling closed in with little light. Her problems had to be something simple, something Ham might be able to correct if he spoke with her. If Zara could convince him that there was a real problem.

But what if Keziah had more problems than they knew? Some of the people Zara had known had suffered delusional thoughts, and there were a few who had chosen death over life. The whole culture had been obsessed with death in various forms.

Had Keziah fallen prey to that kind of thinking? Or did she suffer a malady they could not easily see? What kind of herbs could help broken emotions and a hurting heart?

Chapter
22

Sedeq settled on a cushion opposite Shem, who lounged on the bed. He held a cylinder in his hand, and a parchment from Noah's library was spread out on the table before him. He looked from the cylinder to the parchment, his brow knit in concentration.

"Can you make sense of it?" Sedeq leaned in for a closer look at the pictures drawn on the parchment. "That cylinder came from Methuselah, didn't it?"

Shem nodded. "He gave it to Father right before he died." He ran a hand over his face. "The writing on this parchment is hundreds of years old, and we have improved our communication much since it was recorded. I am glad our ancestor Enoch created this cylinder to help us interpret what's written here."

Sedeq rose to sit beside him. "Perhaps I can help you." She took the cylinder from Shem's hand and studied it, then leaned close to compare it to the parchment. "The pictures of the animals and the heavens are fairly obvious. I think this is a record of the beginning when the Creator made the world."

As Sedeq turned the cylinder, Shem looked from it to the

parchment again. "I think it says, 'Adonai Elohim came . . . garden . . . evening . . . walk. Spoke . . . king . . .' No, not king. There's a picture of a city next to the crown."

"Kingdom? Methuselah spoke of the kingdom of God, didn't he?"

Shem nodded. "I think so. I think these are Eve's memories. See the symbol of a woman? She is speaking of the Creator and the serpent. I believe this is not just the story of creation and the fall into sin, but things Adonai Elohim said to them." He looked at Sedeq. "It will take time to decipher all of it."

"We have plenty of time to do so." She set the cylinder between them on the bed and tucked her knees beneath her. "I wonder what it was like then. You know, to be all alone on the earth with just the Creator. With no evil."

Shem leaned against the wall and intertwined his hands behind his head. "When the ark lands one day and we leave this place, we're going to find out what it's like to be alone on the earth. Not quite as alone as they were, but after living among so many people and animals, it's going to be very different."

She rested her chin on her knees, pondering. "We won't have things nearly as beautiful as they had in the garden."

The ark rocked slightly, and a rumbling came from beneath them.

"I think another fountain of the deep just burst." Shem sat up and tilted his head as if listening. "When we step out into the new world, I don't think we're going to recognize any of it." He held her gaze, his look full of affection. "I'm glad we have each other at such a time as this."

Heat filled her face at the ardent way he looked at her. "I'm glad to be with you as well. I only hope that we can all start again in kindness and love for each other. With Keziah's struggles already evident, I think the problems we are escaping won't be long in rising up again."

Shem took her hand and squeezed. "Sin will always follow

us. I think Ham is completely confused by her behavior. I need to find a way to help him. And if you can find a way to help her, we will be more at peace."

Sedeq looked at their twined fingers, seeing the strength in her husband's calloused hands. He was such a good man. All Noah's sons were good, conscientious men, though she was very glad Shem belonged to her. Ham could get on her nerves sometimes, and Japheth was too much of a dreamer. She had come to love Zara and Noah and Adataneses in the years of her marriage to Shem, but Keziah . . . Why had she always been so hard to love?

"I have never understood Keziah." She pulled his hands to her lips and kissed them. "She is nothing like anyone I have ever known except . . ." Her mother had acted erratically in times past. Why hadn't she seen the similarities until now?

"Except what?" Shem released her hand and cupped her shoulder. "Who are you thinking of?"

"My mother."

Her mother had been so loving when Sedeq was a child, but then her sisters and brother came along and her attention turned from Sedeq to them. But having many children shouldn't have made her favor one over the other, should it?

Sedeq hugged her knees close to her chest again. "I think my mother had trouble loving all of us. She favored my sisters, especially after I came to believe in the Creator. She admitted that she'd once believed in Him, back when she and your mother were friends, but my father changed her thinking. So when I heard Methuselah speak—and later your father—and decided my parents were wrong not to believe, she truly pulled away from me. But even before that, she would say strange things."

"What kinds of strange things?" Shem had heard some of this before, and she smiled at him for his willingness to listen again.

"She would accuse me of things I didn't do. She would especially accuse my father of being unfaithful to her. Many of the things she told me about my sisters I would later find out were not true. I trusted her, but I realized later that she purposely told me things she knew would hurt me. And sometimes she denied me things just because I wanted them. I just realized that Keziah does similar things. She twists the truth or makes things up, and she says things to make herself look good and others look bad. She is never happy." She blew out a breath.

"Keziah seems to be projecting her unhappiness onto all of you. And Ham is enduring more than all of us." Shem raked a hand through his long hair. "We're going to have to talk with her. Show her what she's doing."

"That's not going to change anything," Sedeq said. "I tried with my mother. They don't listen to reason."

Memories of her strongest attempt to convince her mother of the truth flooded her thoughts.

"Ima, I didn't disobey you," Sedeq had said. "I weeded the garden just like you asked." She lifted her hands in a defenseless gesture as her mother stood frowning down at her, arms akimbo.

"Lagina weeded the garden. I saw her out there. You were nowhere to be seen. Where did you go?" Her mother's slap across her face came before she could duck.

Sedeq shrank back, holding her burning cheek. "I didn't go anywhere. I was the one out there. Why don't you believe me?"

The question had fallen on deaf ears, and Sedeq found herself sent to bed without supper before the sun had even set.

"Your thoughts are far off, dear wife." Shem gently touched her cheek. "Tell me what troubles you."

Sedeq shook her head, tears stinging her eyes. "I just had a vivid memory of the time my mother didn't believe me. I spent a lot of nights without supper because she often falsely accused me and then didn't believe me. She wouldn't even check with my siblings to see if I spoke the truth. If not for my grandmother, I would have had no one to stand up for me."

Shem pulled her into his arms and rubbed her back. "You have me now, beloved. I believe you. And I won't allow Keziah to treat you as your mother did. I will speak to Ham if I have to. We cannot begin the new world with the same problems we had in the old. I don't think any of us could bear going through something this massive again."

"There would be no one left, for we would all be too discouraged to keep going." She breathed in the scent of him, grateful for his love. "Thank you for believing me."

Keziah poured feed into the small trough belonging to the finch kind. The golden bird hopped from branch to branch, then landed on the bottom of the cage and pecked at the small seeds and grains now in his trough.

Such a beautiful bird. She found a small amount of joy listening to the songbirds sing their various tunes each day—on the days when she could force herself out of her room. Why was waking so hard on this vessel? And how had her life come to this? When she married Ham, she'd had such hopes, looked forward to a life filled with love and promise.

Deep down, she wondered if the problem was that she hadn't actually believed this judgment would come to pass, despite the years of preparation. Despite the mocking and standing together with Ham's family. Had she really lost everything she'd known, every person in her family of birth?

But of course she had. One look out the window high atop the ladder showed nothing but water. No one and nothing could survive in water other than the fish and animals made to breathe there.

Oh, that she had died with them. The thought did not scare

her as it had the first time. She actually drew comfort in imagining climbing to the roof and finding a way off this ark.

But did she honestly want that?

She moved to the next cage, aware of the other women talking in the large food preparation room behind her. She took her time feeding the birds, not wanting to join them yet. Why did she dislike them so much of the time? Were they the reason she didn't want to be here?

She shook her head. It wasn't like her to question her own behavior or thoughts, despite what others thought of her. She wasn't doing enough, wasn't good enough, wasn't thoughtful enough. They acted as if she was the reason for all the problems between them. If she would change, everyone would get along just fine.

Her jaw clenched as she capped the sack of grain and set it in its niche in the wall beneath the cages. Depression settled over her. Was she as bad as they said?

She turned away from the birds and walked toward the stairs to the roof. She wouldn't climb them as she'd imagined, as no one could stand beneath the covering without feeling the spray of the pouring rain. She would be asked how she had managed to get her clothes wet, and she didn't need to explain herself to them.

Even if she wanted to carry out her wild imaginings, none of the openings were actually large enough for her to fall into the swirling waters. But if she took an axe to chop away one of the pillars . . .

Her stomach dipped. Where did that thought come from? Yes, she'd considered what it would be like to not have to endure this ark, these people, and starting the world anew with just them. The world would be foreign and hostile. Her pulse quickened at the thought of the unknown. None of the people she had known would be there to greet them when they left the ark.

The world would be so silent. Eerie.

Dying would have been easier. Wouldn't it?

But what happened after death? If the Creator did exist, which seemed obvious to her now, then He had made His image bearers eternal beings like Himself. But then, what happened when they died? For eternal or not, they surely would someday.

A shudder worked through her. She wasn't ready to find out. And in that moment, she was mildly grateful that she had been chosen to live on this ark, with these people. Without her, Ham's line would die out, and there would be no one left to tell her future children of *her* family, of her heritage. She couldn't let that be forgotten. Future generations would all know of Zara and Noah and *their* children. But who would remind them of the people who had perished in the flood? Who would tell the stories of the Nephilim and the Watchers, good and evil, and all the amazing things men and women had made?

She stared at the top of the steps to the roof. Turning about, she sat on the bottom step. The women didn't like her much, that was true, but Ham was hers, and she would make him see that he needed her more than he needed anyone else. She would woo him and win him and convince him, especially once they left the ark, that he didn't need his family. Eventually. Once she bore him children and they grew old enough to help him build his own city or kingdom.

Ham could become a king of an empire and she his queen. Much like Cain had ruled his city. Or even like Seth had ruled his. They would not turn away from the Creator as Cain did. But they could move away from Ham's family and the women who might pull him away from her. The women she tolerated.

She could tolerate them, even act kind and charming now and then. Let them think she was happy here, doing her part without complaining all the time. They would begin to trust her then, and when they did, she could keep what they told her until she needed to use it against them. Not today or tomorrow, but someday things would change to the way she wanted them. And she wanted Ham to herself. She wanted him to want her. Only her.

Keziah smiled and stood, smoothing her hands on her robe. Yes. That was exactly what she would do.

Chapter
23

Two weeks passed, and the rain continued. Zara fought lethargy from the constant grayness coming through the roof opening and the dark rooms that remained the same morning and night.

She rose from her bed, tied the belt at her waist, and left her living quarters. Noah's room was already empty. He normally awakened early, took a lamp, and began the work of feeding the larger animal kinds before the others roused. Perhaps he worried about them more.

Their sons worked early as well, shortly after Noah, but the women, who normally would rise first, could not seem to follow the early schedule when everything felt like night.

Zara moved to the area where the food stood in baskets and lined cupboards. She pulled the grain from the sack and poured some into a grinding mill. The men would return after their first shift to eat.

Adataneses and Sedeq approached with Keziah behind them. Zara smiled at each one. "You are all just in time." She turned the handle of the mill to make flour as the women set about making a mixture from the fresh fruit that remained and set out dishes of cheese and onions.

Keziah walked to the plants Zara was growing and tended them. A look passed between Sedeq and Adataneses. Zara glanced from one to the other and then at Keziah's back. She lifted a brow, but the women did not speak, only shrugged.

Keziah returned, smiling. "The plants are looking good. I'll check on the birds, but first I thought I would see if you need me for anything else here."

Zara searched Keziah's expression. "Thank you for asking. I think you can tend the birds. There is not much to do for the morning meal. The men should be back soon, and then we can help with the animals." She placed two loaves of bread into the oven and shut the door. There was always so much to do besides feeding and watering and taking care of their waste. "Adataneses, I think we should begin to check each cage to be sure the animals are healthy. They haven't been confined long yet, but any sign of illness will need to be addressed early."

Sedeq washed her hands and set the bowl of fruit on the table. "We need to be aware of what is normal for each kind in order to know when something is wrong."

"I will examine the night creatures and the larger kinds," Zara said. "Adataneses, you can examine the small land animals. Sedeq, you take half of the midsize animals, and Keziah, the other half. Let's record how they're behaving now so that we can be aware when we see a change." She pulled two loaves of bread from the oven and set them to cool, then placed the last two in to bake.

"I enjoy the smaller animals better. Can I switch with Adataneses?" Keziah leaned on the counter and looked at Zara. "Of course, if you'd rather I work with Sedeq, that's fine. I'm just more afraid of the larger kinds."

Zara held back a sigh. Keziah had been easier to work with

the past week, but she still had a way of changing the plans to suit her desires.

"I don't mind switching with you, Keziah." Adataneses put the last of the onions into a bowl with a garlic spread for the bread. They all enjoyed a mixture of tangy and sweet with their meals, and Zara said a silent prayer of thanks that they could still have these small pleasures.

"If you're sure." Zara took in all three women. Keziah seemed pleased. Sedeq and Adataneses showed little emotion. The two of them enjoyed each other better, so the decision to work on the same level would likely please them. It did irk Zara that her attempt to pair Keziah with Sedeq had failed. She wanted all the women to get along better. But perhaps it was easier for two to be friends than three. Of course, *she* did not fit in as "friend." She was Ima Zara, their mentor of sorts.

But she was failing miserably at mentoring or fostering good relationships with her daughters-in-law. How were they ever going to improve when the conditions they lived in were so dreary, with day after day of sameness? Day after day of darkness and constant swaying. Day after day of thinking of all the people left behind. Lost. Gone.

She shook herself. She would grieve them later. If she gave in to the emotions now, she would accomplish nothing.

"It sounds like you have worked it out, so let's do that," she said to the women. "After we feed the men." Footsteps sounded on the ramp leading to the upper floor. "I believe they are coming now."

Relief filled her. When they were all together, the relationships were better. Keziah doted on Ham and ignored the others, while Noah usually talked about something he'd read the night before in one of the books he'd brought with him. Books about the Creator or about some technique they could use in the woodworking, metallurgy, or blacksmithing rooms on the lower level.

Shem appeared and snatched a piece of cheese from the platter. "I'm starved. Is it ready?"

The others came behind him, and they all sat together. Zara removed the last of the bread from the oven and placed it before them.

"Let us thank the Creator for these provisions." Noah bowed his head. "Adonai Elohim, thank You for sparing our lives in this catastrophic judgment and for making a way for us to have food and every provision we need to survive now and in the world that will be. Help us to please You in all we do. And if any of us harbors resentment or anger or unbelief in our hearts, forgive us. We need You every moment of every day. Thank You for allowing us to pray to You. Amen."

A chorus of "amens" followed his prayer before they broke the bread and passed it around. Zara listened to the conversations moving about the table as she ate. This was the time of day, morning and evening, when she felt most at peace. The dark sky and dim rooms melted away in the company of her family.

Family. She had never realized how precious that word could be. Even Keziah with all her struggles belonged to their family now. Zara loved each woman as if she had borne them from her own body, and she thanked the Creator for finding women who loved her sons and loved Him too.

She was truly blessed, and she must not forget that when the daily trials came. One day there would be grandchildren to join them, and she could only imagine the joy that would bring. Perhaps this new world would also give them a chance to fix the evils of the old one. Perhaps the Creator would look down on them and be pleased, not only with the eight of them but with the many who would come from them. And one day the Redeemer would make all things new. Truly new.

She longed for that day.

Sedeq walked along the lower level of the ark where the midsize kinds of animals were kept. Adataneses moved above her on the bridge, pouring feed into the cages. Were the animals eating enough food? Sedeq studied the way the males and females interacted and approached the food and water troughs. Some of the friendlier animals allowed her to reach through the bars to touch them.

She knelt when she came to one of the cat kinds. The spotted animal was frisky, and she took care not to get too close to its claws. "You are a pretty boy." She attempted to reach past his head to pet his soft fur, but it was clear he wanted to bat at her hand or bite her fingers. "Oh no you don't. You might want to play, but I don't want to be scratched!"

She laughed at the way he flipped onto his back, then turned upright and pounced as the food came through the pipe and filled the trough. "I'll find something to bring next time to play with you." She chuckled and moved to the next cage.

Working in pairs made the work more enjoyable, though each person had over eight hundred animals to care for each day. When she thought about it, the task was daunting. She glanced up at Adataneses. "How are you doing up there? Do you want to trade places?"

Adataneses set the sack of grain in its place and leaned over the rail. "In a bit. I'd like us to move faster, though. I've thought of an area where we can build cages and keep ointments for healing sick or injured animals."

"Sounds good. Hopefully we won't need it anytime soon, as they all seem fine now, but we just began this journey. I wonder how being cooped up in cages for a long time is going to affect them." Sedeq approached the wolf kind, careful to keep her distance. While the cat and wolf were both wild, the wolf did not seem quite so playful. She didn't want to get too close to those sharp teeth.

They continued down the row, and Sedeq jotted notes about

each kind on a clay tablet, which she would transfer to parchment after the evening meal. How would they know how to care for each different kind if they did get sick or injured? Would the male and female fight with one another as humans sometimes did, causing injury?

Noah's library should have something on animal care among the many books he'd brought on board. Over the years men and women had lived on the earth, there had been entire schools devoted to learning the anatomy of people and animals. But though Japheth had a partial knowledge of the animals and Zara particularly seemed to understand the birds, they all had much to learn.

Sedeq moved on, her mind whirling. They would need to make sure the area to treat the sick and injured was fully stocked. They had talked about building this area in the past but had not pursued it, as too many other things seemed more urgent. She quickened her pace. It was time they did, while everything was new and good. They had no idea how long the good would last.

Chapter
24

Adataneses and I found a corner where we could build a small enclosure to help the sick and injured animals." Sedeq dipped her bread into the barley stew, taking in the group with a look. "If we build small cages, we can keep them isolated in case there are more than one at a time that need attention."

"I've been researching some of the writings in the library about herbs that are helpful to animals. Some of them can be harmful, so we need to be cautious." Zara smiled at Sedeq, then directed her attention to Noah. "I think the idea is good and necessary. We can begin to gather what we need for remedies, while you can get to work in the woodshop on the cages and tools we will need."

Silence followed her remark.

She nudged Noah with her foot. "Well? Tell me you agree, my husband." He couldn't possibly disagree with something so necessary. Why hadn't he thought of it sooner?

Noah nodded. "Illness is something we all need to consider. I had hoped the Creator would keep all the animals healthy and without injury during this time, but He did not promise that." He broke a piece of bread and scooped stew into his mouth.

"If Sedeq and Adataneses can describe what they envision, I can sketch the plans for it." Ham glanced at Keziah. "I'm sure Keziah would be happy to add her suggestions."

Another moment of awkward silence followed. Keziah had had nothing to do with this idea, if what Sedeq had told Zara was true. But of course Ham would speak up to include her.

"I think we can all contribute to make this work well," Zara said. "I can use Keziah's knowledge of herbs to help me, and we may need Adataneses to make more jars to hold the tinctures and ointments."

"Why don't you take me to the spot you have in mind after the meal?" Shem looked at Sedeq, accepting a tray of olives from her hand.

"Perhaps we should all go." Keziah linked her arm through Ham's and gazed up at him. "I would like to see what my sisters had in mind without telling me."

Zara bit back the urge to reply. Nothing she could say would be good, but she did not miss Noah's sigh.

He looked at the members of their family. "We will all have time to give our opinions after we study more. We need to continue to read about the treatment of injuries and remedies for illness for the different animal kinds. Most of us don't know enough yet. Let's not worry about who had what idea and just work together to care for these thousands of creatures God has put in our keeping. Can we agree on that?" He leveled each one with a look until they all nodded. "Good." He wiped his mouth and looked at Zara. "I'm going to the library to see what I can find."

He left the table, and Zara and the women began to clear away the food in relative silence. When they finished, Keziah headed toward her room.

Sedeq stepped closer to Zara, and Adataneses joined her. "Ima Zara, I'm not sure I can continue to do as Noah asks. Keziah is growing more difficult to put up with. We have only been on the ark a few weeks, and it's still raining! I'm so tired all the time."

Adataneses folded her arms over her chest. "I completely agree. Every time she steps into a room, I feel tense. My jaw clenches and the muscles in my shoulders tighten. How do we get along with her?" She lowered her voice and glanced in the direction Keziah had gone.

Zara wiped her hands on a linen towel and placed it on a hook to dry. She set the last dish in the cupboard and closed the door. Everything had to be fastened down lest something fall during the rocking of the ark. But this emotional rocking between her daughters-in-law was not something she could fasten down and keep from breaking.

She motioned for both women to follow her. "Let's go down to the next level." She grabbed a long broom and dustpan to carry with her.

Sedeq and Adataneses followed, and they each took one of the brooms on the next level and began to sweep around the cages, following Zara's example. They finished one end of the floor, and at last Zara scooped up the debris from the animals' feed and tossed it into a barrel. The other women did the same.

"You wanted us to come here to work more?" Sedeq leaned on the broom, her expression puzzled. "Could this not have waited until morning?"

Zara looked from one to the other, affection for them rising within her. "I wanted you to see that when we are working together on a task, however simple or complex it might be, we don't need to be at odds with each other. I swept and you both did the same. We didn't speak or say things to upset each other. We just did what we all knew needed to be done, whether tonight or tomorrow."

"Yes, but if Keziah had been here—"

Zara held up a hand at Adataneses's words. "If Keziah had been here, she would have done what we were doing. We would have each taken our section and completed the work." She leaned her broom against the wall and lifted her hands in a gesture of entreaty. "The truth is, we have been called to a difficult task. Each one of these animals needs to be fed and watered, and even though we gather the waste through the piping system, we still have to wash out their cages now and then. As we discussed, they could grow ill or one could injure the other. One of us could grow ill or injured, and then we would need to take up that person's work until they're well. I don't think we realize how vulnerable we are here."

Sedeq straightened and Adataneses seemed to relax. "You're right," Sedeq said. "We have to overlook each other's differences or we won't survive the flood any better than those not on the ark." She paused and looked away, her dark eyes filling with tears. She placed her broom back in its niche in the wall. "I'm sorry. I can't help thinking about our families and . . . everyone." She looked toward the ceiling as though indicating the sky above.

Zara draped her arm about Sedeq's shoulders and gently squeezed. "We all have sorrow over their loss. Not a day goes by that something doesn't remind me of your mothers, our neighbors, even those who taunted us."

"I think of my brothers every day," Adataneses said softly. "Payam was so close to joining us, right at the door, according to Noah. If only he'd swallowed his pride and come inside." She turned about, and Zara saw her shudder. How she longed to comfort these women, but how did one find comfort when there was so much devastating grief?

"What if something happens to one of us?" Sedeq asked. "If we fall ill or die . . . part of the future will die with us."

"I've thought of that too." Adataneses turned back around,

her brow furrowed, revealing lines of worry. "If anything happened to Japheth or to me, there would be no one else for either of us to wed. One-third of Noah's line would be lost."

Zara picked up her broom and dustpan and motioned for the others to follow her to the upper level. Her family could not possibly worry and grieve about everything, but obviously these women did. She faced them. "I do not believe the Creator would go to all this trouble to save us and the animals only to have any of us die on the journey. I think death will eventually come again, but not until God gives us all time to procreate and fill the earth. We can trust Him in this."

"I find it hard to trust Him." Adataneses's voice was just above a whisper, as if the admission brought her shame.

"I do too," Sedeq said. "I mean, we know He keeps His promises, and when He says something, He does it, but it's when we don't have any sure word or promise from Him that I find it hard to trust Him. Like bearing children. Shouldn't one of us have a child by now? We've been wed for seventy-five years and yet none of us has borne a child. What if we can't have children? What if years and years go by once we are off this thing and we still don't give our husbands sons and daughters?"

Zara placed her arm about Sedeq's shoulders again and pulled her close. "Oh, my daughter, do not fear this. I waited hundreds of years to bear Japheth, Shem, and Ham. God has not saved us to leave us without descendants. In this we simply must trust Him because there is nothing else we can do. We can pray, but I think He is waiting until we no longer have to care for the animals to answer those longings. His timing is never wrong." She smiled at each woman.

"I can pray. And trust Him." Adataneses returned Zara's smile as they continued to climb the ramp toward the upper level. "I need to go to my room and relax. Maybe I'll paint one of the jars I made before we boarded the ark. Mark it with a symbol for the animals. I have several jars we can use for that purpose."

"That is a great idea," Sedeq said. "I think I'm going to see if Shem wants to continue our reading. He is quite interested in Eve's memories of the garden and the early years of the earth. I enjoy listening and trying to decipher Enoch's elementary writing."

They reached the upper level. "I hope we can all agree now to work together without looking for things that cause tension," Zara said. "Let us all practice forgiveness, shall we?" She hated preaching to these beloved women, but sometimes her mothering ways rose to the surface. Would they accept her teaching?

"You made your point, Ima Zara. We will try harder to look for the good." Sedeq kissed her cheek, and Adataneses hugged her.

"Thank you," Adataneses said.

Both women returned to their rooms, and Zara tried to decide between joining Noah in the library or settling in her own room to rest. She headed toward her bed as weariness suddenly overtook her. She needed God's mercy to help her survive as much as her daughters-in-law did.

Oh God, please help us.

Chapter
25

Forty days had now passed, and as dawn approached on the forty-first day, Zara awoke to silence. She blinked against the strange lack of sound and sat up, shaking herself. What had happened? And then she knew.

"The rain has stopped!" Her voice carried louder than she intended, for the others were still likely abed. But in a moment, all of them began talking at once, hurriedly dressed, and gathered in the cooking room.

"The sun shines through the opening!" Keziah's joy lifted Zara's spirits even more. Perhaps her ornery attitude had been because of the constant gloom.

"At last!" Sedeq hugged Shem, and soon Zara was caught up in the hugs of each of her family members. Even Noah's smile was wider than she'd seen it in a long time.

"Can we go onto the roof and look out?" Japheth addressed Noah, his arm around Adataneses. "We can return to eat, but I think we're all anxious to see what the world looks like now."

Noah took Zara's hand. "That is exactly what we will do." He tucked her hand beneath his arm, and they all fell in behind him.

187

They reached the stairs, and Noah led them up. Zara's heart pounded with a strange mix of joy and anxiety. What would they find? Would they see the mountains or any trees?

On the roof, they all spread out beneath the canopy. The water reservoirs were full and slowly draining through the pipes below to the lower reservoirs. Zara leaned against the railing beside Noah and gazed into the distance. Water filled her view as far as she could see. No mountains?

She left his side and moved to the opposite end of the ark, but no matter where she went, the view was the same. Water everywhere. Not the slightest hint of dry ground. No one could have survived this. The thought brought another wave of sadness despite the joy of the moment.

"It's covered the entire earth." Shem came alongside Noah, who now stood again at Zara's side. "God has left us alone on the waters."

"How long will it take for the waters to subside?" Ham joined them, and soon the eight of them stood in the middle of the roof.

"The Creator has not told me that." Noah's expression was resigned. "But given the amount of water, I think we can expect to be floating for a long time."

"Water doesn't go away quickly. At least I don't think so." Zara met Noah's gaze, pushing her sadness aside. "I imagine it will take the earth time to absorb so much. Perhaps new rivers and seas will form because of this."

"Possibly so. God alone knows how the earth will look once we finally land." Noah took her hand again and squeezed. "Let us not lose heart. The rain has stopped, and that is cause to rejoice. Now the waters *can* subside. In the meantime, the animals will not be kept waiting much longer."

He led the way back down the steps to the cooking room. Zara and the women quickly grabbed fruit and nuts and cheese. They'd been gazing at the water for too long to take time to bake bread. They would all carry their food with them in pouches as they took care of the animals.

It would be another long day, but Zara could sense a lightness in each person's spirit. The sun was shining again, and the rain no longer beat against their thoughts. She turned toward the lowest level to begin feeding the bear kind, whistling a tune as she went. And in the distance, she heard other family members singing.

"Where will we live once the ark lands on the earth and God opens the door?" Shem picked up the wood he was carving and whittled while the family sat together in the gathering area after the evening meal. The animals had been tended, the chores completed, and the discussion and relaxation always invigorated him. He glanced at his father, who turned his own piece of wood over in his hand, pausing in sanding it.

"It will take months, even years, to build houses as we had in Seth's City. I'm not sure how well the trees will have survived under the water. They may need time to dry thoroughly, so they will not be good to use in building right away."

"We will live in tents, of course." His mother smiled at him. "We should begin weaving them, as we will each need our own tent, or at least one for each couple."

Shem glanced at Sedeq. She was an expert at weaving and even now sat stitching something on a tunic. "Do we have enough material for so many tents?" He had never concerned himself with these domestic things. He and his brothers had spent all their time building the ark and crafting cages and any other wood or metal thing they would need.

Sedeq nodded. "We have stacks of flax to be made into linen, and Ima Zara gathered goat hair from our neighbors and family for many years. We just didn't have time to weave it all before the flood came."

Shem set down the whittling knife and turned to face her. "How long will one tent take?"

Sedeq shrugged. "It depends on how big we make each one. If the waters settle and we land soon, I imagine we will live on the ark until we can finish the tents."

"I don't want to live on this thing one day longer than we have to." Keziah looked up from a list she was making. "I will be happy to give up my work with the animals to weave."

"Sedeq is the weaver in the family, is she not?" Shem touched his wife's knee. "If anyone should devote time to weaving, it should be her."

Keziah huffed. "We all know how to work the loom, Shem. Sedeq simply enjoys it more than the rest of us. But she likes working with the animals best, so why should she give that up?"

His father held up a hand. "There is no need to rush ahead and worry about changing the way we are doing things. It took forty days for the water to rise to its current level. It will take at least that long, probably longer, for it to subside. I'm sure you can all take turns working both looms. And if you need a third, we will build it." He looked at Shem's mother, then met Shem's gaze. "There is no need to worry, my son."

"Your father is right," his mother said. "We can take turns weaving in the evenings, and if we need more time, we can also take turns trading the animal chores for this work. We knew there would be a need to weave and spin and stitch clothing and cloths for various purposes. This is no different." She smiled at Keziah, then at Adataneses and Sedeq.

His mother had learned to appease them all, but Shem still felt the sting of irritation every time he dealt with Ham's wife. The sun had been shining for nearly a week now, but Keziah's sweeter spirit, if he could call it that, had almost disappeared. What was wrong with her?

He swallowed the anger working its way to the surface and

squeezed Sedeq's hand. How thankful he was to have a wife who did not try to manipulate everyone in the family. If Ham had been able to marry that first woman, would life be as it was now? Keziah had been a quick decision, whereas Adataneses and Sedeq had been known by the family for a long time.

Sometimes Shem wanted to speak to Ham about his wife, but something in Ham's demeanor always stopped his words. Keziah had Ham convinced that she was always the one in the right, always the one who suffered the most.

Maybe Ham and Keziah would move far from the family after they landed, as Cain and Hasia had—or so he had read—when God sent them from their parents' home. But in this strange new world his own family was about to discover, could any of them survive without the others?

Shem shook his head to clear his thoughts as the women began talking about how to manage this new weaving project and his brothers brought their father up to date on the animals they had tended that day. He whittled the wood again, carving a hole in the top. The flute he was making from a design he'd found in his father's library would cheer him. Cheer them all, he hoped. And perhaps the music would at least help him and Sedeq deal with the continual dripping of Keziah's complaints and twisted words. He sent a silent prayer heavenward for mercy, to learn to accept this woman and Ham for who they were, not for who he wanted them to be.

Sweat trickled down Zara's back as she lifted the heavy sack of grain and poured it into the reservoir that fed the bamboo pipes into the animal cages. Keziah worked on the same floor halfway down. During the weeks since the tent discussion, things had calmed between the women. But she worried about Ham's relationship with his brothers. They didn't talk about it, but Zara knew that something was troubling Ham. A mother always knew when one of her children suffered. Even if they didn't say a word about it.

She tossed the empty sack onto the pile. They could reuse the burlap for weaving the tents or for some other use. But would the grain hold out for the length of their stay? Would the new earth have enough food for the animals once God let them return to the wild?

She pushed the damp hair from her face and moved to the next group of cages. A few more and she could return to the cooking area to prepare the new dish Keziah had come up with.

"Let me help you lift that, Ima Zara." Keziah approached, arms outstretched.

"Thank you. Have you finished already?" When she wanted to work, Keziah worked hard and finished quickly. Convincing her to enjoy the work was the challenge.

Keziah nodded. "Yes. I'm anxious to try the new soup and to see what the bread baked with the goat cheese on top tastes like."

Zara smiled. "For some reason it feels warmer in here today. Or I should have worn a lighter robe." She was used to the hard work and sweat, but the days of sameness were beginning to wear her down. She must keep up her spirits or she would become as Keziah had been and not wish to rise from her bed.

"Ready?" Keziah emptied the last bag for the day, and each of them gathered a handful of the empty burlap sacks and headed toward the upper level.

"I'm ready." Zara picked up her pace to match Keziah's eager strides. When they reached the cooking area and set the sacks near the looms, Zara released a sigh. She loved this time of day with the family.

She chopped onions while Keziah carved a large yellow squash. They worked in companionable silence. Adataneses soon joined them and began to grind the grain. But there was no sign of Sedeq.

"Have you seen Sedeq?" Zara asked after they'd nearly finished the soup. "It's not like her to stay away after caring for her animals."

"I can check on her." Adataneses put the last loaf of bread into the oven, wiped her hands, and walked down the hall to Sedeq's room.

Zara watched her go, wishing she had been the one to check on Sedeq. She chafed in the waiting as she grated the last of the cheese.

Moments passed, then Adataneses approached, out of breath. "Ima Zara, please come. Sedeq is in her bed."

Zara dropped what she was doing and hurried after her daughter-in-law. In her bed? "Is she ill?" Why did Adataneses not say more?

When they were out of earshot of the cooking area, Adataneses slowed and leaned close to Zara's ear. "She's weeping. I didn't think she wanted everyone to know, but I don't know what to do for her."

Zara drew in a breath. "I'll go to her." *Please, Adonai, let me be able to help her.*

Chapter
26

S edeq curled on her side. The soft bed beneath her did nothing to comfort, and the sobs that rose kept coming until she could barely breathe. *Oh God! Why?*

Visions filled her mind's eye of her ima and abba. Her sisters Lagina and Faustina and her brother Dalton. If only one of them had listened to her. Had they believed before the waters covered the earth, though it was too late to board the ark? Had God shown mercy to them and offered them repentance even then?

Footsteps caught her attention between her gulping breaths. She didn't want to talk to anyone. Why couldn't they leave her alone? She sniffed and brushed the tears from her face.

"Sedeq?" Ima Zara approached and knelt at her side. "What's wrong, dear one?" She touched Sedeq's back. "Do you want to tell me?"

Sedeq shook her head and buried her face in the pillow. Ima Zara rubbed circles on her back as though comforting a small child. The tears slowed. Sedeq unfurled her body and sat up, furiously wiping fresh tears that came when she looked at her mother-in-law.

Ima Zara pulled her into her arms. "There, there. Tell me what happened."

Sedeq held her tightly, then slowly leaned away, arms crossed over her chest to stop the sudden shaking. "I'm cold." Was she ill? No, this was emotional, not physical.

Ima Zara pulled a blanket from the end of the bed and wrapped it around her arms. "Better?"

Sedeq nodded. She drew in several slow breaths. "I don't mean to upset everyone . . . I was thinking of my ima and the rest of my family, and I could see them trying to escape the flood. It was awful, Ima Zara. I couldn't bear the thought that they perished in the waters while we float safely above them."

Ima Zara pulled her close again, and Sedeq heard her swift intake of breath. "I miss them too, my daughter. Your mother was a good friend. I had always hoped . . . She came so close."

Sedeq swallowed back more emotion, her breath quivering in her chest. "Do you think . . . do you think God might have forgiven them if they called on Him in the end? Did they lose their chance when they didn't join us on the ark? Or did they still have a chance until the end of their lives? I have to know that it might not have been too late. Too late to begin again on earth, but not too late to live with the Creator after our life ends here."

Ima Zara held her at arm's length, her expression full of compassion and hope. "I have to believe that God gives us the span of our life to come to believe in and obey Him. Sometimes people reject Him early and come back to Him later in life. Others obey and love Him all their lives. But none of us deserved to be rescued. Rescue for us meant we are living on this ark with the animals. Rescue for those left behind could have meant salvation at the point of death. God alone knows."

"I wish He would give us some kind of assurance," Sedeq said. "It is impossible to think of my family and not fear that they are forever lost. I know the Creator will send a Redeemer

195

one day, but that doesn't mean He might not judge the world again in the future. We can't stop being sinners, so we will always displease Him at one time or another." Sedeq took a piece of linen and wiped the remaining tears from her face. She drew a steadying breath.

"I would like to know for sure what God chooses and doesn't choose to do, but I have learned through the years that it is not ours to know. Did any of Noah's preaching break through to those who listened? Did his words ring in their ears as the waters broke from the deep and the rain poured down? We cannot know." Ima Zara placed an arm about Sedeq's shoulders. "These things are going to cause us grief for years to come. When we leave the ark and it is just the eight of us and the animals, most of whom will run off into the wild, we will remember how things used to be. And I daresay we will miss those things. We will certainly miss the people we loved the most."

Sedeq looked at her hands and turned them over in her lap. There were no answers to her many questions. Grief was going to remain part of her life for as long as she lived, for she had survived when so many others had perished. And she had failed those who were lost. She had not been able to convince even her mother or sisters to believe in the Creator over their false gods. How could she ever stop blaming herself?

She lifted her head and met Ima Zara's gaze. "Do you feel guilty for not being able to convince anyone to join us? I do."

Ima Zara paused. "I used to blame myself, before the flood. I tried to talk to old friends, your mother, and neighbors. I stood beside Noah and Methuselah as they preached to larger crowds. But I watched as people turned away or mocked their words, and I knew that no human could convince another human to change their mind about something. Only the Creator had the power to show a person the way they should take. But they still chose not to believe Him, even when they heard about the great things He'd done or looked at the amazing creation that testified to His greatness all around us. They were willingly blind to Him."

"But they might have seen the truth in the end, right?" She needed to know. Perhaps she just needed to believe it whether it was true or not because perishing was such a horrible thought.

"I have to believe that God can do anything," Ima Zara said. "If He can create the universe, He can show a human being what truth is. He can open their eyes to see, even though they kick against His efforts. I don't think He forces us to believe, but He can be very persuasive. And I don't think He gives up on us until our dying breath. But I think it hurts Him every time someone turns away from Him. He made us for Himself. He had to destroy the world because the Watchers corrupted His creation."

"Could the Watchers have survived the flood? They are not human, after all." The thought sent a stab of fear to Sedeq's heart. "I don't want my children to know them."

Ima Zara stood and offered Sedeq a hand. "The Nephilim could not have survived, as they were part human. The Watchers probably did, as they don't live only on the earth. I cannot promise that your children and future descendants won't be tempted by them. I don't think this judgment was meant to destroy them. All evil will not be conquered until the Redeemer comes." She slipped Sedeq's hand around her arm. "How about we return to help with the food? The men will be back soon, and I think we need to discuss happier things."

"These are important things, though." Sedeq tossed the blanket aside and fell into step with Ima Zara.

"Of course they are. But it does no good to grieve all the time. Especially since we cannot know for certain, and we absolutely cannot change anything." Ima Zara smiled into her eyes. "You are a tenderhearted woman, Sedeq. I am so grateful you married my Shem."

Sedeq returned the smile, though her eyes watered again at the compliment. "Thank you, Ima Zara. I'm glad I married Shem too."

"And I think he'll appreciate it if you feed him." Ima Zara laughed, and Sedeq joined her.

"Yes," Sedeq said. "Shem is always hungry."

Zara stood at the birdcages, watching the different kinds peck at the food she had given them. Light shone through the opening, as it had now for the past forty days. She'd recorded the days on a small papyrus roll, but she had stopped climbing the roof each day to see if the waters had receded at all. The view always disappointed. How was it possible they had already lived here for eighty days?

A sigh escaped, and she turned from the birds to examine the plants growing in soil and the others sprouting in water. It amazed her the way life grew from the smallest seed. How incredible a thought that the Creator had designed life to flourish this way.

"Working with your plants again, Ima?" Shem's voice surprised her, and she turned to embrace him.

"Are you done with the animals so soon, my son?" She leaned away to search his face. "You don't usually wander away from them this time of day."

Shem shrugged. "We have all learned how to move quickly about the chores each day, so they take less time."

Zara nodded. "Well, that is certainly true. I suppose I forget because you and your brothers are usually off working in the woodshop or metalworking rooms."

"Or the library." Shem grinned. "You know I much prefer researching our past. Though I do enjoy the other tasks."

"It's good to gain knowledge and remember the past. You will need to teach your children of all that has been lost in the flood. If we don't teach and warn the next generations, we will fall into the same sins that brought this about." She waved a hand toward the window and the area where they stood.

"That is exactly what I plan to do. Sedeq and I intend to hold meetings with all the children who will be born to share the stories of Adam and Eve and Enoch and the rest of the generations of the human race." He leaned closer to the basil plant, plucked a leaf, and popped it into his mouth.

Zara shook her head. "They taste better when they flavor other food."

He shrugged. "I enjoy food however it comes."

She smiled. "Yes, you have made that quite clear. I've watched you eat raw onion and garlic and bitter herbs. I'm afraid I don't share your strange palate." She shivered at the very thought. "Where are you headed next?"

His brow furrowed, and he rubbed his bearded chin. "I'm trying to avoid Ham right now. I think he's working in the woodshop, so I'll probably work on a few hinges that need reinforcement in the metal shop. Some of the larger animals have pushed against the doors, and they're loosening the bolts and have broken a hinge or two."

"Then you should definitely fix those," she said, concern filling her. "Why are you avoiding Ham?" She wasn't sure she wanted to know the answer. Trouble between her children always caused an unsettled feeling within her. Why couldn't they just get along? Work out their differences and live in peace?

Shem leaned against one of the pillars and looked beyond her for a moment as if considering her question. "We argued about Keziah again. He doesn't see the way she controls him and tries to control everyone else. If he doesn't speak up to her, who will? And then he gets contentious and tells me I think I know everything when I don't. He went so far as to tell me Sedeq doesn't respect me, so I had no room to tell him about his wife when I should deal with my own. There is no talking to him when he gets like this. So I'm staying out of his way until he calms down."

Zara felt like a rock had settled in her middle. This again. *Oh Adonai, if we cannot keep from bickering on this ark, how will we survive once we are all free to go our own way? Will my children leave us because they cannot speak kindly to one another?* She looked hard at Shem, struggling with this son who was so bright and sought so hard to learn yet sometimes lacked the ability to know when not to speak.

She had come to accept Keziah's need to control everything she could. It was her way of keeping fear at bay. She still had not come to realize that none of them had control of anything. Hadn't the flood proven that? God alone was in control of all things. But Keziah tried to keep a tight hold on Ham and her circumstances. When she chose to rein in her emotions, it was a good thing and helped maintain peace among the women. If only her sons could do the same.

"Did you start the argument with Ham?" Zara asked. "Did Keziah do something to make you try to change how he views her?"

Shem did not hold her gaze, looking instead at the wooden planks beneath them. "Keziah upset Sedeq yesterday. I was tired of hearing Sedeq complain about her, so I did something about it."

"So, it's Sedeq's fault for sharing her burdens with her husband?" Zara placed her hands on her hips.

Shem looked up and crossed his arms. "A man gets tired of hearing complaints, Ima. He wants to fix things. You can't fault me for trying to protect my wife."

"I can if you're sowing discord with your brother to do so."

"Keziah told Sedeq she should stop fretting about her lost family. That they got what they deserved. That she should be glad she was spared. Sedeq asked Keziah if that's how she felt about her own mother and sisters. Keziah said yes, she didn't care what happened to them. They never treated her well anyway." He ran a hand over the back of his neck. "How can she be so callous? Sedeq loved her family. Keziah sounds so cold."

Zara lowered her arms, defeated. "Keziah said that?"

Shem nodded.

She'd never known Sedeq to lie or exaggerate, but Keziah had once cared for her mother and sisters. Zara shook her head. She'd had no idea that Sedeq complained to Shem. How often did she do so?

"I don't know why Keziah said what she did, Shem," Zara said. "Surely she doesn't really feel that way. She loved her family. Perhaps she seems cold as a way to cope with the pain of losing them. Keziah didn't come from the happiest home. Perhaps she remembers the painful things and chooses to believe her family deserved judgment. But we all must remember that none of us deserved to be saved. We all sin against the Creator. Even now we can't seem to go a week or sometimes even a day without some irritation or hurt coming between us. The Creator can't be pleased with that."

Shem looked remorseful. "I probably should have kept silent. Ham grows weary of Keziah's control, but I don't think he knows what to do about it. I shouldn't have tried to make him see the way she treats him. I just wanted him to help her so that she doesn't grow worse once we're off the ark and raising families. If she manipulates him now, she will use any children they have to manipulate him more. And she'll use them against all of us. You and Abba most of all, I think."

Zara let the words settle between them, listening to the singing of the songbirds in their cages. "We must pray for Ham and Keziah, that what you suggest doesn't happen. She might seem controlling on the ark, but everything could change once we begin our new life in a new world."

She had to believe that. People could change. God could

help anyone become more like He wanted them to be. He could heal their broken relationships and broken hearts.

"I will apologize to Ham," Shem said, touching Zara's shoulder. "Thank you, Ima. I hope you're right, and I will agree to pray for them. I think we should ask Abba to hold another time of worship. We've been so busy with the animals that we've grown lax the past few weeks. We all need God's help."

She held him close. "You are a good son. Thank you."

Shem released her and walked off in the direction of the woodshop. She silently prayed that he could make amends with Ham. He might try, but Ham was not always quick to forgive.

Chapter
27

Shem slowed his gait after he was away from his mother, taking his time to reach the woodshop where Ham was supposed to be working. Did he mean the things he'd said to his mother? He *should* pray for Ham and Keziah, but he found the effort frustrating. He had tried to seek the Creator on their behalf in the past, but nothing ever changed. He'd prayed for Sedeq's family to believe and join them on the ark, but that had done no good either.

Did God want them to pray to Him? Did He care about the personal concerns of individual humans? Shem had searched the archives his father had accumulated over the years, but few spoke of a close relationship with the Creator other than that mentioned by Eve and Enoch. Did God only hear the prayers of a few? Even his father, whom God had directly spoken to, seemed too afraid of God to ask much of Him. He was quick to obey the Creator, but did he ask the Creator for personal things?

The thoughts tormented Shem, and he turned to take the steps to the roof. Suddenly he needed to look at something other than the inside of the ark. Would God speak to him if he called to Him from above the waters?

He reached the top and gripped one of the pillars as he leaned close to the tall ledge that framed the roof. Water had accumulated in the reservoirs during the rain, but now only water that occasionally sloshed over the side or misted from the air made it onto the roof. Fortunately, they had created plenty of storage jars to hold fresh water for this time and purpose.

He looked to the horizon where sky and water met, longing for a glimpse of dry land. The blues of the heavens were broken up by puffy white clouds, and the darker waters below rippled with the gentle wind.

He lifted his gaze to the heavens, his heart beating with a longing he had never felt before. *Do You see me? Do You see the struggles we're facing here? Do You care about such little things that trouble Sedeq and make me want to lash out at my brother?*

He stared at the clouds moving across the great expanse. Had God even heard him? Silence met his ear, and a sense of defeat settled over him. Had God set them here to be forgotten, floating endlessly on this wooden craft, never to set foot on the earth again?

How was he supposed to speak to Ham and make things right with him when his own heart felt so shattered? He had no answers, no ardent faith like his father's. He'd searched the books for answers to questions that no one seemed to address. His ancestors had recorded detailed drawings for how to build things, along with the histories of his people since the beginning, but his father had not brought along the writings of the philosophers of their day because they had strayed from the teachings of the Creator. No doubt they would not have helped him anyway.

He moved from his post and walked the length of the roof,

in no mood to return to the people and animals below. After eighty days on board the ark, he was weary. And by the height of the water, they had many, many more days remaining here.

He looked again at the heavens, then the water. In the distance, he caught sight of a number of whales blowing air from the holes in their heads. So the water mammals lived. No doubt all the fish in the sea had survived, perhaps even thrived.

He was watching the whales play when another creature caught his attention. The snakelike head rose above the surface, exposing a long neck and the wide curve of its body. It bobbed up and down, and by its expression Shem wondered if animals could laugh. Leviathan. It had to be.

Do you trust Me?

The thought came to him unbidden. He had almost forgotten his earlier desperate prayer. He looked again from Leviathan to the heavens. *Do You see me?* A sense of assurance filled him.

Do you trust Me?

He struggled to answer. Did he trust the Creator?

Trust Him how? He'd obeyed his father when he'd followed God's plan to build the ark. He'd obeyed when his father told everyone to gather on the ark. He'd done everything that had been asked of him. Wasn't doing the work given to them by the Creator a sense of trusting Him?

Why would God ask such a thing? Shem searched his heart. There was still so much to learn of the ways of the Creator from centuries past. From what his father had told him, the Creator had put up with a lot of evil on the earth before He ever decided to stop it. Or perhaps He had already decided but simply waited to give people time to change their ways. To trust Him?

How do I trust You?

He wasn't sure he could. Trust Him to take them safely to the earth again? Or trust Him with something far different?

With the dealings of the human heart? With his problems with Ham and Keziah?

How?

He waited, hoping for more, for a distinct answer or explanation, but nothing came.

The memory of God's words filled his heart and mind. Did he trust Him?

He turned away from the waters. The sea creatures had slipped beneath the surface again, and the heavens held no answers. But he had much to ponder, to study, to understand. How did a man trust the Creator of all? Perhaps his father would know, but Shem determined that if he could, he would discover whatever answer existed on his own.

Ham stood over the workbench, running the blades of a saw back and forth across a thin piece of wood. Why Keziah needed another cupboard in her sleeping quarters, he did not know, nor did he want to. Every week it seemed she came up with a new project she wanted him to complete. He'd stopped trying to figure her out. She always seemed to want new things to decorate or places to keep things she had made out of sight of the others. Why the need for secrecy? Why the need to always have something new?

Of course, she always turned to him to make things for her instead of allowing him the freedom to create something he might want for himself. Or to finish a project he thought would help the animals or please his father.

The thought made him pause. Why did he want to please himself and his father more than his wife?

He shook his head, angry with himself. He thrust the saw deeper into the wood until the piece broke free. He slammed the saw onto the bench and picked up a file to sand the edges smooth. Keziah had been difficult since the day he married her. Why hadn't his parents seen the problems that could arise with her? They'd been in such a hurry to find a wife for him once his choice of Naavah had become impossible. All because they feared no one would want to marry him once they learned of the ark.

He should have been more involved, sought a woman for himself as he had with Naavah.

A sigh lifted his chest, and he tossed aside the piece of wood that would make one of the shelves and picked up another. He should put all of it in a corner and build the new cart the oxen could pull, which would drop waste at the pump and out through the moon pool. Japheth would surely make one first if he didn't start it soon.

He picked up the saw and began again. If Japheth made something before he could, so be it. But a part of him wanted to be first, to be best. Japheth wouldn't care. He didn't seem to be bothered about anything, unlike Shem, who couldn't keep his thoughts to himself. How dare he accuse Ham of being blind to Keziah's ways!

Footsteps barely sounded above the noise of the saw. He looked up and frowned at the object of his reflection. He set the saw down.

"What do you want?" He glared at Shem, unable to keep the disdain from his tone. "Haven't you said enough?"

Shem took a cautious step closer. "I've come to apologize. I shouldn't have interfered. I felt protective of Sedeq and wanted to do something to help her and Keziah get along. I thought you could help, but I didn't go about it very well."

Ham crossed his arms over his chest. "No, you didn't." He studied his brother's expression and saw sincerity in his eyes. But anger still rested beneath the surface of his own emotions. "When I see you've changed, perhaps I can forgive you." He looked away, surprised at his response.

Shem did not speak for a lengthy breath. "I'm sorry you

feel that way, Brother. If you wait for me to change, you might never forgive. I cannot promise I will never say something to upset you again. Is that how we're going to be with each other? If we grow bitter, how will that help us all survive once we're on land again? And don't you think we need one another even now? Cold silence and angry looks will not help our wives or our parents. Is that what you want?"

"So you're lecturing me now?" Ham shifted from foot to foot. Why was it so hard to let this go?

"I don't mean to lecture. I would like to have a friendly discussion." Shem touched the workbench and sifted the wood shavings through his fingers. "I'd like things to be better between us, as they used to be."

Ham looked away again, guilt pricking his heart. He would not please his father by continuing to fight with either of his brothers. He closed his eyes, warring with his thoughts. Keziah would want him to hold a grudge and keep Shem at arm's length. Ima would want him to forgive and get along. No doubt Abba would agree with Ima.

He looked back at Shem. "I appreciate your apology. I can let it go. I would ask that you not speak to me of Keziah again. She has her struggles and I have mine, and you cannot help either one of us. So please don't try."

Did he mean that? He could honestly use advice on how to handle his wife, how to get along with her better. But he had no one to ask. No one he could truly trust with the battles that waged in his heart. If he went to his parents, they would know that he blamed them for choosing Keziah. For not finding him a stable woman like Adataneses or even Sedeq. For not giving him time to search the cities for a choice that was his own. For not waiting—they could have waited decades before he married.

"I won't mention Keziah to you again," Shem said, "unless she and Sedeq cannot resolve their problems and we both need

to talk to them. I hope you will allow me that." He brushed the dust from his hands.

Ham nodded. "I will speak to Keziah about Sedeq. She will listen to me."

By Shem's look, Ham doubted that his brother agreed, but he simply said, "Thank you," and turned about, leaving Ham to ponder whether he understood his wife or himself at all.

28

Chapter

28

Zara rose before the pink light of dawn came through the covered opening. She donned her robe, took a small lamp from her bedside, and left her room. She bypassed the cooking area where she would normally begin the morning meal. Sleep had been fitful, and she felt an inner restlessness. She needed to walk, to think. Perhaps to pray, though she had grown lax in her talks with the Creator of late. Should she climb the steps to the roof to be closer to Him?

She turned instead toward the second level, gliding slowly past each of the cages. Most of the animals still slept. How peaceful they looked, some of them almost tame in their state of repose.

She passed the kinds with leather-like skin and the smaller soft mammals with fur that begged to be stroked. Dare she? She stopped at the rabbit kind's cage and knelt close, but she did not attempt to touch them. She stood. To awaken them would just rouse the others, and she knew better than to begin the work before its time. Just because her mind would not shut down and give her peace did not mean the others didn't deserve to rest.

One hundred days—more than three months—had passed since the flood began. Six of the animals had needed tending for cuts inflicted by their partner, whether in play or in frustration from being caged, Zara and her family could not tell. Separating them had been a challenge, but Noah had added extra connecting cages for the purpose of cleaning the main area, which had proven to be a wonderful idea. For now, all seemed well.

But the concerns of each day's work would not leave her. More than the work, which always involved something new in addition to the sameness, she struggled the most with her own sense of peace.

Why did her sons and daughters-in-law have so much trouble getting along and working in harmony? Peace lasted such a short time before one of them took offense at something another did, and all she did in her spare moments, what few there were, was attempt to be the peacemaker.

She was so weary of the role. She lifted her shoulders, aware of the tension there. Adataneses had grown silent while the women worked together on the tents. Zara understood what had caused her hurt look and unwillingness to speak, and that troubled her most. She sighed as she remembered yesterday's conversation.

"I think we should design something to distinguish one tent from another," Adataneses had said. "Start our new life by giving each family its own colors and symbols. I've already begun stitching ours." She held up a piece of cloth with a symbol stitched in deep blue, with arrows pointing in four directions.

Sedeq smiled. "What a good idea! I must think of something that would please Shem."

Keziah's frown caused a knot to form in Zara's middle.

"You think your family will be larger than ours?" Keziah continued spinning the goat hair they had gathered before the flood. "Aren't you being a little presumptuous?"

Adataneses's brows scrunched, and she gave Keziah a confused look. "Of course not! Japheth's name means 'enlarge,' so I simply designed something to follow that. I have no doubt that God will enlarge all our families to fill the earth as He wants us to."

Keziah humphed and looked away. "Well, *our* symbol will be strong, fiery, something to draw and devour our enemies."

The words had come out almost venomous, and Zara could barely contain her shock. But Adataneses grew quiet. Never one to confront another, she focused on her work, her cheeks growing red, varying emotions playing across her beautiful face.

Sedeq switched the subject to the colors each of them should use to distinguish their tents and eventually their camps. "I think blue fits Japheth well, and Shem should be green. What color do you think Ham should be, Keziah?"

Keziah's mouth drew into a tight line again, her anger still obvious. At first she did not respond, but then she lifted her chin, her gaze haughty. "I think he should be blue, but obviously Japheth would have first choice."

Zara stopped the loom and turned to face Keziah. "I think we can all discuss this without growing angry about it. These colors are not owned by any of us. If you both want blue, pick differing shades. The Creator has made a wide variety of colors to choose from. Why do you argue over something that does not matter?"

The question had finally silenced the discussion, and for a time Zara had worked to the sound of the looms instead of bickering. But the tension between the women had not abated. Eventually they'd brought up the subject again, and Zara had finally left them to work on the food for the evening meal.

What did it matter what colors they made as a banner for their tents or what symbol they thought typified her sons? In naming them, she had never considered a symbol or color. Noah did not possess either one, so why this? Why now?

She continued walking until she reached the lowest level, where she felt the movement of the ark more than she did above. The weariness she'd risen with dogged her steps, and she dreaded returning to their living quarters to face the women again. They'd said little during the evening meal and had all gone off to their rooms without a word to her. Would she face another day of silence or bickering?

Oh Adonai, what am I to do with them? I know You chose to save us because Noah is righteous and You are pleased with him. And I know You have heard my prayers in the past, though You do not always grant my requests. Memories of her prayers for Vada and some of her other friends and family members left behind often haunted her.

I don't know how we're going to survive the new world if You don't help us. You have carried us these hundred days on the waters in safety, so I have to believe You will be with us when we finally land. But will You change the hearts of our children to seek You instead of their own ways? Already I see them thinking more of themselves than each other. They want their own good, not the good of the whole group. What am I to do?

The prayer filled her heart, and she could not stop the sting of tears at the thought that one day her children might become like those who did not believe. Maybe not her own children, but what of her descendants? In time, would there be anyone left who remembered the judgment of God on the evil of sin? When the Redeemer finally came, would He find faith on the earth?

Sedeq found the cooking area empty when she rose, surprised that Ima Zara was not already at work. She lit a fire in the oven and took the grain from one of the sacks, poured it onto the grinding stone, and turned the handle. Adataneses soon joined her, though Keziah was nowhere to be seen. Sedeq poured the grain into a bowl, mixed it with oil, and began to knead it.

"You're alone?" Adataneses picked up a knife and began chopping onions for the cucumber sauce.

Sedeq nodded. "I don't know where Ima Zara is. I didn't look in her room as I passed. Did you notice? Is she still abed?"

Adataneses shook her head. "She's not there. The men left to begin the rounds of feeding and watering. I haven't seen Keziah."

Sedeq leaned closer. "I would not mind if we didn't see her at all today." She glanced about, thankful that there was no sign of the woman.

"I don't fault you for that. She was hurtful yesterday, and I didn't know what to say to her." Adataneses tossed the onions into a bowl and began chopping the cucumbers. "I think we upset Ima Zara more than we realized, though. I've never seen her walk away from us like that."

Sedeq shaped the first loaf and placed it into the hot oven, then set about to knead the second loaf. The work went quicker when all four of them helped. What could have happened to Ima Zara?

"I'm sorry I didn't make things easier." She looked at Adataneses. "I should have changed the subject entirely to talk of the animals or what we wanted to grow first when we land. I didn't realize choosing colors and symbols would turn so contentious."

Adataneses touched her arm and smiled. "It's okay. I need to be kinder in the way I say things. I wish I could make Keziah see that I'm not her enemy. She has a lot of good ideas when we're able to speak civilly."

Sedeq glanced around again. Still no sign of Keziah, but something in her spirit prickled at the thought that she could be nearby. She held a finger to her lips and walked quietly around the counter to the hall. Keziah was leaning against the wall between the cooking room and the sitting area.

"Keziah! There you are. Come and help us." Sedeq smiled, though she wanted to scream at the woman. Had she been listening the whole time?

Keziah startled, then straightened her shoulders and walked ahead of Sedeq. "I know you were talking about me," she said as she entered the cooking room. "I know you don't like me." She grabbed cheese from one of the cupboards, sliced it, and placed it on a plate. "If it was just us, I would have nothing to do with any of you, but for Ham's sake and his mother's, I won't mention this to her. I was not trying to be hurtful to you, Adataneses. You are simply much too sensitive. You ought to be able to discuss something without acting so hurt." She tipped her chin up, and Sedeq caught a hint of a smile, though it held no kindness.

Keziah could not see that she was no different. If any one of them said something she didn't like, she held it against them. Or she tried to make them change their mind, like she'd done with Adataneses about the color. Whatever it was, Keziah's way was always right, and she easily twisted others' words.

Sedeq met Adataneses's gaze behind Keziah's back. Adataneses simply shrugged, while Sedeq bit her tongue to keep from lashing out at Keziah. Where was Ima Zara? But perhaps it was better that she was not with them at the moment. Apparently, yesterday's quarrels were not yet resolved, and Sedeq did not want a repeat of that.

She took the bread from the oven and continued grinding, grateful that the noise drowned out the words pounding in her head.

Chapter
29

Zara entered the area near the birdcages, close to the cooking room, in time to hear Keziah's bitter comments to Sedeq and Adataneses. Had all her prayers been for naught? She lingered with the birds, taking time to feed and water them, in no mood to join her daughters-in-law just yet. This arguing had to be related to the many days of being inside the ark with no end in sight. Had God forgotten them?

She must address this with them, but she was just so tired.

The voices coming from the cooking area quieted, and Zara drew in a deep breath, grateful for the silence. It was better than contentious words. She finished with the last birdcage—the pure white doves—then headed toward the food area.

"Ima Zara, there you are!" Sedeq hurried toward her and offered her a brief hug. "We wondered what had happened to you. Are you all right?"

Zara nodded and returned the embrace, then looked at each woman, her ability to say nothing evaporating. She released a deep sigh. "I am better now, but I must speak with all of you."

The others looked up from their food preparation, their expressions curious. "What about?" Keziah asked.

"I have been deeply troubled by the way you're all treating each other." She paused, but no one else spoke. "Yesterday . . . I have never seen any of you so hurtful toward each other. You can all blame someone else for a problem, but I daresay we can all learn to be kinder to one another. We have lived in these close quarters for over three months, and it may take a year or more before the land is fully dry again. Or the Creator could make all the water disappear tomorrow. We can't know. But we have to accept the fact that He might make us wait until the land has time to absorb so much water and rearrange itself into new rivers and seas."

She moved closer to the workbench where they prepared the food and leaned against it. "I cannot bear to see my family tearing themselves apart when we have not even been together here for that long yet. We must be ready when the land is dry again to go out into the world together, to work *together* to rebuild what has been lost. No single family unit will be able to survive alone. This is not like Eden when the world first began. We have no idea what we're going to find, but I can tell you it is not going to be easy."

Sedeq lowered her head, and Keziah would not meet Zara's gaze.

Adataneses nodded. "I will try harder to speak of things that are pleasing, Ima Zara. I think we can all admit that we could have handled yesterday differently."

Keziah looked at Adataneses, and for once Zara did not see an arrogant tilt of her head or a smirk on her face. "I'm sorry to be so disagreeable sometimes."

"So am I," Sedeq said. "You're right, Ima Zara. We need to prepare ourselves for a shock when we leave the ark. We are safe here, but out in the world, we won't be safe anymore."

A shiver worked down Zara's spine. She hadn't considered the fear of safety. They would have no human enemies, but once the animals multiplied—or even before that—would the predators among the animal kingdom fear them or turn against them because of their lengthy captivity?

"I was thinking," Zara said, taking some of the bowls of food and setting them on the table. The men's voices could be heard coming closer. "After we care for the animals today, why don't we each take some time for ourselves? We've been working hard on building the tents and other items we will need, but I think we need to do something we enjoy."

They'd taken rests in the past, but the concern of having the tents ready in time had caused them to cut short that needed respite. Surely they could afford to take breaks from the weariness of the work they did each day. They might not be able to rest from caring for the animals, but the Creator had established a day of rest from the very beginning. It was time they observed that, at least in part.

"I plan to record some of the things we've learned from each of the animal kinds for future generations," Zara said. "Tell me, what will each one of you do with an afternoon to yourself?"

"I think I will paint." Adataneses smiled. Of all the things she enjoyed doing, and there were many, painting her pottery seemed to bring her the most joy.

"I will read. I'm still trying to decipher the symbols on Enoch's cone." Sedeq carried the bread to the table as the men approached.

"What's this I hear?" Shem caught Sedeq about the waist and squeezed, kissing her cheek. "My wife is going to discover Enoch's secrets before I can?"

Sedeq laughed and playfully smacked his chest. "No, of course not! But I'm going to try."

Keziah took her seat beside Ham and passed him the food before Noah sat and blessed it. She did not meet Zara's gaze. Zara listened to the men talking without really hearing them.

"What are you planning to do, Keziah?" she finally asked after the men had dispersed and Sedeq and Adataneses had left to finish their work. "I would be happy to have your help with my records if you have nothing else you prefer to do today." Did she sound sincere?

Keziah looked at her, emotion evident in her dark eyes.

"What's wrong, dear girl?" Zara attempted to step closer, but Keziah held up a hand.

"I know you are trying to be kind, Ima Zara. I know I'm not your favorite and the others don't like me much. I don't know how to be different. I don't know how to be what you want me to be." She spoke through gritted teeth and stood erect as though barely holding herself together.

Zara held back a sigh, longing to understand this woman who seemed beyond understanding. "I do want you, Keziah. I'm trying to help us all."

Keziah swiped at the moisture in her eyes and looked beyond Zara for a lengthy breath. "I have so many feelings I cannot explain," she said, her voice barely above a whisper. "I am always angry inside . . . and . . . afraid." She held Zara's gaze then, looking more vulnerable than Zara had ever seen.

"What do you fear the most, dear one?" Zara dared not move lest she break this fragile moment.

Keziah rubbed a hand along her temple. "I don't know. I fear everything. I've been afraid all my life. I had hoped marrying Ham would take that away. All this time we've prepared for the worst thing that could ever happen, and now it has. If there was another woman in the world Ham could have, I know he would leave me for her. My only consolation is that he has no choice but me."

Zara risked touching Keziah's arm. When she didn't pull away, Zara opened both arms to her. Keziah walked into her embrace and rested her head on Zara's shoulder, weeping.

Zara rubbed her back in slow circles and held her, praying that God would give this woman rest from her struggles and take away her fears. "I will not reject you, Keziah. You have nothing to fear from me. I love you." She whispered the words into Keziah's ear.

Keziah pulled away and covered her face with her hands. Embarrassment filled her expression, and she turned and walked quickly away. Had Zara not said the right thing? But perhaps Keziah just needed time alone after such emotion.

Zara put the rest of the food away alone, grateful Sedeq and Adataneses had not been witnesses to her talk with Keziah. She must find a way to break through to the woman. Perhaps a talk with Noah was in order. If she could figure out what to say.

Noah tested the new lock they had added to the cage of the tyrannosaur kind. He had underestimated the strength of these animals, and one had pushed too often against the door and loosened the bolts. Satisfied that the cage was now secure, he walked on to glimpse the others of similar kinds, checking locks as he went.

"Father, there you are." Shem approached with Japheth in tow, both smiling.

"I'm glad to see you are both in good moods this morning." He walked with them as they headed toward the lower level to empty the waste. "Did you want something or just my company?"

Shem laughed. "Well, a little of both. We would like to take the tame animals out of their cages and walk them along the ramps to give them some exercise. And if we could get a noose around the necks of the wild ones, perhaps we could risk taking some of them out as well."

Noah looked from one to the other, disbelieving. "You aren't serious."

They both nodded. "We thought it could be helpful, and a little entertaining," Japheth said.

"And not at all safe for the animals," Noah said. "What if one gets free or attacks you?"

"The sheep and goats are used to being removed from their pens. What could it hurt to let them out for a time?" Japheth tilted his head and gave Noah his telltale pleading expression. "I know they have the larger cages since there are fourteen of each of them, but isn't that all the more reason to let them free to stretch their legs?"

Noah glanced at the ceiling and sighed. He should have known his sons would grow weary of the work and try to find diversions. He continued walking, checking the locks while the two followed him. "It's not like we can take the sheep and goats to pasture. They would be at risk of falling if the ark shifted. They are surefooted on land in craggy places, not on smooth wooden planking."

"Then let us go into the cages to care for them as a shepherd would." Japheth didn't let a subject die easily, and his tone grew more persuasive.

"Only sheep and goats need a shepherd," Shem said, coming up alongside Noah. "You're right, Father. But we want to study the animals up close. I've read how Eve used to ride on the backs of the lions and run with the cheetahs. We can't do those things, but might the Creator change the behavior of the animals after the flood to make them more like they were in Eden? If we treated them well, in a friendly way, perhaps we could even tame those that are now wild."

Noah stopped walking to face them. "If you try to tame those that are wild, what do you think will happen once we set them free? Do you think the lion or wolf will lie down with the lamb in peace? No, my son. You cannot take the wildness out of them. They changed when our ancestors brought sin into the world. Those that live in the wild kill others to survive. If you try to make them tame, will you teach them to eat only plants the rest of their lives? How will you do so? They eat the grain and other food we give them now, but this is for a specific time. After a while, and God knows when, they'll return to what they once were."

"You're saying that if they were allowed to choose their food even now, some would kill the tame animals rather than eat what we give them?" Shem rubbed the back of his neck, looking disappointed. "The cats are Sedeq's favorite, and I had hoped we could tame at least some of their kind for her sake. She would love to hold one and pet its soft fur."

Noah touched Shem's shoulder, moved by the desire in his eyes. If only he could give his children what they wanted. Hadn't Zara expressed such a longing when she passed the rabbit kind's pen? He slowly shook his head. "I wish we had the freedom to do as you ask. I wish we could change the nature of the animals, but I doubt we will ever see these creatures interacting with humans on friendly terms. Perhaps someday in the distant future as they mate and produce after their kind, there might be some who enjoy human company. Be glad the sheep and goats and even the donkeys and cattle allow us to touch them and use their strength and other resources for our good." He turned and led them back up the ramp toward the second level. "Come. We have work to do. Put your minds to working on building the pens we will need for the sheep and goats once we are on land again. We can take the cages apart for such use, but there will be much to figure out even then. And if you want to be entertained, play your music for us, Japheth. Surely you can find something to do besides watching the animals slide down the ramps."

He shook his head as they both protested that he had misread their intent. Sometimes he felt as though he was still raising them instead of counting on them to be the men he knew they were coming to be.

Chapter

30

Zara walked with Adataneses to visit the cages of the rodent kinds. A week had passed, yet the waters did not seem to have gone down at all. Zara fought the discouragement that came with counting days and sometimes hours, marking them on her clay tablet. Perhaps keeping track of the time only made the waiting harder. But she could not seem to stop herself from doing so. One day, when they told the story of the flood to future generations, they would want to know the details, and that included how long the flood lasted and how long they had lived on the ark.

"Up here. This is the cage I wanted to show you," Adataneses said, drawing Zara's attention back to the problem at hand. "This one has a small wound." She unlocked the cage and pulled a chipmunk from where it rested on a nest of wood chips. Careful of its claws, she pointed to the right paw. "See?"

Zara took a close look. "Some comfrey should help that. Let's take him to the healing center." She locked the cage while Adataneses gently carried the tiny creature in her hands.

"He's so cute, isn't he? I wonder how he rubbed the skin

away." He squirmed in her hands, and she struggled to hold him. "I think we need to make a carrying bag to transport them. He's trying to get free."

"Don't let him go." Zara quickened her pace, anxious now. If they lost the chipmunk, they'd never find him, as he could hide in a thousand places throughout the ark. His mate would be alone and their kind would die off. They couldn't let that happen.

"I'm holding him. There, there, little one. Don't be afraid. I'm not going to hurt you." Her tone lifted like Zara's used to do when she talked to her infant sons. What was it about humans that they spoke in higher pitches to people and creatures that were small?

They reached the top level and quickly set the chipmunk in one of the healing cages. Zara gathered the jar with the comfrey mixed with oil. Together she and Adataneses applied a small amount to the area and wrapped a tiny piece of linen over the wound.

"Let's hope he doesn't chew it off and eat the linen." Adataneses stroked his head through the bars of the cage.

"No doubt he will try. But hopefully not before the comfrey has a chance to help him heal." Zara did not risk putting her finger through to pet him. "Be careful he doesn't bite you."

Adataneses pulled her hand back. "I don't think he would. But he's quick. And scared."

"Let's go and check on the others. I'm hoping this is just a scrape and not something that they're passing on to each other between the cages." Zara's heart quickened at the thought. The Creator wouldn't allow the animals to die on the ark. He wouldn't have saved them from the flood just to have illness overtake them. She need not worry.

"I didn't see any others with problems yesterday. I think this one just rubbed his paw on something to irritate it, though I can't imagine why. Unless the animals are just growing as weary of the ark as we are." Adataneses glanced at the chipmunk once more, then followed Zara as she headed back to check on the other animals.

"It is possible, I suppose," Zara said. "I did wonder whether the Creator would keep the animals calm, even cause them to sleep during this time, but as we've seen, that is not the case. He has protected us, and I'm grateful we are all well. But we must not underestimate that these animals can still injure themselves or each other or contract an illness. We must pray they do not but be prepared in case they do."

How would life have been if the animals had all hibernated during this entire time? Zara and her family would have had less to do and more time to get on each other's nerves. God had given them charge over the animals, and apparently that meant caring for all of them as if they were caring for a flock of sheep. She hadn't even known the Creator had made so many kinds until they began to show up at the ark!

"This has been good," she said, looking at Adataneses. "We are learning much about the animals of the earth, and if we record what we learn, future generations will not be surprised when they come upon a kind they rarely see. I'm glad the Creator has entrusted us with their care."

The realization surprised her, but despite the monotony of the same chores each day, she was coming to appreciate the different creatures God had made. Some made her laugh because of their appearance. Some were just lovable to look at, begging to be cuddled. Others were slightly terrifying but thankfully kept at a safe distance.

What would life be like when her family opened the cages and set the animals free? She wanted to know. But a part of her was glad that day was not yet.

Sedeq finished her morning chores and hurried to the lower level with the larger animals. She wanted to visit the cat kind again. She suspected the female was pregnant, as the middle of her body had grown bigger in the past few months. They hadn't expected the animals to give birth on the ark, but it was certainly possible. And if the female was carrying young, she would give birth soon. She didn't want to miss it.

"Where are you rushing off to?"

Sedeq turned to see Keziah running after her.

"I thought we were going to work together on the second level," Keziah said.

Sedeq stopped and waited for her. "I'm sorry. I should have told you." Keziah had been easier to deal with in the past week, and Sedeq didn't want to upset that fragile balance. "I think the female cat kind is going to give birth today. Come!" She motioned Keziah closer, and they walked quickly toward the animal's cage.

"How can you know for sure?" Keziah's eyes were alight with excitement, matching the joy in Sedeq's heart. She loved the cat kind and hoped she was right in her estimation.

"I don't. With cats being in the wild, we can't know how long they carry their young, but I've been watching her since we boarded. Cats are my favorite."

Keziah gave a slight nod. "I like the horse kind. They're so strong and majestic."

"They are. It's hard to have a favorite. I think Ima Zara favors the rabbits." Sedeq liked their soft fur as well. But the cats had a way of looking at her that seemed so intelligent and yet . . . affectionate.

"I wonder if any of us will conceive before we finally land on the earth again," Keziah said as they stopped in front of the cats' cages. "I find it strange that we have not already borne many children, don't you?"

Sedeq knelt and looked up at Keziah. "I have wondered why the Creator has not given us sons and daughters yet, but He must have a reason. I do hope He doesn't keep us from bearing children much longer, though. A baby or two or three would definitely keep us from thinking about the monotony of life here, wouldn't it?" She coaxed the female with her hand and a quiet call.

Keziah knelt at her side. "I think it could happen soon." She reached out a hand to cautiously stroke the cat's fur. "They don't bite, do they?" She pulled her hand back when the cat's mouth came near.

"They can. And scratch. But so far, this one has been gentler than I expected in the beginning." She met Keziah's gaze. "What do you mean, you think it could happen soon?"

Keziah's cheeks pinked, and shyness crept into her expression. "I'm a few days late. It might mean nothing, so please don't say anything. I've been late before. But I've been hoping . . . and praying."

Sedeq leaned back on her heels and searched Keziah's expression. She saw no guile there. They all hoped for a child, but to hear Keziah say she had prayed for one surprised her. She'd never known Keziah to think much about the Creator, at least not to speak of Him. "I'm glad you asked the Creator, Keziah. I hope He grants your desire. You would be the first, unless Adataneses is in the same place. She hasn't said so, though, at least not to me."

"Or me." Keziah brushed the hair from her face and smiled, something Sedeq rarely saw her do. "I haven't said anything to Ham or to anyone. I could be wrong."

"I hope you're not." Sedeq longed to become a mother, a desire she'd had since she wed Shem. But Ima Zara had assured her that sometimes God caused women to wait, as He had her. Sedeq had learned to be content with waiting—as content as one could be. But for Keziah to be the first to conceive . . . She was the youngest among them. Would God answer her prayer before He did the longings of the others?

Then again, who could know the mind of the Lord?

"Apparently the cat does not want our company," Keziah said, drawing Sedeq's thoughts back to the animal.

"She appears to want to hide," Sedeq said as the cat tucked herself into the secluded corner of the cage. "I think that means her time is near." Her heartbeat quickened. Would the cat allow them to help her, or would she be angry at their presence? It wasn't like she could stop the birth once it came, but Sedeq did not want to make her uncomfortable either.

"Perhaps we should watch from a distance. I suspect she wants her privacy, and I don't think she would allow us to help her." Sedeq stood and stepped away from the cage.

"Do you think we should wait or go ahead and feed the other animals? We can always return later to see her babies." Keziah stood as well, and again Sedeq was surprised by her humble manner. Perhaps she was with child. Could pregnancy make a woman kinder?

"I only hope she doesn't have any problems. I don't want her to lose any of her litter, and if we aren't here, we won't know." Sedeq touched her chin, contemplating.

"I can begin without you," Keziah said. "Why don't you stay a while. If nothing happens, you can take over and I'll come and watch her."

Sedeq pondered the thought. It would be hard to accept if Keziah was the one to see the birth while Sedeq missed it because of her chores. But dare she sit here all day when the mother might not give birth until evening? Only God knew how the wild animals birthed their young. No humans had witnessed such a thing, as far as she knew.

"Let's get Ima Zara and ask her. Perhaps she knows how long the cat should take. Maybe we can all take turns watching her so that everyone can participate." Sedeq looked closely at Keziah, trying to judge her reaction. She saw no sign of frustration as she had so often in the past.

"I think that's wise. I'm sure we would all like to witness

this. Perhaps we can call to the others once we see the kittens coming." Keziah smiled again and turned to go. "I will find Ima Zara and send her to you, then begin the chores. Go ahead and stay with the cat for now."

Sedeq thanked her and watched her walk away, her step light. She seemed so sincere. It was not something Sedeq was used to, and she could not stop suspicion from sneaking into her heart. Could she trust Keziah? Or was she acting different for a purpose that was still ultimately trying to control them all? But to what end?

Perhaps she was simply being too cynical. She didn't have a good reason to doubt Keziah other than past behavior. And if she truly was pregnant, she might have found the happiness that always seemed to elude her.

Sedeq turned her attention again to the cat, watching her belly quiver and move as though the kittens were jostling inside her. Surely the time was soon. When it came, would one of the kittens allow her to hold it?

Perhaps not right away, but she hoped so. The thought cheered her.

Chapter

31

The kittens came hours later, and Sedeq leaned against Shem's arm, holding back the desire to squeal at how tiny they were. "Look!" She kept her voice low. "They can't even open their eyes."

"But they can find the nourishment they need without a problem." Shem's arm came around her, and he kissed her cheek.

"I wish I could hold them." She wasn't sure why she longed for such a thing. They'd seen plenty of ewes and nanny goats give birth over the years, and she'd never wanted to cradle their young in her arms. Sheep wouldn't scratch the way a kitten could. "I've just never seen anything like this."

Shem nodded, pulling her closer. "This is a wonder to watch. I think we've been blessed beyond what we realize or deserve."

She looked at him, recognizing his moments of reflection. "You are thinking of those God judged."

"Yes." He looked toward the ceiling. "Abba said that God did not want to judge us. His heart was broken by our rebellion.

230

I never thought of the Creator as having a heart that could break like ours does."

She looked from him to the kittens, wondering if the animals could feel emotion like humans did. Probably not. "We are made in His image, so perhaps that's one way that we are like Him. We feel because He feels. Perhaps that is the greatest kind of love."

He bent to kiss the top of her head. "Perhaps it is." He clasped her hand. "Have you watched them long enough for now? There is nothing we can do for her or them. They seem to be doing well."

"I could sit and watch them for hours," she admitted. "But we do have other things to do."

"And I'm hungry." He grinned.

"You are always hungry!" She laughed, and they walked together to the upper floor. When they reached the third level, she stopped, spotting Ham and Keziah ahead of them, deep in conversation. "I don't think I want to become part of their discussion," she whispered.

Shem led her the other way toward their rooms.

"I should begin preparations for the meal, since you are *always* hungry." She pulled him close and kissed him. "Though we could take time for a different kind of hunger." His ardent look warmed her to her toes. "I do wish the Creator would grant us a child soon. If we have to live on this ark much longer, it would make life more interesting."

He searched her face. "Or to hear my ima tell it, you might feel worse and have trouble doing anything. The motion of the ark, even slight, could cause discomfort."

She brushed his comment aside with a wave of her hand. "It would be worth it. I am very ready to give you a son." She leaned her head on his shoulder. "We could close the curtain."

He pulled her toward his bed, not needing any more coaxing. Sedeq had not told him that Keziah thought she had already conceived. She did not want to be in competition with her sisters-in-law. But surely they wouldn't live on the ark forever, and the sooner they began to replenish their families, the sooner they would fill the earth.

Shem closed them in and pulled her to him. Perhaps this time.

"Are you certain of this?" Ham gently gripped Keziah's shoulders, searching her face. "You have wondered before."

Her gaze skipped beyond his, and his chest tightened in worry. He'd thought she was changing, no longer trying to twist things to get her way. But what reason would she have to get his hopes up about a child if she didn't know for sure?

"I'm later than I've ever been. I won't know for another month, but I needed to tell you, Ham. I need someone to be happy for me." She lifted pleading eyes to his. "Aren't you a little bit excited at the idea of becoming a father at last?"

He released a sigh, then wished he'd held it back. By her look, she was not pleased with his reaction. "I simply want to be sure, Keziah. I cannot rejoice with my father and brothers until you are certain."

"I thought you would want to rejoice with just me until we are sure." A pout formed on her beautiful mouth, causing him to feel manipulated again.

His hands fell to his sides. "Of course I want to rejoice with you, but would it have hurt to wait and not get my hopes up?"

"You would have me keep this all to myself? That's not fair. And I'm not trying to raise your hopes falsely. You're twisting my words."

He was twisting *her* words? Anger flared for a moment, but one look into her vulnerable gaze stopped it. What if she was telling the truth? What if a babe truly did reside within her? He shouldn't discount the possibility just because she'd been wrong before.

He pulled her close, allowing her to rest her head against him, grateful that she could not see his confusion and frustration. He lost patience with her so often. Was he part of the reason she seemed to want him to agree with her, always be with her, focus on her? He couldn't tell.

"I will be glad to tell our family once you're certain," he said softly against her ear. "Perhaps check with my ima if you have doubts. She will know the signs to look for."

Keziah leaned away from him. "I told Sedeq. But I said I wasn't sure. I will ask your mother in a few weeks."

"I'm glad you felt comfortable enough with Sedeq to share this with her." This was a good sign, wasn't it? He could not remain her only confidant. Maybe he had misread her earlier. Perhaps she was just anxious and hopeful, while he kept looking for her attempts to control him.

"Thank you. I think Sedeq likes me a little. She is kind to me." Keziah stepped back. "I should go help prepare the food. I'm sure you're hungry. You can help me if you want to."

She wanted him to prepare the food? He chewed on the thought a moment, then shrugged. "I suppose I could chop something for you."

A wide smile creased her face, reaching her eyes. Why had he never noticed how beautiful she could be when she was happy? But then, he'd rarely seen her happy.

He laughed. "I don't know if Ima will shoo me away from the cooking area, but I suppose none of us should think we are above helping with anything. Just please don't ask me to weave. I'm not meant to work a loom."

She took his hand, and her laughter rang out as they walked to the cooking room. Maybe he should do things with her more often, "domestic" or not. They all had to eat, and the women did all the things the men did to care for the animals, so why did they expect the women to feed them?

He followed Keziah, determined to find out what was so

special about cooking food. If women could do it, surely men could too.

Noah climbed the steps to the roof a month later, Zara following. He offered his hand and steadied her as she reached the final step.

"That wind is strong!" Zara tightened her belt and clung to his arm. "It's making the waters churn."

He gripped the railing and turned to face the wind, relishing the feeling. His hair whipped behind him, and he closed his eyes against the onslaught. "Perhaps we should stand away from the edge."

She followed him beneath the shelter of the roof. "Things feel different," she said. "Not just the wind, but I'm not sure what it is."

"The waters of the deep have stopped releasing, and God has sent this wind to help dry up the land. He has remembered us." Noah rested an arm about her shoulders as they watched the churning waters and felt the wind.

"Do you think He ever forgot us?" She lifted a brow in question.

Noah shrugged. "Not exactly. I meant that for reasons only He knows, He allowed enough time to pass until He was satisfied that the earth was cleansed. Now He is ready to move us back onto the land."

Zara looked from the waters to him. "I think it's going to take the wind some time yet. We can't even see a hint of land from the tallest mountains."

"True." Noah shaded his face and turned about until he had seen the waters from every angle. "It will still take time. But we will not be here forever. That is reason enough to rejoice."

He couldn't tell her that he'd grown discouraged of late. All the years of building the ark had kept him singularly focused. But when the waters rose and everything on earth died, he'd struggled. He knew God was just and had every right to judge the wickedness of the earth, especially because of the Nephilim who were destroying the human race. But the loss had never seemed real in the building years.

Care for the animals had taken so much time, and there were so many records to keep, things to mend, and disputes to settle that he'd given little thought to why he felt disquieted. Now he knew. God had not told him how long they would remain on the ark, and the waters never seemed to go anywhere. He had envisioned living here for years.

Zara touched his chin and turned him to face her. "Your mind is far away, my husband. What troubles you? We have news to celebrate!"

"We do." He rubbed his face and grasped her hand, kissing her fingers. "I've been fearful that the Creator would keep us here too long. I didn't tell you, but I feared we would run out of food before we landed."

She squeezed his fingers and smiled. "So you are like the rest of us, despite that strong demeanor you show us."

He nodded. "You have found me out, dear wife. I have obeyed everything He told us to do, but once the flood came, I felt so unworthy to be spared. Then I felt guilty to be spared. Then I wondered if we would ever be free to live the life He spared us to live." He laughed. How ridiculous he sounded now.

She laughed with him. "We have all wondered the same. I'm sure being so cooped up has put us all on edge, though at least we can walk around and are not in cages like the animals." She linked her arm through his. "How long do you estimate it will take now that the wind has begun? Has the Creator told you anything?"

Noah shook his head. "If only He would. But He has not spoken since He told us to board the ark. I simply sense and know in my heart that only He could have sent the wind, so I think we can begin to hope it will be soon."

"In that case, we have tents to finish and, I suspect, garments to make." Zara's smile held a secret. He could always tell, for she loved to play this game with him.

"Garments to make?" he asked, playing along.

"For the coming babes. Just today both Keziah and Sedeq told me they think they are with child." She clapped her hands together and laughed again. "Hopefully they will be born on the earth and not the ark."

He smiled. So God was beginning to replenish the people. After one hundred and forty days so far, they finally had something hopeful to look forward to. "I think we will be off the ark long before the little ones are born." He took her hand. "But let's go below and tell the others of the wind. It will cheer them to know why the ark is swaying more."

"There is much to celebrate today."

He kissed her, silently thanking God for sparing them all. And for the promise of the children to come.

Chapter
32

Ten days later as they all gathered around the evening meal, the ark jolted and tilted. Zara grabbed the pot of stew to keep it from sliding, while the others steadied the other food and tableware. Another jolt leveled them back. But the ark no longer rocked with the perpetual gentle motion of the waves.

"We've landed!" Shem exclaimed.

"Yes!" Japheth raised his arms above his head in a gesture of worship.

Ham jumped to his feet. "Let's go and look." He took Keziah's hand and led the way as the rest of them followed.

Zara let go of the pot and looked at Noah as he walked around the table. "I think they're going to beat us to the roof." She smiled. "I'm glad they're so excited. I didn't think we would land so soon." A few more small jolts made her nearly lose her balance, and she gripped the table. "I hope that's the last one." She looked into Noah's smiling eyes.

"Shall we?" He offered his hand, and she took it. "I doubt there will be many more jolts. I think we are fairly level now."

"I hope we're not perched on the edge of a cliff." She gave him a wry look.

"I hope not too." They quickened their pace to ascend to the roof.

"We're on top of a mountain," Shem said. "I can barely see the land where we stopped, and there are no visible trees or other mountains. Only water as far as I can see."

The others gathered around Zara and Noah. "I wish we could see more," Japheth said, pulling Adataneses close. "It feels a little eerie knowing we're somewhere but we can't see it."

"At least we're level." Ham pulled a tablet from his robe and jotted something down. "Exactly five months since the rains began, we're settled on land again."

"Just not very dry land," Keziah said, leaning closer to him. "I will be glad when we can get off this thing." She shivered. "I don't like not being able to see more than water. What if there's a long walk to find suitable land to set up our tents once we leave?"

"I agree," Sedeq said. "I hope we don't have to pick our way down a mountain on some narrow, rocky path. I've never climbed a mountain, but from a distance they didn't look inviting."

"Especially in our condition," Keziah said, sharing a smile with Sedeq.

Zara watched Adataneses, wondering how long it would be until she too conceived. By her furrowed brow, she sensed Adataneses wondered the same. How well Zara could relate. Hadn't she longed for children for years and years?

"I suspect the Creator landed us in a good place to make it easy for the animals, especially those with young, to go safely into the wild again," Noah said. "Though I know most have no trouble with walking in craggy places." He walked to the edge facing north and looked out.

Zara joined him. "Do you think another ten days will show as much progress? I hope we can be ready to leave that soon." The tents were nearly finished, but they still had much to do, though most of the things would just come with them off the ark.

"There is no way of knowing. The wind is still blowing, but there's still so much water," Noah said, sighing, though she knew their landing brought him joy. "I know we're all impatient to see the Lord bring us out," he added, "but let's not think about it too much. The more we want something, the longer it seems to take."

She leaned against the railing, allowing the wind to whip the hair from her face. The water sprayed up, and for a brief moment it gave her the sensation of sailing, as she had with her father years before on the Euphrates.

She turned to Noah. "Do you think the Tigris and Euphrates will still exist? So much will have changed. One day I would again like to see the place my father loved." Nostalgia washed over her, and suddenly she missed both of her parents more than she had in years.

"I suspect the whole earth will be different, yet I think the Creator will have kept some of it the same," he said. "I doubt we will know for a long time because we will likely live on this mountain until we grow larger in number and feel safe enough to be a good distance from the ark." Noah took her hand and led her toward the stairs as the sun turned the sky a beautiful array of oranges and pinks.

"You don't intend to take the ark apart and use the wood to build other things? I always thought you would." Zara motioned the others to join them.

Noah led the way down the stairs. When they reached the bottom and were all together again, he looked at her. "Other than the cages, I don't intend to dismantle the whole ark for other uses. We will need to come here to use the woodshop and metalworking shop, and we will have no other place to store the books until we can build a library for our descendants. We will preserve our history here until we can build cities as we had in the past." He looked at their sons and daughters-in-law. "It's going to take years for your children to grow up and have children and many generations to follow."

"I wonder if we will live as long as we did before the flood." Shem's question caught Zara off guard.

"Why wouldn't we?" She couldn't imagine anyone not living for hundreds of years as they did now.

"The atmosphere has changed. Can't you feel it when we're on the roof? The air is thinner since the canopy of waters fell upon us. Will that affect us in some way?" Shem addressed the question to his father.

Noah lifted his hands. "I have no idea, my son. The Creator has said nothing of our years upon the earth. We will all know in time."

"Well, if we are going to be leaving here soon, we'd best get some rest," Zara said. "We have much to do tomorrow."

She turned to head to her room, her mind spinning. She spotted the table with dirty dishes and the food not put away and turned to do that work instead. She was too awake to rest in any case.

Adataneses woke to the telltale signs of another monthly cycle. Her emotions plummeted, and she longed to stay abed and not speak to anyone. Why had the Creator blessed Keziah and Sedeq yet seemed to have forgotten about her? Would Japheth's line die out because she could not conceive?

She closed her eyes, not wanting to acknowledge the truth. Of course the Creator would bless her. He would not want one of Noah's sons to be without descendants. A troubled sigh escaped her, and she slowly forced her legs over the side of the raised bed and rose.

"You're up early," Ima Zara said as Adataneses dragged herself into the cooking area. "But you don't look like you want to be."

Adataneses shrugged. Tears stung her eyes.

Her mother-in-law set aside the bread she was kneading and came to her, wrapping her in her strong arms. "There, there. What troubles you, dear one?"

Adataneses clung to her a moment, then leaned back, brushing away the moisture from her eyes. "I learned this morning that I have not yet conceived. I don't even want to tell Japheth."

"Then don't. He doesn't need to know. It will only cause both of you more angst." She cupped Adataneses's shoulder. "I know exactly how you're feeling. I waited hundreds of years before the Creator saw fit to bless us with three sons, one right after another. Trust me. The Creator will not forget you. For some reason He is simply waiting."

"I don't see a good reason why." She drew in a ragged breath, mentally telling herself all would be well. Ima Zara was right. God would not forget her forever.

"He doesn't give us answers to those questions." Ima Zara motioned her to help with the bread. "Unfortunately, most things in life do not have answers. We wait and wait for blessings that others seem to have without effort. We lose out on things we thought He meant to give us. We pray and we still suffer. I wish I could change this for you, my daughter. Waiting is no easy task."

Adataneses picked up the grinding stone as Sedeq and Keziah joined them. "No, it is not," she said, then turned the stone to drown out any more words. She did not understand the Creator. He had kept all of them from bearing children before the flood. Now He began to bless, but she was left out like one born at the wrong time.

She blinked back the emotion that fought to surface again. She would not cry. Not in front of Keziah. And with Sedeq also pregnant, she could not even share her pain with her closest sister-in-law.

She focused on her work, half listening to Ima Zara converse with Sedeq and Keziah, not wanting to join in. She couldn't keep herself from them or the men. She couldn't leave the ark or hide in a corner or curl up beside the lambs. No. She must do as Ima Zara had said, which truly was the hardest thing she had ever done.

Wait.

Chapter
33

Zara carried a sack of nuts to Noah where he worked in the metal shop. They had nearly enough pegs made for the tents, which now sat in a corner of the weaving room, but Noah said they needed more. She rounded the corner, entered the metal shop, and set the sack on a table near Noah. He picked up a peg with long metal tongs and set it aside to cool.

"Another one complete." He wiped his hands on a linen cloth and picked up the sack, popping a handful of nuts into his mouth.

She sat on a stool beside him and looked over the shop. "If you can construct the outer shell of a building, you have all you need to move this shop to the outside world. How hard can it be to build the structure, especially if you take from the beams you already have cut here?"

Noah's brows lifted. "You still want me to dismantle the ark? You know how I feel about that, Zara."

She lifted her hands in a defenseless gesture. "I'm not suggesting you take it completely apart, but once we leave, what

243

need will we have of it? You're already planning to take the animal cages apart. We can use that wood to build the shops you need. The ark could still stand. It would simply be empty. Is that so bad?"

Noah set the sack on the table. He looked beyond her a moment, then met her gaze. "I think part of my feeling is simply not wanting to destroy what took us so long to build. The other fear is that we might need it again. What if the Creator decides to flood the earth a second time? What if in a few generations we become as evil as we were before the flood, and He tells us to build another ark because we've taken this one apart? I don't want to go through all that work again, and I don't want our descendants to have to do so either. If we keep this intact, our future descendants will have it as a place of refuge and remembrance should they need it."

She searched his face. "Do you think the Creator would put future generations through this again? I mean, I am grateful He rescued us, but is this something to fear? By the look in your eyes, I think you do." She'd rarely seen him show fear, so why now, when they were nearer to leaving the ark than they'd ever been?

Noah looked away as if embarrassed by his admission. "I have no reason to fear such a thing. The Creator has not said what to do with the ark once we're living on the earth again. He has not spoken to me at all. Perhaps that's why I worry."

She stood and took his hand. "Why don't we go to the roof to see the progress of the water? Perhaps it will lift your mood." She tugged on his hand, and he rose. Two and a half months had passed since they'd landed on top of a mountain, and she was anxious to visit the roof to see how much more the water levels had dropped.

He looked back at his work and snatched the bag of nuts. "I'm not in a bad mood, dear wife. I'm just thinking of all we might encounter once we leave this place. I've gotten used to it here."

"Well, I've gotten tired of it here." She smiled as they neared the steps. "I love how well you built it, but I want to breathe the clean air and feel the dirt beneath my feet again."

Was Noah right? Should they keep the ark intact and near them in case the Creator sent another flood? He wouldn't really do that, would He?

Noah stepped ahead of her and climbed to the roof. When they reached the top, she hurried to the railing. The sun coated the clouds in gleaming white, and the sky was blanketed in a vivid blue.

"It's beautiful," she said, barely above a breath.

"Yes. And look." Noah pointed to the west. "Mountains."

She turned in that direction, and there, not far from where they stood, the tops of a range of mountains rose above the waters. She leaned forward and looked below. "More land is visible beneath us as well!" She whirled about and embraced him. "Soon, my husband! We will step again on the earth."

He laughed before he kissed her. "It won't be long now."

Together they hurried to find their children to give them the good news. Two hundred and twenty-five days they had waited for this moment. Surely they would see the waters flee away and the rest of the land appear within another month or so.

She breathed a silent prayer. *Please, Lord?*

Zara met Adataneses near the cage of the sheep several weeks later. "You wanted to see me?"

Adataneses had requested the meeting after the others had left the gathering area to feed the animals. But why here?

Adataneses looked up. "This ewe is about to give birth. I thought you would like to see it. If she delivers soon, that is."

Zara had watched many sheep give birth over the years. She gave Adataneses a curious look, wondering why this one was so special.

"I know," Adataneses said. "You're thinking, why would I want you to see something so ordinary?" A slow smile graced her lips.

"You are pregnant at last!"

She laughed. "Yes! I wanted to tell you as soon as Japheth knew, but not with the others. And this seemed like a good way."

Zara pulled her close and held her. "I'm so glad, my daughter. I know how much you have longed for this moment."

"I'm thrilled that we will all be leaving the ark carrying the next generation of your children. I admit, I felt left out of the joy."

"I know you did." Zara released her, and they crouched low to better see the ewe. "Soon it will be all three of you bearing young, and I will be there to help bring them into the world."

"I wouldn't want it any other way." Adataneses had not often shared her feelings, so the admission surprised Zara. "I'm glad God chose me to marry into your family. I would not have wanted to miss all of this, despite the lonely days and hard work."

"I'm glad you love my son and he loves you. There is nothing a mother wants more than to see her family getting along and loving each other. And to see your marriages grow strong." Zara's heart lightened, joy filling her.

"I can't wait until we can begin to build anew and replenish the earth." Adataneses touched her middle where the babe was just beginning to grow. "I wonder how many children God will give us."

"I suspect, like Adam and Eve, you will all need to bear enough for them to marry their cousins or siblings. It's not what we were used to in times past, but there will be no other way until the earth is populated once again." Zara pointed to the ewe and leaned close to Adataneses. "She is restless. It won't be long now."

They watched the animal lie down and stand up again and again, until at last the lamb emerged from the womb. The ewe cleaned it off, and a short while later the lamb stood to nurse.

"I wish our children could walk when they are born, but I suppose that would make birthing them even more painful," Adataneses said. "I'm glad babies are small." She stood, and Zara rose with her.

"I'm happy you told me first. Almost first." Zara touched Adataneses's shoulder. "Tonight we will have even more to celebrate."

"I'm going to send a raven out to see if the waters have gone down enough for it to land," Noah said at the morning meal the following week. "If there is no place to land, it should return to us."

"Are you sure about that, Father?" Japheth broke off a piece of his flatbread and dipped it into a fruit spread. "The raven is an adaptable bird. It may even find food in the water and rest on anything that might float there. I'm not sure it would return."

Noah took a drink of water. "The raven is also a hearty and intelligent bird, and I think it has a better chance of survival than the other kinds. Especially if the water has not abated enough."

"But if it doesn't return, how will you know anything? Why not try the dove?" Japheth didn't usually argue his point, and Noah had to hold back his irritation at being questioned.

"If it doesn't return, I will send the dove." He rose from his cushion on the floor. "Does anyone want to watch as I release the bird?" He didn't wait for a response but turned and walked toward the birdcages.

Why did Japheth's question irritate him? His son understood the animals better than most of them. Was he wrong to send the raven first? What if the bird didn't return?

He looked at the doves perched on branches in their cages. God had sent more of them than the ravens because they were clean. If one was lost, wouldn't it be better to keep the raven with its mate?

He shook his head. No. He had made this decision days ago, and the raven was the smarter bird. More resourceful. It could survive better should land be hard to find. The dove could wait.

He took the raven from its cage and slowly climbed the ladder to the window. Footsteps sounded below, and he glanced down to see his family surrounding the ladder.

Noah undid the latch, then pulled the window inward. A soft, cool wind caught him in the face, and the raven lifted its feathers, obviously anxious to be set free. Noah reached through the window and released the bird, watching it fly with ease against the wind. The Creator had not stopped the wind since it began months ago. Perhaps the waters would be gone when the wind stopped.

He watched the bird fly until he could no longer see it. He closed the window. The bird would make its presence known when it returned.

But why had the air cooled? Before the flood, they had known only a steady, pleasantly warm temperature. A chill worked through Noah as he climbed down the ladder.

"The raven will know where to come if he can't find a place to land." He looked at his family, their eager expressions showing their longing for change. "Let us pray he finds dry ground and returns to let us know. I think we'd best feed the rest of the animals, yes?"

His sons left to do so, and his daughters-in-law turned to clean the eating area.

Zara slipped her arm through his. "I know Japheth's comment upset you," she whispered. "He was only trying to help. Do not hold it against him."

"I don't." Noah looked at her briefly, denying the irritation he still felt. Why was he so bothered by his son's disagreement? "Did you feel the chill in the air when I opened the window?" He was more disturbed by that than Japheth's opinions.

She shook her head. "I didn't notice. But you didn't keep the window open long." She tilted her head. "Do you think the weather has changed since the waters fell and burst from the deep?"

He scratched a sudden itch on his arm. "I think we should prepare for cooler weather. We can't know whether we have landed in a lush, warm climate or one that requires more heat."

"I will begin weaving more blankets and heavier clothing today. But Noah, if we leave soon, I won't be done in time, even if all of us work together." She touched his shoulder.

He shrugged. "I'm sure the Creator will help us to survive in whatever climate awaits us outside the ark. He's brought us this far, after all."

"So you no longer worry about what is to come?"

"I didn't say that. I have work to do." He kissed her cheek as her brow lifted in question. She knew him too well. Knew his hidden fears. And she wasn't fooled any more than he was.

Chapter

34

A week passed and the raven had not returned. Zara worked steadily at the loom, devoting her time to weaving while the others took care of the animals. Sedeq would join her at the second loom when she finished her work while Adataneses and Keziah spun the goat hair and wool for clothing. They knew of Noah's concerns of cooler weather, but no one knew how deeply he worried.

She worked the threads in and out, pondering the thought. Noah had always seemed so strong. In all the years she had known him, his faith had never wavered. He obeyed the Creator and did all he could to please Him. But beneath it all, did he fear *displeasing* Him? Was that why he wasn't sure he wanted to dismantle the ark and feared that God would judge the earth again?

She glanced behind her at the sound of voices. Noah and her sons approached. She stopped the loom. "What is it?"

Noah motioned her to join them. "I'm going to send a dove out. Japheth may have been right. The raven is resourceful and could have found a way to survive even if the ground is still covered in water. The dove will not be able to stay until there is enough dry land or trees in sight."

Zara saw acceptance in his eyes. Good. He did not hold grudges, for which she was grateful. No doubt he'd seen the wisdom in Japheth's words days ago and finally gave up waiting.

She followed the men toward the birdcages. Noah took one of the doves from its cage and held it gently in his hands. Again he climbed the ladder, opened the window, and let the bird go.

"Now we wait," Noah said, climbing down again. "Hopefully she will return soon."

"Should we wait by the window for her?" Zara glanced up the ladder. "She will tire quickly if she can't find a place to land."

"Ima is right," Japheth said. "Perhaps we should take turns waiting near the window to watch for her."

"I'll leave that to the rest of you." Ham raised a hand as though passing the idea on to the others. "I don't particularly enjoy the birds."

Zara faced him. "Your wife seems to find pleasure in them. I'm surprised she hasn't convinced you to do the same."

"Keziah has her opinions, and I have mine. This is not something on which we agree." Ham's lips formed a thin line, and Zara got the sense that he was talking about more than birds.

"I need to empty the waste into the waters," Shem said. "Are you coming?" He looked at Japheth.

"I'm coming." Japheth didn't sound as though he wanted to leave. No one enjoyed that chore, but they all took turns with it.

Noah looked at Zara. "If you hear the dove at the window, let her in. I'll be in the library for some time. I don't think she will return immediately."

He left Zara with Ham, who surprised her by staying. "Is there something troubling you, my son?" she asked.

Ham so rarely talked to her alone. He kept most things to himself or discussed them with Keziah, at least as far as she could tell. She felt the pull of the loom calling her back to work, but she realized how rare time with Ham had become.

"You could say that." He looked beyond her. "Can we talk, Ima?"

"Of course." A feeling of foreboding came over her, but she told herself not to fear.

They settled on the cushions where they usually ate their meals. The women were off caring for the animals. "Tell me." She laid her hand over his.

Ham looked at their hands, then lifted his head. "It's about Keziah."

Zara nodded. She'd suspected as much.

"I found an idol among her things the other day. I was just looking for a tablet I thought I'd misplaced when I found this image. At first I thought she had made a new kind of pottery." He paused, and his cheeks reddened. "She's been learning to sculpt like Adataneses does." He pulled his hand from hers.

"I've seen her at the wheel." Zara searched his face.

"She's made a few small containers," Ham said, "but this was not like that. It had no opening. It was in the shape of a woman, like the cult worshipers used all over the world before the flood."

"Which began in Cain's City." She'd seen such an idol in Vada's shrine.

He nodded. "She has begun to paint it. I know she needs things she enjoys. Even with the babe coming she is often sad. So I was glad when she found something that seemed to make her happy again, though I thought preparing for the babe would be enough."

Zara's heart skipped a beat. Why hadn't she noticed what Keziah was making when she worked at the pottery wheel?

"Ima, why would she do this? God has just destroyed every living thing on the earth because of our disobedience, idols, violence, and more. I can't allow her to keep it, but if I destroy it, she might just make another. And it would upset her. A lot." He ran a hand over his face, looking far older than he was. Such a burden he bore, and he'd tried so hard to please his father. Noah would be furious if he knew.

"It's possible she remembers their use in childbirth, as some type of charm to help women giving birth and to protect the child. They are simply tools of the evil one, but you're right, we cannot allow her to keep it or to make more. She will bring destruction on us before we even begin to rebuild." Zara felt an overwhelming ache in her middle. How could this happen before they were even off the ark?

"Should I confront her now? Or wait until we are on land again?" His voice wavered, and Zara longed to pull him into her arms and comfort him as she had when he was a young child.

"Do you want me to talk to her?" What would she say, though? Keziah would think Zara had gone through her things, but she would *know* Ham did if he confronted her. And she would be angry and unreasonable either way. *Oh Adonai, what are we to do?*

Ham rested his face in his hands, and Zara touched his head, praying for wisdom and comfort. At last he looked up. "I will find a way to talk to her. I don't know how, but I will." He stood and offered her his hand, pulling her to her feet. "Pray for me?"

"Always," she said, thrilled that he had asked. To be needed, even in such a small thing as listening and praying, warmed her heart.

But as she pondered the reason for his need, the warmth left her and she shivered.

Noah stopped outside the eating area, listening to Zara and Ham talking softly. He had intended to check the window again, realizing that the dove could return sooner than later, but what he heard made his blood run cold. Keziah had made an idol?

He covered his face with his hand and rubbed his jaw, attempting to dispel the sudden tension there. To walk to the window now would draw their attention, which he did not want to do. Neither could he pull himself away.

How was this possible? He knew Keziah had her problems, but she had never, in all the years they had been building the ark, shown signs that she worshiped idols. How had they not seen?

He heard the shuffle of feet and moved farther away. Ham left in the direction of the animals, while Zara headed toward the loom. He met her on the way.

"Noah! I didn't see you there." Her distressed look did not surprise him. She was shaken by Ham's admission, as was he.

"I heard your discussion. I was headed to the window but stopped when I heard the word 'idol.'" He took her hand and pulled her toward the window in case the dove returned. They were less likely to be overheard there.

"I didn't want you to know," she said, her voice a mere whisper. "I'm trying to understand why she decided to do something she knows angers the Creator and would upset the rest of us as well. But I will admit, I've never understood her motives for the way she has acted since she came into our family."

"Ham might as well have married the woman from Cain's City if his Sethite wife is going to practice their ways." Ham had not known Naavah well, but even Noah had been moved to pity her by the way her father had treated her.

"I agree. But we must not see her that way. She may have made the object as a decoration. Or perhaps she thinks it will bring her fortune and protection when the babe is born." Zara glanced toward the window, and her face brightened for a moment. "The dove has returned."

Noah followed her gaze, then quickly climbed the ladder and drew the bird back into the ark. He settled her safely in her cage and returned to Zara. "She could find no place to land, obviously. No trees grow on the mountain peaks for her to nest in. Perhaps the raven settled on the ground."

Zara nodded, but by her troubled look he knew she was not thinking of the dove or how soon the water would finally abate.

"I don't know what we can do about this problem," he said, taking her in his arms. "We will let Ham talk to her to see if that helps. If we must, we will bar her from using the pottery wheel, but Zara . . ." He held her at arm's length. "If someone wants to worship something other than the Creator, they will use anything to replace Him in their hearts. It does not have to be a creation of wood or stone. An idol can be anything we place above Him as the most important thing in our lives."

"I know that." She searched his face, and he kissed her forehead. "I'm just rather heartbroken that before we can even feel dry ground beneath our feet again, the evil that destroyed the world is already among us once more."

"I fear the evil never left us, beloved. Our hearts are sinful from birth, and not one of us is good in God's eyes." He sighed, wishing it weren't so.

"Then why did God spare us? Surely He looks on you with pleasure." Her brows drew down in confusion.

"That does not mean I am good. It only means that I believe Him and want to please Him. Future generations of our children will face the same evils that the Creator destroyed, and one day it will destroy them again." He wasn't sure how he knew that, but deep down he did. "It's why God must send us a Redeemer, as He promised Eve. But that day of His coming is not yet."

"I hope one of our grandchildren will be that Redeemer, so that the earth will be filled with people who love Him." She leaned her head against his chest. "I grow weary of it all."

He rubbed her back and rested his chin on her head. "As do I, dear wife. As do I."

Chapter

35

The following day, Noah called a family meeting. Zara watched him closely, fearing he would tell everyone of the idol before Ham had the chance to talk with Keziah. *Please, Adonai, do not let him do that. It will make things worse.*

She held her breath, waiting for the others to quiet. When they did, Noah spoke. "It is time we offered our worship to the Creator as we did in times past. When we leave the ark, we will build an altar to the Lord and offer a proper sacrifice, but for now, I want all of you to join me in prayer and adoration, that we might give our devotion to the Creator and not to ourselves."

"An excellent idea," Shem said, glancing at Sedeq. "We were just reading about how Adam built an altar to the Lord and sacrificed every year for the forgiveness of their sins."

"And we must continue to do as God instructed Adam, lest we become like Cain," Zara said, looking at each one of them.

Ham looked slightly uncomfortable, but a moment later he nodded. "I agree. Let me be the first to say how thankful I am to the Creator for seeing us safely through this storm. Soon we will walk again upon the earth, and I will be even more thankful when we no longer have to take care of animal waste."

Soft chuckles followed his remark.

"I am also thankful the Creator spared us," Sedeq said, smiling at Shem, "and that He saw fit to bless each one of us with the promise of new life before we leave this place. Our children will not know what it was like to live with the animals, but I'm glad we had the chance to know them."

"He is worthy of all honor and praise," Japheth added, wrapping an arm about Adataneses. "He did not have to spare us. But if He hadn't, He would not have been able to keep His promise to send a Redeemer. We serve a God who keeps His promises."

The comments continued until all had spoken, though Keziah only said, "I am grateful to be part of this family." Nothing about the Creator, which dampened Zara's spirits. Did she no longer believe? How could she not after she had seen all they had lived through?

Noah ended their worship by praying for each one of them, for each child in the womb, and for God to forgive them where they had failed Him.

Zara pondered his words after the others had gone to their work and she sat at the loom once again. If only forgiveness was not necessary. She would have loved to know the Creator as Eve did and not have the wall of sin separating them. But would she have been able to live with herself if she knew she had caused the whole world to suffer?

She shook her head and picked up the shuttle to begin weaving the weft into the warp. No. Life was better being who she was, living in the time in which God had placed her. She did not need to know supreme goodness and beauty and then never see it again. The opposite had been her experience. She'd known supreme evil and ugliness on an earth that no longer existed.

She now had the privilege to help carve a new life with the Creator for herself and her descendants.

If only she could help Keziah see that the Creator was worth worshiping, and that idols of wood or stone or anything else were worthless.

Ham walked into Keziah's room later that night. "We need to talk." He sat beside her and took her hand.

"Talk about what?" She gave him a curious look, but no hint of guilt filled her eyes.

He drew in a slow breath. "About the idol you made and have been painting. The woman you made out of clay."

Keziah's eyes widened. "You looked through my things?"

"I was looking for a tablet I misplaced."

"You thought I took it?"

"No. I thought I misplaced it and perhaps it got mixed in with your things."

"You could have asked me."

"You weren't here. Nevertheless, I found the idol. Show it to me." He opened his hand.

She stared at him. "Why should I? You've already condemned me."

"Because I'm your husband, and I asked to see it." He frowned, giving her his sternest look.

She crossed her arms over her chest. She was not going to make this easy.

He lowered his tense shoulders. "Please, Keziah. I need to see what you've made."

Again she stared at him, and he was certain she would not comply, but a moment later, she reached into a basket beside her and pulled out the idol. She placed it in his hand. "There. See? Are you happy now?"

He turned it over, examining it. "Why did you make this?"

She looked away, her telltale sadness creeping into her face. "I thought it would be something pretty to decorate our home once we are off this ark. It's not an idol. I don't worship it. I just started working the pottery wheel, and this took shape in my hand. It's like one of Adataneses's vases, only it came in the shape of a woman. That's all."

He looked from the image to her. "It has no use, Keziah. No place to hold ointments or food or anything. It looks like one of the idols from the world God just destroyed."

"Well, it's not." Her lower lip jutted forward in a pout. She reached for the image, but he closed his fingers over it. "Why can't you allow me even the simplest pleasures in life? It is not an idol."

"It looks too much like one. I can't allow you to keep it." He set his jaw, giving her his most determined look. He could not let her control him in this as she had so many times before.

"You can't *allow* me? You can't stop me!" She raised her voice, then quickly lowered it. "Destroy it if you want. I will just make another." Her words were a mere whisper, but they held an edge.

"Keziah." He gentled his tone, tamping down his frustration with her. "Please understand how important this is. I do not want our children to grow up believing in other gods as our ancestors who were judged did. Do you really want to bring the Creator's judgment on our family?"

She looked away again, and her cheeks flushed pink. Tears slipped down her face, and he forced himself to remain strong.

"I'm sorry, Keziah. We have to destroy it."

She nodded. He stood and left her room, then walked to the ladder, climbed to the window, and threw the object into the world below.

Seven days later, Zara walked with Noah to the window as he released the dove again. "Do you think you've given the earth enough time?" She took his hand once he reached the bottom step. "A week almost doesn't seem long enough. It's hard to keep getting our hopes up and discovering not yet."

"I have to keep trying." He squeezed her fingers and released them. "Despite our worship and prayers, we are all growing anxious. You know that."

She nodded. "We have had some tense moments in the past week. I'm glad Ham settled things with Keziah."

Noah nodded. "Let's hope her heart has changed, for if she harbors bitterness there, she will find a way to make another idol or something else she can worship. I fear for Ham's children."

Zara walked with him toward the steps to the roof. They climbed to the top, attempting to see the dove. "She has flown too far away and is too small to see against the vast mountains below."

"She won't be gone long. If we can see the mountaintops, which are even more visible now, surely soon." Noah shaded his eyes with his hand. "I cannot see trees yet, but that doesn't mean the waters haven't receded more in the lower places."

"We will wait for her return. I have weaving that beckons me."

"And I must help our sons with the animals. I fear I've grown lax of late and allowed them to do most of the work." They descended the stairs, and he kissed her. "I will return soon. If you hear the dove before then, come for me."

"I will." She watched him walk away before beginning her work. Though she had prayed often, her heart yearned for the Creator again. *Please, Adonai, let it be soon.*

Part 2

Then God said to Noah, "Come out of the ark, you and your wife and your sons and their wives. Bring out every kind of living creature that is with you—the birds, the animals, and all the creatures that move along the ground—so they can multiply on the earth and be fruitful and increase in number on it."

So Noah came out, together with his sons and his wife and his sons' wives. All the animals and all the creatures that move along the ground and all the birds—everything that moves on land—came out of the ark, one kind after another.

Then Noah built an altar to the LORD and, taking some of all the clean animals and clean birds, he sacrificed burnt offerings on it. The LORD smelled the pleasing aroma and said in his heart: "Never again will I curse the ground because of humans, even though every inclination of the human heart is evil from childhood. And never again will I destroy all living creatures, as I have done."

Genesis 8:15–21 NIV

Chapter

36

Sedeq bent over the small body of a lamb that wasn't thriving as quickly as it should. She hadn't expected any of the animals to have trouble nursing here, but this one seemed to need a little extra help. She moved into the pen, made sure the ewe had milk to give, then placed the lamb near its mother and guided it to her to nurse. She held her breath, waiting, and was relieved when the kid began to suckle.

Thank You, Adonai.

The Creator would protect the animals until they could repopulate the earth. She wondered if the kinds God had made in the beginning would continue on forever as long as there was an earth on which to live.

She watched the small lamb, keeping her distance, then slowly backed away when all was well. She closed the latch on the cage.

"What are you doing?" Keziah's voice came from behind her. Sedeq whirled about.

"Trying to keep this little one alive." She pointed to the lamb. "He had trouble latching on to his mother."

Keziah nodded but said nothing else for a lengthy breath.

"Is something wrong?" Sedeq asked. Keziah wasn't usually so quiet, and by her look Sedeq knew she was troubled.

"Is everyone talking about me?" Keziah crossed her arms over her chest as if warding off a blow.

"Talking about you? Why would we?" Sedeq lifted a brow.

"Because of the pottery." She looked beyond Sedeq, and her face darkened.

"Pottery?" Completely confused now, Sedeq walked toward the third floor to their living quarters. Keziah came up with some of the strangest things, and no doubt she feared something that was nothing. "I don't know what you're talking about."

Keziah slowly followed, and for a moment Sedeq wondered if she would say any more.

"I made a piece of pottery," Keziah said at last. "Ham thought I'd made an idol, but it was just a decoration. He took it and threw it out the window." She frowned. "He didn't believe me."

Sedeq forced herself not to react, though the words surprised her. Perhaps shocked was a better word. An *idol*? If Ham thought it was an idol, he must have had a good reason. And why was Keziah telling her this? Shouldn't it be something kept between her and Ham?

She glanced at Keziah. "What did it look like?"

"It came out in the shape of a woman. I didn't think I was capable of making something like it, but I was pleased with it. I had begun to paint it when Ham found it." She crossed her arms again and took a step back. "I've said too much. I just wanted to be sure he wasn't telling everyone about it to make me look bad. It *wasn't* an idol and he shouldn't have destroyed it."

Sedeq's mind whirled. Bitterness dripped from Keziah's words. This was not good. Could they not even get off the ark before their family fell apart and became like the world used to be? She fought a sense of despair.

"Perhaps the image simply reminded Ham of the idols he

had seen all around us, and he might have feared displeasing the Creator. I would have feared such a thing. Surely that thought crossed your mind, didn't it?"

Keziah lowered her gaze. "I hadn't really thought about it. But you're right." She looked up. "I should have remembered the images my mother worshiped and considered what I was doing. Tell me you don't think ill of me."

"Of course not! We are all going to do things we shouldn't. We can't escape displeasing the Creator because only He is perfect and good."

Why was she assuring Keziah when she wasn't truly sure how she felt about this news? But she couldn't bear to leave her sister-in-law with a reason to fall into a depressed state again.

"Thank you." Keziah fell into step with her again.

Relief that she seemed to understand filled Sedeq. "Let's just put it all behind us."

"Yes. Let's."

But Sedeq doubted Keziah could do as she'd suggested.

Noah left Shem and Japheth in the midst of caring for the larger animal kinds to see if the dove had returned. Zara hadn't called him, but a part of him needed to be there, whether the bird had enough time to explore the earth or not.

He rounded the corner near the birdcages and met Zara. "I expected you to be working the loom. Is she back already?"

"And I expected you to be working with our sons. But I see that we're both anxious." She smiled as he climbed the ladder to check.

He opened the window and peered out, and there, coming toward him, was the dove. "She has something in her beak!" He stretched his hand through the window, and she landed in his palm. "It's an olive leaf." He pulled her into the ark and descended the ladder.

The bird released the olive leaf, and he took it in his other hand, then placed her back in her cage. She rested on her perch.

"She wore herself out," Zara said. "But she found what she was looking for."

Noah nodded. "This is good. The waters have definitely receded from the earth. In another week they should be down even more. I will send her out again then."

"She might not return next time."

"That is my hope." He turned the olive leaf over. It was fresh and green. "Perhaps the earth will not look so very different than it did when we entered the ark. At least we know the trees have survived."

"I suspect it will have all the same plants as before, but the way things look—don't you think it will be rearranged? I wonder if where we've landed is higher than the hills we once knew." Zara walked with Noah toward the library, where he set the leaf beside his parchments. He would record this new development, as he had everything else during their time here.

"I do believe the waters will have moved the land around. Water is a powerful force. Nothing is immune to what it can do." He looked at her. "I don't know if we will live long enough to explore the many ways the earth has changed. But then, we didn't know much more than our few cities and the waterways of the Tigris and Euphrates. I suspect the earth is much larger than we knew even before the flood."

"I'm sure you're right." She turned to leave. "I'd best get started on the evening meal. I will leave you to your writings."

He absently watched her leave, then sat at the table to record all that had happened in the previous week. Hopefully someday his descendants would find his writings and learn from them. If those who came after him did not learn from what had come before, they would forget God just as easily as the people born after the fall. He must not let that happen.

A week later, the whole family watched as Noah let the dove go again. "The air isn't as cool as it was when I sent the raven. Perhaps with the water receding, the air will be warmer."

Zara moved toward the cooking area, the others following. "I think we are safe to go about our chores. The dove might not return for some time, especially if the waters are gone." She sent a silent prayer that they were. How she longed to have God open the door and let them out of this place.

She watched her sons and Noah head off to care for the animals, while the women gathered around her. "I think we should go through our things and make sure we have what we need for four tents, including ropes, pegs, and poles. I think we have enough rugs to lay on the ground inside them."

"I'm sure we do," Adataneses said. "I counted the ones in our rooms. If we need bigger tents, we can always weave and spin once we are off the ark. But should we have a separate tent for the looms? I think we should protect them in case it rains again or the sun is too hot."

"Or too cold," Sedeq said. "I agree. I think we've made enough tents for the four families, but let's quickly weave one to house the food and one for working."

"I've already begun one for keeping the food, and we can begin a garden with the plants we've started here as soon as the ground allows." Zara moved to the loom to show them the last of the pieces she was sewing together for a cooking area. "I will have the men move our oven outside so we can bake. It will take time to build another one. Meanwhile, we will share a joint courtyard once that is built."

"It's starting to seem real." Keziah smiled for the first time Zara had seen since Ham discarded her idol, or whatever she was calling it. "I've been sewing clothing for the babe." She touched her middle, which was barely bigger than it had been when she first told them. She had plenty of time for such things. Why would she focus on that instead of things for the group at large?

Zara stifled a sigh. She'd given up trying to figure Keziah out. The woman had her struggles. "Yes, it does seem real at last. I will admit, I'm excited to see the earth again."

"I'm going to dig my feet into the soil and twist my toes until they are covered in earth," Sedeq said, laughing.

"I think I might just kiss the ground," Keziah added.

Silence followed her comment, but a moment later Adataneses said, "And I will pick the first flower I find and sniff it and breathe deeply of the air. No more animal smells!"

Zara joined them in laughter that time. "I think we will all be happier outside than in. Why don't we get busy so we're ready when that day comes?"

They chattered and left her to do the things they needed to. Zara sat near the loom to finish sewing the cooking tent. Surely Keziah had meant nothing by her comment. To kiss the ground wasn't to worship it. Someday perhaps Zara would ask her what she'd meant. But for now, she would believe the best.

Chapter
37

That evening as they sat together for the meal, Noah joined them after checking the window again.

"Any sign of her?" Zara asked, already knowing the answer.

He shook his head. "I left the window open so she can come inside if she needs to. But I don't think she will be returning." His smile showed relief that matched Zara's feelings.

"This is the first day of the first month of your six hundredth and first year, my husband. A day to truly celebrate!" Zara's heart lightened as she listened to the laughter and excitement of her family. These were good times. Despite all the trials of living on the ark, she would miss these moments of family closeness. Once they began to fill the earth, how often would they continue to come together? How long would her children and grandchildren and future descendants live in unity as they did now, at least most of the time?

"We will take the covering off the ark tomorrow," Noah said, drawing her attention.

"Why not do it now?" Shem's face held the eagerness they all felt. His brothers nodded in agreement.

"The sun has not yet set. It will take time to dismantle the covering, so why not get started while we can?" Japheth wiped his mouth on a linen cloth and stood. "I'm ready, Father."

"I agree." Ham jumped up and Shem stood as well, all of them looking like young boys ready for an adventure.

Zara looked at Noah. "Listen to your sons, Noah. We are all anxious to glimpse the earth, even if we have to do so as the sun sets."

Noah looked at them all, then stood. "All right. Let's get started."

"We will put the food away and join you." Zara gathered the plates and Sedeq helped her. Adataneses and Keziah carried the leftover food and tucked it away in the appropriate cupboards.

"Let's hurry!" Sedeq wiped off the last plate, and Zara placed it on its shelf in another cupboard.

The four of them walked eagerly toward the stairs and joined the men on the roof. The covering had already been removed from a third of the roof. Zara gazed at the heavens, mesmerized by the vastness of the sky and the sight of the setting sun. The colors mingled in blues and golds of varying shades, taking her breath.

"It's beautiful," Sedeq said, coming alongside her. She slipped her arm through Zara's, and together they walked toward the edge to look out over what they could see of the land.

"It's dry!" Keziah's squeal startled Zara, but she couldn't blame her.

"It does indeed look that way." Zara called to Noah, and the men stopped their work and joined them. "It's growing dark, but can you see any water?" She strained to see into the distance.

"I don't see any," Japheth said. He leaned far over the edge, causing Zara's heart to skip a beat, but she refrained from telling him to be careful. He was old enough to know how safe it was.

Japheth stepped away and wrapped Adataneses in his arms. "We will be able to tell better tomorrow, but I think it's truly dry."

Noah nodded, stepping beside Zara. "I thought I saw patches

of water here and there when the first part of the cover came off. But those could be brooks or streams. We will see better by light of day."

"Which means we should probably finish this tomorrow." Shem pulled Sedeq toward him. "I'm as excited as the rest of you, but we also need to rest. There will be much to do in the few days we have left here."

Zara stood with Noah, watching their children descend the stairs to their rooms. Noah held her back and tucked his arm about her shoulders, turning her toward the sunset.

"God is very good." He lifted his gaze heavenward, and she followed it. As the sun dipped below the horizon, the stars broke out across the sky, displaying their shining glory. "It's as if the heavens are playing a melody of their own."

"The lights are appearing a few at a time as though they're different notes in a symphony," she said, marveling. They hadn't seen the stars in such brilliance even before the flood.

"You're remembering the musical accomplishments of our ancestors."

"Yes. It will take us years to duplicate such things, even though we saved many of the instruments they used."

He nodded and held her closer. "Great is the Lord and worthy of praise. Let all the earth be silent before Him."

She pondered Noah's praise, her heart lifting in songs of her own. *God truly is good.* He had brought them through the hardest trial anyone could ever face. He forgave them even though they were no better than anyone who had perished. They had simply believed in Him and obeyed Him.

She looked out at the land below, void of any human or animal life. Why had most of humanity found it so hard to trust the Creator? All they had to do was look at creation to know He existed and He cared for His creatures.

Oh Adonai, may we never look away from You again. You

truly are God and Lord of all. You alone control all things. May we always worship You.

Nearly two months passed before the ground held no hint of water that was not a river or stream or, in the distance, a larger sea. Zara wearied of the anxious checking and finally waited for the others to look out on the earth. What had seemed so dry that night when they first removed the ark's covering had proven to still be muddy in places. Too muddy, from what they could see.

As dawn broke on the twenty-seventh day of the second month, Zara ground grain, again wondering how long. A sigh lifted her chest as Noah entered the cooking area. She glanced at him and stopped grinding at the wide smile on his face.

"What is it?" Hope rose within her, but she dared not let it rise too high.

"I've heard from the Creator. He said, 'Come out of the ark, you and your wife and your sons and their wives. Bring out every kind of living creature that is with you—the birds, the animals, and all the creatures that move along the ground—so they can multiply on the earth and be fruitful and increase in number on it.' The day has finally come!" Noah leaned his hands on the board in front of her. "Let us eat quickly. Bring the flour with you for later. We will eat nuts and dried fruit and get started."

She nodded and quickly poured the flour into a smaller container. "Girls, come and help me!" Her voice rang out as Noah left to call their sons. "The day has come!"

Suddenly everyone was talking at once. "Gather the tents and poles and pegs first," Sedeq said to Adataneses. They filled a cart Japheth had built for them while Zara and Keziah filled another with rugs and bedding.

"Wait for us to leave the ark with the tents before you release the animals," Zara called to Noah's retreating back. "I don't want to have to wait for them or be trampled trying to share the space."

Noah and their sons turned about and walked back toward her. "We will help you," he said. "We don't want to wait to step outside of the ark either. Let's get the tents outside and pick the area. You can be setting them up while we let the animals go."

"Grab something to eat as you work," Zara said, placing one of the pillows at the top of the full cart. "We will take these out, find a place to set them up, and return for the rest."

"What if we can't find suitable ground on this mountain?" Worry lines appeared along Keziah's brow. "How far will we have to go?"

"Hopefully not too far. At least for the night." Zara stopped, and Japheth nearly ran into her with the tents.

"What's wrong?" Adataneses asked.

"Keziah makes a good point." She looked to Noah. "What if we have to travel a distance for level ground? Perhaps God doesn't want us to come out of the ark completely yet. What if we still need to sleep here tonight?" The thought did not please her, though their quarters were surely more comfortable than sleeping on the ground would be.

"I'm sleeping outside under the stars even if I have to do it without a tent or a bed!" Sedeq's emphatic tone lightened the moment. "You don't think the Creator would tell us to leave if the ground was not ready for us, do you? It is early morn. We have all day to set up a home outside." She motioned Zara to move the cart, and Zara did not argue.

"You're right. We will sleep on dry ground tonight. Let's go, for we have many trips to make." She lifted the handle of the cart, but Noah took it from her. She slipped into the cooking area, grabbed several baskets of food, and motioned for the others to do the same. "Let's take as much as we can. I don't want to make that trip back and forth any more than we have to."

"I can't wait to see what the earth looks like." Shem grabbed a heavy sack of grain, and Ham took another.

"On that, my son, I think we can all agree." She smiled at each one and hurried after Noah and Japheth.

The ramps seemed to stretch on forever, but then they were at the door. Noah stopped the cart and undid the latch. He pushed it open. Light poured into the opening, and the rising sun nearly blinded them.

Zara blinked, adjusting to the daylight. "It's a good thing this door is on the bottom level. It's still a step down."

Shem was the first to jump to the ground, followed by Ham and Japheth. They gathered large rocks that littered the earth and piled them near the door. "Let's remove the door. It can be the ramp for the animals and for us." Shem climbed up again, and Japheth joined him.

Ham took the baskets from Keziah's arms, then helped her down. Zara held back her impatient desire to have been ahead of her children. Did it really matter? But it irritated her that Keziah was the first of the women.

She watched Keziah do exactly as she'd said she would—bow to the ground and kiss the dirt. She jumped up, and Ham twirled her about, laughing.

Shem, Japheth, and Noah worked to remove the door from its hinges, laid it on the edge of the opening, and dropped it at an angle to the ground. A perfect fit.

Japheth tested the door by pushing the cart over it and walking down it to the ground. Suddenly they were all touching the earth, setting their burdens down, and hugging and laughing. Sedeq dug her toes into the soil. Adataneses plucked a flower and took a long, deep breath. Apparently they all meant what they'd said.

Zara leaned against Noah and looked into his eyes. "God is very good."

He smiled down at her as their children danced around them. "Indeed, He is."

Chapter

38

"Everything is so different." Sedeq looked from one end of the land to the other. Though the flat area was large enough to hold their own tents and many more, they were not far from where the mountain sloped upward and the cliffs led downward. "Do you think we will stay here long?" She turned to Ima Zara, who was helping Adataneses unfold her and Noah's tent.

Ima Zara lifted her gaze to Sedeq's. "I imagine we will want to move to lower ground eventually. I don't want my grandchildren falling down one of these steep cliffs."

"I agree." Sedeq glanced at the one she had edged closest to and shivered. Though it was some distance from where she now stood, she could imagine young children walking too close out of curiosity. She held her end of the tent Keziah had unfolded and helped set the poles in place. "We will have time to relocate after all the animals are out of the ark and we've moved everything out that we need."

"I think the men are going to want to stay close to the ark for a while, and I agree with them," Adataneses said, poking her head out from behind the tent. "They're going to need the workshops for a while until they can dismantle the cages and build permanent structures here." She glanced heavenward. "And what if the Creator sends rain again? If it rains hard, I'm going to want to run back to the ark for safety!"

"Do you think He would do that?" Keziah stood from where she had been pounding a peg into the ground. "I hope not! I never want to enter that thing again."

Sedeq straightened and rubbed her back, turning at the feel of the earth shaking slightly. "They're letting the animals out. Look!" The birds were flying high above them, squawking in their various languages, while the larger animal kinds hurried down the ramp and moved past them toward the forests and rivers below.

"They seem as glad to be set free as we are," Ima Zara said. After watching them a few moments, she moved on to the next tent with Adataneses's help. Sedeq and Keziah did the same.

Sedeq couldn't wait to make their tent cozy and inviting for Shem. It would feel strange to sleep on the hard ground, but she would never grow tired of the smell of the earth. The trek to the river would take a little effort, but thankfully, a smaller brook ran behind their encampment and would be sufficient for their basic needs.

"How is it going?" Shem's voice behind her startled her.

She whirled about, caught in his embrace, and accepted his quick kiss.

"I only have a moment," Shem said, "but I wanted to tell you that Abba wants you to keep the pairs of clean animals near the tents. He has kept back the clean birds and the rest of the clean kinds for a sacrifice. But we don't want the sheep, goats, and cattle running off."

"I assume you're going to build pens for them by tonight. I do not wish to sleep with them in our tent," Ima Zara said, arms akimbo.

Shem laughed. "As soon as we feed those still on the ark and release the last of them, we will build enclosures for the animals." He pointed to the sheep coming down the ramp toward them. "Just keep your eye on them so they don't wander off."

Sedeq crossed her arms over her chest. "Humph." She shook her head. "Perhaps you should have built the enclosures first."

He shrugged, then looked about. "Where is the sack of nuts we carried out?"

She tilted her head. "You're hungry again?"

He gave her a sheepish look. "I just need a handful."

She laughed, then walked over to the sack, untied it, and scooped some nuts into her hand. She offered them to him.

"Thanks." He grinned, kissed her cheek, then turned and ran off toward the ark.

Noah walked out of his tent the next day and went to the pen they had built to house the sheep. He selected two male lambs, two male goats, and two of the male cattle kind. He set them apart and then called his family together to meet in the central area between their tents.

"Is there a problem, Abba?" Shem rubbed a hand over his face and yawned. They had been up late building pens for the clean animals and carrying the birdcages out of the ark.

"We are going to build an altar to the Lord." He looked at his sons, who were all struggling to awaken. He should have waited, but the desire to sacrifice to the Lord had troubled him throughout the night. He needed to do this before another day passed. "I know you're tired, but this is important." He glanced at Zara. She had been aware of his restless night's sleep.

"Your father is right," she said. "He barely slept with the concern of this, so while you help him, your wives and I will prepare food for you." She shooed them toward Noah. "Go with your father."

Noah led the way, thankful when he did not hear grumbling. They all needed to have humble attitudes toward the Creator, especially now that they were free of the ark. They still needed His protection and help if they were going to survive and keep from angering Him again.

No, not just angering Him. They'd broken His heart. Noah had sensed it in the way the Creator had spoken to him in years past. None of this was supposed to be this way. If only God had not given them a choice. But then they wouldn't have been made in His image. They wouldn't have had the chance to truly know Him in a way that no other created being could.

He glanced heavenward. *Thank You.* Could he ever grow tired of praising the Lord for all His kindness and goodness? They must never forget His great love for humanity. If not for His love, He would never have promised a coming Redeemer. He would not have given humans a chance to repent.

"We would have been like the Watchers." He stopped at the area he had chosen to build the altar.

"What did you say, Father?" Ham came alongside him. "Did you mention the Watchers? Do you think they survived the flood?" His wide eyes matched the horrified looks of his brothers as they all gathered around him.

"I was thinking out loud of how good God is to give us another chance when we sin. He did not give a second chance to the Watchers." Noah spread his hand to indicate where they stood. "We will build an altar of stone here. Gather as many large rocks as you can find, but do not attempt to cut them. We will fit them together without using any tools on them."

"You didn't answer Ham's question, Abba," Shem said. "Do you think the Watchers will be a danger to us still? Did they survive the flood?"

Noah looked from one to another. "I don't think the evil shining ones can die like that. God can destroy them because He can do anything, but I don't think that was His reason for the flood. He destroyed their demon-human offspring, but they are spirits. They will return one day. But hopefully they will not be welcomed by humans again, which allowed the mating that nearly ruined the race of humanity."

"So we will still need to be watchful of them?" Japheth's brow creased in worry. "I had hoped we were free of them."

"We should have stayed on the ark." Shem glanced toward the ship resting on the mountain behind them. "Though I am very glad to be off of it."

"If we obey the Lord and you teach your children and grandchildren to obey Him and keep the sacrifices, they will not be a threat to us," Noah said. "If we walk with the Creator and find favor in His eyes, they will fear us. Do not be troubled, my sons."

Had they ever experienced the Creator the way he had? When God had appeared to him, he'd never feared the evil ones. They could not stand in the presence of the Lord. Surely he and his family were safe if they stayed near Him.

"I hope that's true, Abba," Shem said. "It seems to me that Adam and Eve tried to do that very thing, but our children and future descendants could still end up walking away." He turned to search for the heavy rocks Noah had requested. Ham and Japheth did the same.

Noah found a stick and drew the area where they would lay the stones, pondering Shem's words. How long until the evil they couldn't truly escape crept back into the new world they were making? *Oh Adonai, don't let me live to see Your wrath against evil again.* He wanted to live, but he couldn't bear to watch his family fall into the sins that had hurt God in the past. If only they could put sin behind them for good!

Perhaps the sacrifice would help. He would feel better once he knew that God was pleased with them.

A few hours later, Zara and her daughters-in-law joined Noah and their sons around the altar. The animals destined for sacrifice stood near, and the cages of the birds sat on the ground, surrounding Noah.

"Today we sacrifice to the Lord our God, Creator of all, to praise Him for seeing us safely through the flood," Noah said. "He has been very kind to our family and to the animals. He would have extended that kindness to anyone who perished in the flood if they'd believed, and we can only hope that in the very end, some of them did." He lifted his eyes to the heavens, then faced his family. "Each of you take one of the animals, a sheep or goat, and place your hands on its head."

Zara and Noah shared a lamb, as did Shem and Sedeq. Japheth and Adataneses shared a goat, and Ham and Keziah did the same. Noah prayed, then gave each of them time to silently confess their sins.

Forgive me, oh Lord, for the sin that is always knocking at my heart, Zara prayed. *Help me never to complain against You again or grow impatient with You. Help me to trust You always and be the example I should be to my children and coming grandchildren.*

Zara lifted her head and held a clay bowl beneath the lamb's neck. Noah slit the animal's throat. Each of their sons did the same, then poured the blood on the altar. Time seemed to stand still as her sons and husband placed the pieces of each animal on the altar one by one, then also sacrificed the cattle and birds. Fire rose to the heavens, and the women stepped back.

A sense of sadness filled Zara as she was reminded again of what most of the world had forgotten before the flood. No one was good. Not even one. Compared to the holiness of the Creator, they were not pure. They could no longer come to Him as Adam and Eve had in the beginning. Sin always brought separation. She knew that but struggled with understanding it all sometimes. Would the world sacrifice animals for as long as the earth lasted? Or would the Redeemer somehow change that? What would have to happen for their guilt to be forever removed and their souls restored to a rightness with the Creator that they could not achieve now?

Would that ever happen? Perhaps not. The Creator had not explained anything about the Redeemer other than the fact that He would crush the serpent's head. But how?

She looked at the plume of smoke rising heavenward, the scent of roasting meat filling her senses.

Suddenly the clouds parted, and a voice called to them from heaven. "Never again will I curse the ground because of humans, even though every inclination of the human heart is evil from childhood. And never again will I destroy all living creatures, as I have done. As long as the earth endures, seedtime and harvest, cold and heat, summer and winter, day and night will never cease."

Silence followed the remark, and Noah fell to his knees, face to the ground. Zara and the rest of their family did the same.

The voice came again. "Be fruitful and increase in number and fill the earth. The fear and dread of you will fall on all the beasts of the earth, and on all the birds in the sky, on every creature that moves along the ground, and on all the fish in the sea. They are given into your hands. Everything that lives and moves about will be food for you. Just as I gave you the green plants, I now give you everything.

"But you must not eat meat that has its lifeblood still in it. And for your lifeblood I will surely demand an accounting. I will demand an accounting from every animal. And from each human being, too, I will demand an accounting for the life of another human being. Whoever sheds human blood, by humans shall their blood be shed. For in the image of God has God made mankind.

"As for you, be fruitful and increase in number. Multiply on the earth and increase upon it."

Another silence, and Noah slowly rose and lifted his gaze to the heavens. Zara and their family followed his example. The brilliant light still parted the clouds. Would God speak again?

Zara jumped as He spoke, louder now. How thunderous was God's voice!

"I now establish My covenant with you and with your descendants after you, and with every living creature that was with you—the birds, the livestock, and all the wild animals, all those that came out of the ark with you—every living creature on earth. I establish my covenant with you. Never again will all life be destroyed by the waters of a flood. Never again will there be a flood to destroy the earth. This is the sign of the covenant I am making between Me and you and every living creature with you, a covenant for all generations to come—I have set My rainbow in the clouds, and it will be the sign of the covenant between Me and the earth."

Suddenly a glorious bow of myriad colors stretched from horizon to horizon. Zara's breath caught at the beauty, and gratitude filled her, joy bubbling to the surface. She barely contained her desire to shout Adonai's praise.

"Whenever I bring clouds over the earth and the rainbow appears in the clouds, I will remember My covenant between Me and you and all living creatures of every kind. Never again will the waters become a flood to destroy all life. Whenever the rainbow appears in the clouds, I will see it and remember the everlasting covenant between God and all living creatures of every kind on the earth."

The light shifted slightly, focused on Noah.

"This is the sign of the covenant I have established between Me and all life on the earth," God said.

Suddenly the light disappeared, and the sky returned to its blues and unparted puffy white clouds.

"We never have to fear the rain or any storms God sends," Noah said, turning to face them.

His face shone with a radiance Zara had never seen. Did they all look like that? When she glanced at her family, she saw that only Noah carried the brilliant touch of God.

"It's a relief to know that God won't put us through that again," Shem said, glancing heavenward, then drawing Sedeq into his arms. "I think we would have all feared a flood with every drop of rain."

"So it will rain again," Ham said, slightly frowning. "I had hoped it would not be necessary."

"The waters no longer mist the earth from below," Noah said. "Rain will be the only way for plants to grow. We will need it for food and drink, lest the streams and rivers dry up. The waters of heaven will be a good thing." He looked at the altar. "The Lord was pleased with our sacrifice. Now we will do as He said—be fruitful and multiply and subdue the earth."

"Perhaps we could rest a moment and eat the midday meal first." Zara smiled at him. "Your face is glowing."

"It seems only yours is, Abba," Shem said. "I do hope the Creator will be pleased with all of us. But I'm glad He is pleased with you best."

"I don't think the Creator loves me best, Son. He called me first, and His covenant is with me *and my descendants*. He doesn't show favoritism." Noah came alongside Zara and turned her toward the camp, clearly wanting to take the focus off himself. "I am no better than any of you," he added.

Zara tucked her hand beneath his arm. Noah *was* favored by the Creator, but maybe it was his humility about that favoritism that drew the Creator's attention.

Help me to be the same.

283

Chapter
39

ONE YEAR LATER

Zara rose to the sound of a baby's cry. She could not hold
back a smile. Three grandsons had been born to them since
they had left the ark, and already Sedeq suspected she was
expecting again. God was indeed good.

She dressed quickly, left their tent, and poked her head into
Sedeq's tent. "How is our Aram today?" She took the fussing
baby from Sedeq's arms and hugged him close.

"I don't know what else to do for him." She lifted a haggard
face to Zara. "I've nursed him and he seemed fine, then he
just started to cry. Did he wake you? I'm sorry."

Zara brushed the comment aside. "I was awake. We have
all grown accustomed to having little ones cry in the night and
early morn. But let me take him for a bit. You're tired. Rest a
little. Then you can come and help me."

Sedeq gave her a grateful half smile and crawled back onto
her pallet. Zara took Aram outside. His cries weakened as he
looked about. He was only six months old, but he was already
crawling and loved to push himself to try new things. Though

he was a challenge to watch, Zara loved mornings when she could spend time with him like this. She would do as much with Ham's Cush and Japheth's Gomer, but Keziah and Adataneses were not pregnant again yet and didn't seem to want her help as much.

She released a small sigh. Did that make her a bad grandmother? She loved all her grandsons, but there was something about Aram's curiosity that reminded her most of raising her boys. Though Cush was a month older, he was not as curious, and Gomer was still too small.

"Would you like to see the lambs?" She carried Aram toward the pens, where Shem was unfastening the latch to take the sheep to the fields.

"And who have we here?" Shem tickled his son's belly, eliciting a giggle from him. Shem leaned close and kissed Aram's cheek. Pride shone in his eyes. "Is he giving Sedeq trouble again?" He opened the gate and called the sheep to follow him.

"He was crying even after she fed him. He just wants to see what's going on outside the tent. I let Sedeq rest." Zara walked with Shem as he led the sheep toward a small field not far from their tents.

"Thank you for helping her," he said. "She hasn't been feeling well since before she learned she was carrying another babe. We didn't expect her to conceive again so soon."

"You are taking 'be fruitful and multiply' seriously." She met his grin with one of her own, then kissed Aram's soft dark curls. "She will feel better in time. And I'm happy to help. Speaking of which, I need to return to begin grinding the grain. I will bring you some flatbread later. You took enough food with you, yes?"

He patted the pouch at his side. "I have learned to be prepared."

She laughed. "Perhaps Aram is going to be as hungry as you are. Your poor wife will never get any rest."

"I would help her if I could."

Zara patted his arm. "No you wouldn't. But you mean well."

She turned to take Aram back to the center of the camp, listening to Shem's laughter as she went. Aram acted as though he wanted her to put him down.

"You can't walk yet, little man. But Savta will set a blanket on the ground beside me as I work. You can watch me grind the grain. But don't go anywhere!" She stopped at her tent, grabbed a soft blanket, and returned to the courtyard area. She spread the blanket on the ground and sat beside Aram with the sack of grain and grinding stones.

Adataneses emerged from her tent, her baby in a basket she had made, and joined Zara.

"Good morning, my daughter." Zara smiled at her, noting the exhaustion also in her face. Had she been as tired when her own sons were born? Or had the differences in the earth and atmosphere affected them somehow? She couldn't remember.

"Good morning, Ima. Gomer had me up a lot in the night. But I will nap with him later." She took fire from one of the torches and lit the wood and dried animal dung in the central firepit. A three-pronged griddle stood to the side, and she set it over the flames once they had died down to a manageable level.

They worked in silence to make the flatbread for the others. Keziah soon joined them with Cush and placed him on a blanket beside her. He had begun to push up on his hands and knees but then quickly fell to his stomach again. "He's growing so fast," Keziah said. "I can barely keep up with him." She yawned and glanced about. "Where is Sedeq?"

"She's resting. She's weary with the new pregnancy." Zara mixed oil with the grain and poured it onto the hot griddle.

"I would love to do the same," Keziah said. "I think I might also be expecting another, though I won't know until the next new moon."

Zara lifted her hands to her face, overjoyed. "Another so soon? I'm happy for you."

Adataneses shook her head. "I'm happy for you too, but I'm glad it's not me yet. Gomer is too young. I hope I have more time."

They continued to talk of birthing and the care of the babies while Zara made the food and looked from one grandson to the other. She was blessed. So very blessed.

Thank You, Adonai. I am thrilled that we can celebrate the joy of children again.

She didn't expect Him to respond to her, but from the joy in her heart, she suspected He agreed.

TWENTY-FIVE YEARS LATER

Zara walked across the compound, carrying a basket of sweet breads, and followed the sound of pounding. The dirt path had been smoothed out and leveled to make way for the buildings that had risen in the years since the flood. How grateful she was that they no longer lived high up the mountain but had found a place on the plains. Noah and their sons and some of the older grandsons had helped to dismantle the shops inside the ark and used the wood to make new, sturdier shops of wood and stone in the city they were creating. If they could call it that.

"Ima, wait a moment."

Zara turned at the sound of Sedeq running toward her. She stopped. "Did I forget something?"

Sedeq slowed, a hand to her pregnant belly. Despite already having ten children—five sons and five daughters—Sedeq had not stopped bearing. Her own sons had married their cousins and were due to give Zara great-grandchildren soon. Keziah had four sons and four daughters but had seemed unable to bear in many years, while Adataneses, who had feared she would never bear, had surpassed them all with seven sons and seven daughters.

"Should you be running in your condition?" Zara looked Sedeq up and down.

"I'm fine." She drew a breath. "I brought curds to go with the sweet bread. Shem likes them together." She smiled.

"I'm glad you thought of it." They continued on toward the site where the library was being constructed. "I never thought we would build a city again."

Sedeq glanced at her. "It's still rather barren to be called that, isn't it? I mean, we have our houses and the metal shop and woodshop and now the library, but that wasn't any different than what we had on the ark. When we're large enough to have a government and shops to sell things to more people, maybe then I would call it a city. It feels more like a large family camp."

Zara nodded. "Yes, you're right."

They arrived where the men were working. The pounding stopped as Noah and Shem noticed them.

"Food is here!" Shem called to the others. It was only a midday snack that Zara had begun to bring them, but all of them seemed to appreciate it.

Shem's sons Aram and Arphaxad hurried to them, kissed their mother's cheek, and accepted the food from both of them.

"Like father, like sons," Zara said, smiling at Shem, who was close behind.

"Of course," Shem said, taking his portion and stepping aside so the others could take their turn.

When they had finished, the men returned to their work while Zara and Sedeq walked back toward their houses and tents. They neared the vineyard Noah had planted shortly after they'd moved to the plains. The grapes were not quite ready for harvest.

Zara walked closer, Sedeq at her side. She plucked a grape

and tasted it, her mouth puckering at the sourness. "They need a little longer, I think."

Sedeq took one and said the same. "Yes, I don't think we want sour wine or sour grape juice for the children."

"The raisins will be sweeter as well if we wait a little longer. At least this year we are better prepared for the harvest. Last year we could have used a second vat to squeeze the grapes after the great harvest we had."

They walked among the vines, Zara noting how the Creator had allowed everything they'd planted to flourish. And now that they lived closer to the wider branches of the rivers, watering the fields had not been as difficult.

"We should plan a great harvest celebration when everything is picked and stored. Enjoy the fruit of our labor." Sedeq again placed a protective hand over the babe. "He or she will be born right around that time, though, so I wouldn't be much help to you. But do you think it's a good idea?"

Zara took Sedeq's arm and led them back toward their homes. "I think it's a wonderful idea. We could make it a time of sacrifice to the Creator in thanksgiving for all He has done for us, then feast together from the good food He has allowed us to produce. He has sustained us for twenty-six years beyond the flood, which still amazes me. The time just keeps going by so quickly, and yet none of us except the children seem to be getting any older." She laughed. "At least I don't feel older yet. I suppose we should."

Sedeq squeezed her hand. "Nonsense. God has given you a long life, like our ancestors. I wonder if our descendants will live as long as those before the flood. I can't imagine being six hundred and twenty-six years old like Abba Noah is."

Zara sighed. She wasn't much younger, and in comparison to twenty-five-year-old Aram, Cush, and Gomer, she seemed ancient indeed. How many more descendants would she see born into the world?

"Harvest is in a few months," she said. Food was a better subject than wondering how long she would live. She would enjoy the time God had given her. "I will speak to Keziah and Adataneses, and we can plan a special meal and sacrifice. Of course, you can give your suggestions as well. Just because you will be nursing a babe doesn't mean you won't be part of this."

She was grateful for Sedeq's smile. Before they partook of the fruit of the vine to celebrate, remembering the Creator might keep her sons and grandsons from overindulging. Nothing good had ever come of such imbibing before the flood. She must be sure they remembered that and kept them from falling into such sin. It could only lead to trouble.

Chapter
40

Ham walked beside his sons Cush and Canaan to inspect the fields of grain they had helped his father plant. The wheat had grown to nearly half his height and seemed free of the tares that he'd seen often creeping into the grain before the flood. A blessing from the Creator to be sure, though he wondered how long such blessings would last.

"The wheat looks good, Father," Cush said. "The thorns and thistles we've seen in the gardens don't seem to be a problem here."

Ham nodded. "Perhaps it's a sign of God's favor."

"Wouldn't the Creator also favor Savta Zara and Ima, who planted the gardens?"

Canaan's question caught him up short. Had God favored him above his wife and mother? He dared not think so.

"Of course He would, my son. I don't know why the wheat has been spared. Let us be thankful for this blessing." He smiled at his youngest son, wondering not for the first time why Keziah had stopped bearing once the last of his daughters was born. She had expressed anxiety over Adataneses's and

Sedeq's ability to keep having children while she seemed to be denied. Had his wife somehow displeased the Creator?

They walked the length of the wheat field and came to the barley field Shem and his sons had planted.

"Why are we inspecting our uncle's fields, Father? Wouldn't it be best to leave that to him?" Cush asked.

"I'm simply checking all the fields. You know we can share the work." In truth, he wondered if Shem's fields had been so blessed as his own. When he noticed the barley had grown taller and heartier than his wheat, he frowned. No weeds had grown up to choke out Shem's plants either. Apparently God had blessed his brother even more.

He turned, determined to check on Japheth's spelt, though he questioned his own foolishness. When he noted the same favor on Japheth's fields, he reversed course toward the pens where the cattle waited. But suddenly he did not want to take the cattle to pasture. Questions arose within him, and he needed answers.

"Go on ahead and take the cattle to graze among the grasses," he told his sons. They took off running toward the stone enclosures while he walked back toward the camp. A sudden feeling of disquiet filled him as he headed toward his home.

He entered, careful not to draw attention lest Keziah still be home, and closed the door behind him. "Keziah?" There was no answer. "Keziah?"

He was relieved when she did not respond. He walked into the room they shared and stood there, memories of the ark surfacing. He shouldn't look among her baskets as he'd done then. He hadn't lost anything and had no reason to suspect her of returning to crafting the idol she had once made.

But why would her garden have an abundance of thorns and his wheat not fare as well as his brothers' grains? The old competitive spirit rose within him, and he could not shake it. He didn't want his brothers to find more favor with God than he did. And there was nothing he was doing that should lose that favor.

Was it Keziah? Or one of his children?

He walked slowly toward Keziah's baskets, glancing here and there to be sure he was truly alone. No sound came from the house other than that of his heavy breathing. Why was he fearful of what he might find?

After drawing in a deep breath, he slowly released it, willing himself to calm. He would take a quick look.

He carefully moved aside a garment she was stitching, lifted the spindle with yarn attached, and pulled aside scraps of fabric. Nothing. Relieved, he placed everything back and straightened, looking around. In the corner near their bed he saw a robe that had fallen off the peg. It wasn't like Keziah to leave it there. Perhaps she didn't realize it had fallen after she'd left the room.

He lifted it and hung it on the peg where it belonged. Would she notice? Would she ask him why he'd moved it? They often fought when she got suspicious of him, and though living on the earth again had helped her mood, she had not lost her desire to control the people around her, especially him.

He took the robe from the peg, put it back on the floor, and stopped, leaning closer to the wall. A small object was wedged between the wall and their bed.

His heart pounded as he leaned down and picked it up. When he turned it over, he stared at an exact replica of the idol she had made on the ark.

A knot formed in his middle, churning his gut. No. She had promised she would not bring this upon them again. She knew, especially with each glimpse of God's rainbow, that to anger the Creator had dire consequences.

But what was he to do about it? If he destroyed this one, she would secretly make another. If he exposed her to shame in front of their children and their entire family, what then? He couldn't divorce her. There were no other women to marry, and she would die alone.

Or his children would take her side.

The thought sickened him as he continued to stare at the object. He should pray. That was what his father and Shem would do. Perhaps Japheth did as well, though Ham had never found talking to the Creator something he enjoyed or understood. It wasn't like the Creator spoke in return.

The sound of the door opening jarred him. He shoved the idol back into its hiding place, glanced about the room, and stepped into the main area of the house. Keziah stood at the door, a basket of vegetables in her arms.

"You're home! I thought you would be with the cattle." She looked at him, her brows lifted in surprise. "Why are you here?"

"I was looking for something, but it isn't here." He had rarely lied to her, and he forced himself to hold her gaze lest she suspect.

"What were you looking for?" She walked into the area where they prepared food and set the vegetables on a wooden counter. She glanced at him, innocence in her gaze.

"One of my tools. I thought I brought it home last night, but I must have left it in the woodshop." He needed to leave her presence before she pulled the truth from him. "I have to go."

She searched his face, seemingly satisfied. "I hope you find it."

"Yes. So do I." He turned without another word and left the house, heart racing. She hadn't pushed him for more. Did she recall how he'd searched her things on the ark? It had been so long ago. Why had he even thought to do so now?

And should he care that she'd made the idol? She probably thought it would bring her fortune in conceiving again since she'd had trouble for years. She was competing with her sisters-in-law as much as he was with his brothers.

Perhaps he should wait. The pottery didn't look that old, so perhaps it was a recent creation. He should see if the object really did help her conceive. But if it did, what then?

Warnings stirred within him, and he knew that allowing her to keep falling into idolatry would not have a good outcome.

After so many years of marriage, discovering she had not changed at all brought on a mixture of anger and defeat. Discouragement set in as he slowly walked toward the field where his sons had led the cattle to graze. Perhaps he should check on his other sons at the woodshop instead. It would give him some basis in truth for the lie he had given Keziah, if she asked.

He couldn't tell her what he'd done. He couldn't deal with the fallout of her reaction again. Sometimes a man just grew weary of being controlled. He needed space away from her, but that was impossible.

He turned toward the woodshop and told himself to forget it. Perhaps the Creator would not see, and if He did, perhaps He would forgive. Ham glanced at the heavens. *Please forgive her.* Because he knew in that moment that he would not be able to stop her from creating and perhaps even worshiping idols.

Birdsong greeted Zara as she walked toward the gardens she and Keziah had planted. Trees lined the area near the stream not far from where they had planted the seeds they'd saved from before the flood. Every year they saved some of the seeds to plant the next season, but unlike before the flood, mist did not rise from the earth to water the ground. They had to carry buckets of water—a laborious task—to keep the plants moist each day, lest the sun scorch them.

If only there was an easier way. Perhaps they could pipe the water to the gardens as they had with the food for the animals on the ark. She must speak to Noah about building such a thing.

She looked up as the stream drew near, drawn by the sound

of the water chasing itself over rocks and clay down the mountain. The dawn always beckoned her to see it from this vantage point, and she could water the garden before gathering water for the morning meal.

The sound of voices caught her attention as she came closer, startled that anyone else was up at this hour.

"I know you think it's wrong, my son, but that is your father's and grandfather's thinking." Keziah's voice drifted on the breeze. "Before the flood, my mother worshiped the goddess. I just want you to know of my heritage as well as your father's."

Zara stilled, heart in her throat. What was she talking about? Why would Keziah try to convince her son that her past was something to be remembered?

"But Ima, didn't the flood come because of the worship of your ancestors and even my father's ancestors?" Canaan's voice carried to her.

"Yes, of course it did. But I'm telling you about these things so you will know why the Creator brought the flood. This goddess is a reminder of what we must avoid. I made it to teach you."

Did she really mean that? She sounded so convincing.

"I don't think I need to see it, Ima. I believe you without seeing it."

Canaan's comment gave Zara a hint of hope. Keziah was trying to influence her children and probably even her husband to resurrect the things God had destroyed. But why? And what was Zara to do with this knowledge? She couldn't let Keziah keep misleading her grandchildren. Did Ham know of this?

Indecision warred within her. At last she stepped toward the stream and walked to where they stood, bucket in hand.

"Keziah. Canaan. What has you out here so early?"

Keziah jerked about to face her, guilt surfacing on her expression then just as quickly disappearing. "We came to enjoy the sunrise. I love the water and Canaan wanted to join me. I see I should have brought my bucket, though. How forgetful of me. Canaan, run home and get it for me, would you?"

"Canaan, stay a moment," Zara said to him. "Keziah, show me the idol you've made." She set the bucket down and held out a hand for it.

"I don't know what you're talking about."

"The idol you have in your robe. You were talking to Canaan about it. Let me have it." She waited, barely breathing.

Keziah held her gaze, unflinching, a hard look entering her dark eyes. "It is no business of yours."

"It is very much my business. You're bringing back things the Creator destroyed, and it's not the first time. You will destroy it now or I will tell everyone in the camp what you're doing." She should tell them anyway, but in that moment she could think of nothing else to say.

Keziah didn't move.

"Give it to Savta, Ima. You know you should."

Canaan's words surprised her, endearing the boy to her.

Keziah frowned, but a moment later, she pulled the object from her robe and threw it at Zara's feet. "Have it if you want it so much. I have more."

Zara did not move to pick it up but instead crushed it with her foot. "And if we find them, you can be sure the whole camp will destroy them. You will bring judgment again on us all!" Her voice rose, and she told herself to calm. She did not want to wake the camp.

"She won't make any more, Savta. She knows Abba doesn't like it." Canaan took Keziah's hand. "Come on, Ima. Let's get the buckets to help Savta draw water. Forget the idol." He tugged her arm, and Keziah followed in silence.

Zara did not breathe until they were out of earshot. But she hadn't missed the look of hatred in Keziah's eyes. What on earth was happening to her family? Why would Keziah suddenly want to worship idols and be so hostile? Had someone offended her? Had the evil ones returned to tempt her?

The troubling thoughts would not abate, and Zara's heart pounded as she filled the bucket. Her peace shattered, she could think of nothing but what God would do the next time He was forced to remove evil from the earth. Oh, that the Redeemer would come first.

Chapter

41

Noah bent over the clay, carving pictures into the wet surface to record the season's yield of grain. The harvest had been fruitful indeed, and the grapes were ready for pressing. He looked back at the records from years past, pleased to see that God had blessed them even more now than He had then.

His family had expanded as well—his sons had children and grandchildren of their own. Soon they would need to spread out to give their growing flocks and herds more room to graze. This area of the valley could barely hold them all.

Noah's heart lightened at the thought that they had kept God's laws, making yearly sacrifices. Though he had to admit, Keziah's desire for making images was still a problem. His only consolation was that the rest of his descendants seemed to be following the ways of Adonai Elohim.

Gratitude and a desire to celebrate filled him. He pressed the sharp knife into the clay and carved the symbol for "celebrate," adding the fruit of the vine and a basket of produce. They would continue the thanksgiving feast Zara and Sedeq had begun years ago. They had so much for which to be thankful.

First they must offer another sacrifice. He still carried a healthy fear of God's wrath, even though he knew God was pleased with him. One of his descendants might have sinned in their hearts. He desperately wanted all of them to remain true to the Creator, not stray like the descendants of Adam had.

But was that even possible? The flood had not erased the sin each one carried in their heart. He himself was flawed in ways he couldn't even share with Zara. But he knew his heart, and it troubled him whenever he argued with one of his sons.

Memories surfaced of his last argument with Ham. How could he have let it get to that point?

"I've taken care of the idols, Father," Ham had said. "Keziah will not make them again. There is no need to expose her to the entire clan." He crossed his arms over his broad chest, looking down at Noah, who was a head shorter than his son.

"You said that on the ark, and yet she managed to make more than one, according to your mother. If she didn't care that your mother crushed one, you can be sure it's because she had others, as she said. Why didn't you bring them to the central fire and burn them to show her that not only you but all of us disapprove?" He couldn't stop the irritation in his tone as he frowned at Ham.

"And subject her to public shame? She doesn't see them as idols. She just enjoys making pottery and painting them." His tone held defiance, causing a shiver to work down Noah's spine.

"You know they are idols. Has she convinced you they're nothing? You know better!" He was nearly shouting now, and Ham took a step back.

"I did what I thought best as her husband. I don't appreciate you telling me what I should have done. You don't have to live in the same house with her. She will have her way with or without me, and there is nothing I can do beyond what I've already done."

He'd stormed out of the woodshop, and the conversation still irked Noah. Where was the respect Ham had always held for him? Ham, the son who had seemed so eager to please him during the building of the ark, no longer took his advice. He had pulled away in the many years since they'd left the ark. Keziah and his children and grandchildren now filled his life, and if Noah wasn't mistaken, he'd glimpsed disdain from Keziah and even Ham now and then. Had he done something to cause these feelings in his son? Wasn't he, as the leader of their clan, supposed to lead them to worship the Creator?

He shook his head, his thoughts troubled. He was so weary of dealing with conflict. His whole long life he'd dealt with the degradation of his culture. Now he faced the disrespect of his own kin. He lifted his gaze to the ceiling. He couldn't see the heavens inside this building, but his heart turned heavenward.

A sacrifice was definitely needed. Would Ham even come? Could Noah force all of them to sacrifice?

Of course he could. He was their father, their leader. They would follow him if he insisted.

"We're going to meet in three days to sacrifice burnt offerings to the Lord," Noah said at a gathering of the entire family.

Zara glanced at her descendants to see whether they showed acceptance of Noah's declaration. Most of them nodded, but here and there, among Ham's children, she caught sullen looks.

Was Canaan frowning? What had happened to the younger man who had told his mother that idols were not good? How long ago that had been now. Had he secretly accepted her teaching? Zara glanced at Keziah, whose neutral expression revealed nothing. She looked to Adataneses and Sedeq, both of whom seemed eager to do as Noah said.

"Purify yourselves," he said, interrupting her anxious thoughts.

"Wash your clothes and bathe in the river. Then choose spotless animals for the sacrifices. Are there any questions?"

Zara met his gaze in passing as he took in the entire group.

"We will do as you say, Father," Shem said, placing his arm around Sedeq.

"Will we celebrate after the sacrifice, as you mentioned to me earlier?" Zara asked, watching for reactions to that as well.

"Yes. We will give God our best and then eat of the meat, produce, and fruit of the vine."

At that, the crowd cheered and began talking at once.

Noah made his way over to Zara. "I suppose I should be grateful that they want to celebrate. I only wish they were as eager to sacrifice."

She touched his shoulder. "Sacrifice is something they do not fully comprehend, especially those who didn't live before the flood. They do so to please you."

"They need to do so to please the Creator, not me."

"You represent Him to them."

"They don't respect me enough to please either one of us." He sounded petulant, and Zara gave him a curious look.

"Of course they respect you. Of what do you speak, my husband?"

They walked together toward the sheep pens as Shem and his sons took the flocks to the fields.

"I was remembering my argument with Ham a few days ago. I think Keziah has turned him against me. Against the truth of the Creator." Noah's look held sorrow. "There was a hint of disdain in his tone."

Zara's heart sank. Keziah had been a problem for years, and since landing on earth again, she had grown bolder, especially after God gave her more daughters. Did she secretly think the goddess had given life to her womb?

"The evil one is still at work among us. We can never escape him or the sin in our hearts." She linked her arm with Noah's.

"Ham is just trying to make life easier for himself. Keziah controls him, and he doesn't know how to stop her. He never has."

"I know that." He looked into her eyes. "I'm glad you have always been at my side and believed in the Creator and never tried to control us like that."

Zara chuckled. "Well . . . that isn't entirely true. Most women control their men a little bit. We just don't do so as blatantly as Keziah. We must pray for her."

He gave her a thoughtful look. "I've been lax in that. When did we stop taking prayer as seriously as we should?"

She lifted one shoulder in a half shrug. "I'm not sure. I talk to the Creator daily, but with so many of us now, I forget to pray for each of our descendants by name. Sometimes I can't remember their names!"

He laughed, the sound a relief after the burden he carried. "You are not alone in this. Yes, we must pray for Keziah and Ham. I miss the son he used to be."

"Perhaps you should tell him that."

He nodded. "Perhaps I should."

Three days later, Noah's descendants gathered as families around the altar he had first made when they left the ark. They'd climbed the mountain to reach it with the animals in tow, and at last they all stood before him. As each one of them placed their hands on the heads of the bulls, sheep, and goats, they all spoke quietly, confessing their sins to the Creator. The many voices sounded like a low rumble.

Noah stood with Zara and prayed, "Oh merciful Creator, look down on Your people and forgive our many sins against You. We want to please You, but we do not have the strength within us to always live a righteous life. Grant us Your grace, we pray, and forgive our many sins against You. Make us right in Your holy eyes again."

Zara followed with a prayer of her own. When they had finished, Noah slit the bull's throat, caught the blood in a bowl, and poured it over the altar. His sons and grandsons and older great-grandsons did the same. They each cut up their animals and placed them one by one on the altar, setting aside a small portion to share in the celebration feast afterward.

When the last animal's flesh had turned to ash on the altar, the clouds parted above them. Noah looked up into the bright light of the heavens, greater than that of the sun. He smiled. For now, at least, they had pleased Him.

"God has accepted our sacrifices," he said to the group, stretching his arms out before them. "Let us go down the mountain now and celebrate the Lord's goodness."

Sedeq lifted her voice in a song of praise to Adonai. "Blessed are You, oh Lord, maker of heaven and earth. Blessed are those who learn to worship You and walk in Your light. Great are You, Lord."

The others picked up the song as she repeated the words. Noah led the way down the mountain, carrying the meat they would cook for the feast.

Zara came up beside him. "You did a good thing, my husband. God is pleased with us again. Now we can live in harmony. At least for a while."

She smiled up at him, and peace filled him. Perhaps Ham would respect him now and his sons would get along better than they had in recent years. Perhaps even Keziah would change now that she had confessed her sins.

But had she confessed? Only God knew.

Chapter

42

Zara hurried to her tent, gathered the food they needed, and carried it to the central court. Why Noah had preferred to remain living in a tent when his descendants were building homes baffled her, but he seemed to like the ability to pick up and move, should God call them to do so, more than he enjoyed the comfort of a permanent home.

The women met her in the expanded courtyard, all talking at once amid grinding grain and mixing different dishes to have with the roasting meat. Zara pulled the wine from holes in the ground, where it was kept cool, and set it near the eating area.

Dusk neared, and at last the meat was ready. Stones were set in a large circle, and the men and women took turns eating, feeding the children in between. Zara and her daughters-in-law moved among the men, making sure everyone had enough to drink and the plates were full.

At last Zara sank onto the rock she normally occupied and took a helping of food herself. Laughter filled the air, and she sat back, taking it all in. How she loved watching her family interact. Especially when they weren't competing or fighting in some way. The tension was always less after a sacrifice.

She looked up as Ham took the skin of wine and poured more into the cups of his brothers and Noah. The sack no longer bulged, obviously empty. How was it possible they had finished nearly all the skins she'd been saving for this occasion? Only a few were left in the holes in the ground.

She attempted to rise, but Sedeq's hand on her arm stopped her. "What is it, Ima? Let me get it for you."

"I was going to get more wine. It seems we've finished all of it."

Sedeq shook her head. "I think they've had enough. Look. Noah is slurring his speech. We don't want them all to overimbibe. They might sin against the Creator, and then the sacrifice will have been for nothing."

Zara noted the concern in Sedeq's eyes. "You're right." She did stand then. "I think I'd best get Noah to our tent." She walked over to him and took his arm. "I need you to come with me, my husband."

Noah laughed. "We're just getting started, dear wife. Don't ruin our fun."

Ham chuckled, obviously enjoying Noah's intoxication. "Father is right, Ima. Bring more wine. We're just getting started!"

Zara noted a strange gleam in Ham's eyes. "You can see he has had too much," she whispered to him, leaning closer. "Why do you push for more?"

He lifted his hands in a defenseless gesture. "I wanted Father to enjoy himself for once, Ima."

Keziah appeared at Ham's side. "He only wanted to see if the righteous Noah could handle his wine."

Zara bristled at the edge in Keziah's tone. "'Righteous Noah'?" She looked from Ham to Keziah. "Why would you call him that?"

"Because that's what he is." Keziah's eyes were wide, as though she too had drunk more wine than she could handle.

"That's enough, Keziah," Ham said, giving Zara an apologetic look. "We meant no harm."

Zara turned her attention again to Noah, who was laughing at something. Had he heard her conversation with Ham? Shem and Japheth were sitting close, talking to him, so perhaps not.

She stepped closer to Noah. "Come, my husband. You've had enough for tonight." She tugged on his arm, but he pulled back.

"I think I'll know when that happens." His slurred speech said otherwise.

"Come on, Father. Ima is right." Shem joined her, and together they got Noah to his feet. "You're tired. We're all tired. I think it's time we go to bed, as the sun has set."

"You're wrong. I'm fine." But this time he submitted as they half carried him to his tent. Shem left, and Zara tried to help Noah into his nightclothes.

He pushed her away. "I can undress myself."

Had he ever acted this way? She couldn't recall him ever drinking too much.

"Fine. I'll be back. You rest." She backed out of the tent, making sure he was changing his clothes, then went to clean up the food.

"Is he all right?" Sedeq asked her. "I've never seen him drink too much."

"He never has. But perhaps he's weary of the struggles and didn't realize what it would do to him."

A weight settled inside Zara. Would becoming drunk displease the Creator? She'd seen Noah try so hard all his life to do what God required. He drank wine, of course, but never this much.

Her family began to disperse, leaving only her sons and daughters-in-law.

"Father showed a new side of himself tonight," Ham said, chuckling. Hadn't he said he'd meant no harm? "I didn't know he had it in him."

Zara met his gaze. "I don't think this is something to laugh about. And you didn't help matters. Your father made a mistake. He misjudged how much he was drinking."

"Well, I think it shows he's just like the rest of us. Not quite so righteous, perhaps?" Ham held up his hands to deflect her response. "I wasn't trying to cause a problem, Ima. It was all in fun." He moved toward Noah's tent. "I will go and check on him while you all finish cleaning up."

He walked toward their tent, still chuckling. Zara's irritation spiked at the sound.

A moment later, Ham returned, outright laughing. He avoided her and walked toward Shem and Japheth. He leaned close to them, but she didn't miss his words. "Father is lying on his mat naked! Apparently he passed out before he could finish dressing." He bent over laughing.

Horror filled Zara's belly at Ham's reaction, and she saw the same feeling reflected on Shem's and Japheth's faces. They looked at one another.

"Bring me a blanket," Shem called to Sedeq.

She hurried to their house and returned with a blanket. Shem and Japheth draped it over their shoulders, walked backward into the tent, and laid the blanket over Noah. They returned, expressions grim, and looked at Ham.

"You should be ashamed of yourself," Shem said.

"Why? I didn't pass out naked!" Ham, still laughing, took Keziah's hand, and together they left the group.

"Go home and get some sleep," Zara told the others.

"What will Father do?" Shem asked.

"Only God knows. And morning will tell," she said. A shudder worked through her. She had a feeling she knew.

Zara slept fitfully on her pallet near Noah, unfounded fear coursing through her during the night. Or was it unfounded? Noah had fought with Ham about Keziah's idols, and the pleasant relationship they'd once shared had strained over the years. What would he say when he discovered what Ham had done?

She rose when Noah stirred, holding his head in his hands. "Ohhh." He moaned.

Zara filled a cup with water, added some white willow bark to it, and brought it to him. "Drink."

His hands shook as he took the cup from her. "What happened?"

"You drank too much wine last night at the celebration. We brought you to your tent."

He looked at her, then lifted the blanket. His face blanched. "Why have I no clothes on?"

Zara drew in a deep breath. "You wanted to change into your nightclothes yourself. I left you to do so. But you must have passed out on the mat, undressed."

"So you covered me?" His look held appreciation.

She paused, then slowly shook her head. "Ham came to check on you and found you naked. He told Shem and Japheth, who walked the blanket backward to cover you without seeing you."

Disbelief and horror filled his expression, and his face reddened. He forced himself up and got dressed. "Cursed be Canaan!" He paced the room.

He would curse Ham's son for this? Why?

He left the tent, and Zara hurried after him. "Cursed be Canaan!" he shouted, drawing everyone from their homes. "The lowest of slaves will he be to his brothers."

Ham approached him, his sons at his side. "You would curse my son, Father?"

"Your sons, all of them, follow after their mother and you do not stop them. And you have disdained your father and profaned the name of our God by your actions!"

Zara watched Ham's expression darken, his hands fisted.

God did expect them to honor their parents, and though they had nothing written in stone to tell them that, He had made His will plain over the years. And none of their sons had ever treated them with anything but love and respect. What was happening here?

Ham opened his mouth to speak again, but Noah cut him off. "Praise be to the Lord, the God of Shem!" he shouted. "May Canaan be the slave of Shem. May God extend Japheth's territory. May Japheth live in the tents of Shem, and may Canaan be the slave of Japheth."

The curse could not have been clearer or more potent. Ham put his arms about Canaan and Cush while Keziah grabbed two of her daughters' hands. Every one of Ham's children and grandchildren turned and walked away.

Noah stood watching, shaking.

Zara fell to her knees, rocking back and forth. What had Noah done? Would Ham leave their encampment?

A feeling of spiraling downward filled her, and she wasn't sure she would ever recover from the blow.

Chapter

43

A week passed, then a month, and though the atmosphere had strained considerably between Noah and Ham and between Ham and his brothers, the work continued and nothing more was said of Noah's curse.

Zara worked alongside Keziah, pulling prickly weeds and tenacious vines to keep them from choking the produce. But their words were stilted and few.

Zara lifted a hand to block the sun and wiped the sweat from her brow with the belt of her robe. She glanced at Keziah across the rows, her back to Zara. *Oh Adonai, what can I say to make things better between us?* Every thought that came to mind was quickly discarded. Noah had not retracted his curse, and she knew he never would.

She bent lower to attack another nasty weed, praying. Surely there was something she could do to redeem what seemed so broken.

The sun continued to rise as they worked in silence. At last Keziah stood and rubbed her back. She carried the pile of weeds to a nearby pit where they would be burned. She returned for another pile, and Zara stood as well.

"We accomplished much today," Zara said, desperate to break the silence.

Keziah stopped and faced her. "Yes." She stared at Zara a moment. "There is nothing you can say to change things, Zara." It had always been "Ima Zara" before, but apparently no more. "Noah has wounded Ham beyond repair. To curse our son, who did nothing to Noah, simply because Ham laughed at Noah's drunkenness is unforgivable. We will be leaving your camp soon. I will take our portion of the vegetables with us." She turned about and walked toward the last pile of weeds.

Zara watched her, feeling as though her daughter-in-law had just kicked her in the gut. Did Ham agree with her? Would he tell Zara so if she asked? If Ham would apologize, surely Noah would retract his words. And if she could convince Ham, perhaps Keziah wouldn't be able to see her proclamation come true.

Was Keziah behind the desire to leave them? Or was it Ham, who carried his wounded feelings close to his heart?

She must find Ham and talk to him. Make him see the danger in leaving the group. Though his clan had grown large through the years, she couldn't bear the thought of losing her youngest. Where would they go? Would all his descendants follow?

She gathered her own pile of weeds and carried them to the pit, then left Keziah. She had no words to say to the woman who seemed too glad to be getting her way with Zara's son.

Lifting her skirts, she hurried down the path toward the woodshop, where she suspected she would find Ham. Something must be done.

Ham stood over the workbench, cutting a long piece of wood into sections to make a cart. He would need many if they were going to move away from his family.

Anger rose within him as he relived the moment his father dared to curse his son. If that was how his father felt about him and his family, then he had no use for them. He'd already built six carts, working night and day. They would be fastened to donkeys and make transporting goods easier. Once he finished this one, he had one to go. He couldn't work fast enough.

Footsteps drew his attention, and he looked up to see his mother standing in the doorway. He continued working, ignoring her.

She stepped into the room and stood opposite him. "Ham, my son, please look at me."

He hesitated, already suspecting what she was going to say. He pulled in a steadying breath, telling himself the curse was not her fault. He lifted his head to meet her gaze.

"Ham, my son. My dearly loved son. Keziah has told me you're planning to leave us. Please tell me this is not true." Her pleading tone held emotion, and he sensed she was on the verge of tears.

He felt a sudden twinge of compassion for her. "I have nothing against you, Ima. I will miss you." He paused as she watched him, heart in her eyes. "But my father has forgotten how much I've done to please him all my life. For one wrong thing he would curse my offspring? Then I curse him as well. I won't stay near him and have my descendants live knowing that the man I once respected and even revered hates us."

His mother's quick intake of breath told him he'd said too much. "Your father doesn't hate you, Ham. He spoke in the heat of anger. He felt you disrespected him because you looked on his nakedness and didn't simply cover him and keep it to yourself. Instead, you laughed at his weakness. If you would apologize—"

Ham held up a hand. "I will not apologize, Ima. He made a fool of himself, and it was humorous. I did nothing wrong."

313

He looked away at the tears in her eyes. He'd never handled tears well, especially from his mother.

"I don't want you to go. If you could just talk to your father . . ." She did not finish the sentence as he shook his head.

"That's not possible. We're leaving as soon as I can make enough carts to carry our goods. We will move to the land of Shinar. I know you won't follow since you won't leave my father, and I will miss you, Ima. But this is what I have to do for my family." His heart pounded. The words were more than he'd wanted to say to her.

She stood staring at him, tears tracing a path over her worn cheeks. He hated what this was doing to her. Would he ever see her again? But he couldn't go back. He wouldn't apologize because his father wouldn't care. The curse would still stand, and blessings and curses carried too much weight. His father would never change his mind. He would think he had spoken for God. But God hadn't told his father to drink too much. His words were not from God. They were his own, and they hurt too much to ever forgive.

His mother stood watching him, making him uncomfortable. But at last she came around the bench and pulled him into her arms. "I will always love you, Ham. And despite what he said, your father loves you too. I hope someday you will find it in your heart to forgive him and come home."

Ham patted her back. He would never come home. Of that he was very sure. But to appease her he said, "Maybe someday."

When she left him, he sank to the stool and put his head in his hands. He suddenly felt sick and hollow inside. If he were honest, he didn't really want to leave the only home he had ever known. But Keziah would never let him change his mind. She would fuel his anger every single day until he did what he'd rashly said he would. She wanted this more than he did. And whether his mother realized it or not, he could better

314

live with disappointing her than Keziah. Keziah was just too hard to live with otherwise.

A month later, Zara stood beside Noah, flanked by Shem and Japheth and their families, as Ham and his entire clan prepared to lead a caravan of donkeys pulling overloaded carts to the east, toward Shinar. Ham kissed Zara goodbye, along with his brothers, but barely acknowledged Noah, the father he'd once cared so much to please.

"Go with God, my son," Noah said, surprising her.

Ham at last looked at his father and gave a curt nod. But he did not smile. Ham's sons and daughters came to bid them farewell, and most of them also kissed their grandfather, except for Canaan. Keziah remained with the rest of her family. How could she have lived with them on the ark for over a year and not even bid her sisters-in-law farewell? But Keziah had her own family now, and she no longer needed them or their approval, nor did she need to control them. She had many, many descendants to whom to teach her idolatrous ways.

A sigh lifted Zara's chest as she watched the donkeys move forward. Some of Ham's grandsons had taken their cattle, sheep, and goats on ahead of the others. Ham had been the last. Had he waited, hoping something would cause him to change his mind? But nothing had been said between him and Noah, and now, as Ham's family dwindled from sight, Zara's heart ached with grief so strong she wasn't sure she could survive it.

Noah turned and headed toward the library, his sanctuary. Shem and Japheth hugged Zara, then headed off to care for the animals. The sun was barely up, but the work must continue, with or without a third of their family.

Sedeq and Adataneses stepped closer. Sedeq pulled Zara into her arms. "I will miss them too, Ima."

The words brought the ever-present tears to Zara's eyes. "I can't believe they really left."

"Keziah has wanted this for years," Adataneses said. "She's never been happy among us. Even before the flood."

"And now she's gotten what she wanted," Sedeq added. "I think she was plotting to convince Ham to leave for a very long time. They just couldn't do it safely before all the children were born."

"If only Noah had not said that . . ." Zara could not finish.

"It would have been something else then, Ima," Sedeq insisted. "Noah just gave them the final reason to do what they'd wanted to do. Don't put all the blame on him. He was disrespected by his son in a most personal way. Ham should have handled things differently."

"But if they had just talked it over, perhaps things would be different." Zara could not let the longing for reconciliation go. "I fear neither one was willing to do so."

"Why don't we make a special meal today," Adataneses said. "Or go to the stream and rest in the shade for a while. We all need to rest from the tension we've been feeling for months." She motioned for Zara to follow, and Sedeq tugged her forward.

"The stream would be nice," Zara said at last. She loved the peace she found there. "Perhaps we can make Noah's favorite sweet tonight. But we won't be drinking wine. Water will suffice."

Sedeq and Adataneses chuckled, lightening her mood. "We will all make sure Noah isn't given as much as he was that night," Sedeq said. "I saw Ham continue to fill his cup. Perhaps he wanted to see his father drunk and wondered what he would do if he was."

"Now we know," Adataneses said. "But let's not look at this as a bad thing. We won't have to deal with Keziah anymore. And maybe God will soften Ham's heart and bring him home again soon."

"It is my constant hope and prayer," Zara said. But she doubted that this was a prayer God would answer with a yes.

Chapter

44

Zara walked about the camp, arm linked through Noah's. Shem's and Japheth's descendants worked more fields, and the flocks of both had grown almost beyond number. Many years had passed since the day Ham had taken his family to the east. Shinar, he had called it, though there had been no actual name for the place until he voiced it. How large it had grown since then.

"I hear that Cush's son Nimrod has made quite a name for himself," Noah said as they waved to Arphaxad, one of Shem's sons working in the wheat field. "They say he is a mighty hunter before the Lord and has built many cities in Shinar."

"I hope 'before the Lord' means that Ham has taught his sons and grandsons of the Creator. Perhaps he has not forgotten all he once knew." The thought always troubled Zara. Occasionally a family member traveled to Shinar and returned to tell them what was happening, but there had been no word from Ham himself.

"I wonder." Noah guided her around a large rock in their path. Fields stretched before them, wildflowers waving in the breeze. "Shem's descendant Eber said that the last time he was there, they were building a tower to reach to the heavens. Apparently, the story of the flood has caused the leaders among them to decide to build something that could rise higher than the mountains to protect them from any future flood. They're even using bitumen for mortar to keep water out."

"Humph! All they need do is look at the rainbow and remember the promise. The Creator isn't going to send another flood. How foolish!" Zara bent to pick one of the wildflowers and sniffed the heady scent.

"They also don't want to be scattered over the earth. They want to make a name for themselves." Noah released a deep sigh.

She looked at him, brows lifted in surprise. "The Creator said to 'be fruitful and increase in number and fill the earth.' I would have thought Ham would remind them of that."

"I wonder how much influence Ham has over any of them anymore. He is no longer young, and remember, Keziah's teaching countered ours. They probably consider the teachings of the past to be myths and legends, just as those before the flood did. And they don't live near the ark to see that the flood truly happened." He glanced up the mountain where the ark's shell was still visible. They had emptied it of anything useful but had left the boat intact.

"They wouldn't *deny* the flood, would they?" Zara couldn't imagine that day. The flood was still too real to her.

"The story will be told, but the memory will fade and the succeeding generations will one day wonder if the whole thing was just a story. It's pretty amazing that it actually happened, when you think about it." He took her hand and kissed her fingers. "I don't know how long we will live or what more we will see happen on the earth, but in the last few hundred years, we have proven what has been true since the fall. Men's and women's hearts are only evil continually. It's what made the Creator's heart break in the first place."

"And we will continue to break it." The thought saddened her, for she knew that she was no better than her children or their children or the generations that were still to come.

"Let us be grateful for what we still have here with Shem and Japheth. The time will come when even they will leave us, I'm afraid." Noah's look grew thoughtful.

"Have they said anything?" The thought set her heart pounding.

Noah shook his head. "No. But I sense it in their descendants. I hope I don't live to see it."

"You've never gotten over Ham leaving." She touched his arm.

He met her gaze. "I will always blame myself for that."

But it was too late to change anything, wasn't it?

They turned and headed back toward their house. One of Shem's sons, Aram, came running toward them from the field.

"Savta. Saba. You must come at once!" He stopped before them, out of breath.

"What is it, my son?" Noah asked.

"There is confusion in the camp. Come." He turned around and raced ahead of them. They hurried to follow.

"What's happened?" Noah stopped near Shem in the center of the camp where they gathered for their meals, Zara clutching his arm.

She looked from Shem and Sedeq to Japheth and Adataneses. "Tell us."

"They can't understand us," Shem said, horror in his eyes. "Do you understand me, Abba?"

Noah nodded. "Yes, my son." He glanced at Japheth but saw only confusion in his eyes. "What happened?"

Shem stepped between Noah and Japheth, looking from

one to the other. "We were talking about the upcoming harvest, and suddenly Japheth began to speak in words I couldn't understand. We made hand motions to each other and came home. Sedeq can understand me and Adataneses can understand Japheth, but it seems that our families now have different languages, because we can only understand our own descendants, not each other."

Japheth gave Shem and Noah a blank look and lifted his hands toward the heavens. He shook his head, turned to Adataneses, and spoke quickly in a tongue that made no sense to Zara. What in the world?

"What are we going to do if we can't understand each other, Abba?" Shem hadn't been near tears since childhood, but Zara heard them in his tone now. He'd been close to Japheth all his life. Why were their languages suddenly so different?

"I don't know," Noah said, sitting on one of the stones about the central fire. He took a stick and drew in the dirt. Japheth sat beside him, and through a number of drawings he seemed to understand what Noah was saying.

At last Japheth stood and led Adataneses toward their house.

"Saba!" a voice shouted from the road coming from Shinar. Eber was running as fast as a gazelle and came to a stop near the fire, out of breath.

"What is it, my son?" Shem stepped to him and placed a hand on his shoulder.

"Everything is in chaos. I was in Shinar two days ago, and the tower was getting higher and higher when suddenly no one could understand each other. And I couldn't understand a single one of them anymore. God has confused the languages, and the sons of Ham are moving away from each other to stay with those they understand." Eber's words came out between gasps. Sedeq handed him a skin of water, and he gulped it down.

"This is judgment for building the tower," Noah said. "But

why Japheth? Why make it impossible for us to understand him and his kin?"

"Because God wants all of us to separate and fill the earth," Shem said. "Even we are not immune to His command." He faced Noah and Zara. "He has kept us together and is sending Japheth away. I wish it were not so." Shem hung his head, and Sedeq pulled him close.

Zara leaned into Noah. For hundreds of years they had been a family of five, then eight. Then the grandchildren and the great-grandchildren came until they numbered more than Zara could count.

But until Ham left in anger, they had not separated to fill the earth as God had commanded. What was it about humans that made them want to stick together? Did they do so to build one another up or to stand against the Creator?

The thoughts troubled Zara, and her mind whirled as she looked at the two children who were left to stay with her and Noah until they passed from the earth. Shem and his descendants would be the only humans they would know the rest of their days.

What would happen to Ham's children and Japheth's? Where would they wander, and would God go with them? She couldn't even tell Japheth, "Go with God," as Noah had said to Ham all those years ago, since Japheth could no longer understand her words. But she could hold him close. And Adataneses. And his children and their children down to the third and fourth generation from the flood. And they would remember the Creator and the flood of judgment. Japheth was a good son, and he would make sure of it.

The thought brought little comfort.

Within the week, Noah and Shem had helped Japheth and his sons prepare to leave the area, motioning with their hands and drawing pictures in the dirt. Zara and Sedeq had attempted the same with Adataneses and her daughters, but the struggle exhausted Zara.

She stood now, watching this beloved son and daughter-in-law weeping, holding each other close, and at last moving out to head northwest, opposite of Ham's people.

"I wonder what will become of all of us," she said to Noah, Shem, and Sedeq. "Obviously God has a plan and a reason for scattering us over the face of the earth. How far can we travel? How big is this earth God has made?"

"I have a feeling it is much larger than we can even imagine," Noah said. "On the ark we could see water stretch from horizon to horizon. Now, with the earth where the water once stood and the seas stretching beyond our vision, only God knows its size."

"I hope they all take the truth of the flood with them as they go," Sedeq said, taking Shem's hand. "I hope we all never forget why the Creator sent the flood in the first place. I hope each group of people remembers."

"They have God's rainbow in the clouds to remind them of the covenant." Zara looked up at the clouds, watching the rays of sun peeking through. "Every time it rains."

"Yes. That's true." Sedeq lifted her gaze heavenward as well. "Look." She pointed at the clouds, and though there was no rain yet, the sun burst through and created a vivid rainbow. The longer they watched it, the more it stretched from horizon to horizon in a wide double bow. "How could anyone forget when they see that?" Sedeq asked.

How indeed? Zara's heart lifted for the first time in weeks. As long as God set His bow in the sky, there was always hope. All anyone on earth had to do was look up whenever it rained and see the rainbow, the covenant of God.

Epilogue

I am an old woman now. The years since the ark have made the time we spent caring for the animals and each other seem like a distant dream. I know it happened. But time has a way of dimming our memories.

Shem and his family have remained with us since the earth was divided, during the year his great-great-grandson Peleg was born. That was when God confused the languages, not only in Shinar at the tower they now call Babel, but also right here in our home near the ark, when Japheth's family was sent from among us.

I'm told that Japheth's descendants spread to the northwest and some have become skilled in shipbuilding and roaming the seas like my father. I take pleasure in knowing that.

Ham's descendants left the east and traveled south and west of us, to a land named for Ham's son Egypt. His children are many, and their children have scattered and gone on to build other great cities that I can no longer remember. I have often wondered how Canaan's children will serve Shem and Japheth. Only God knows.

Time has taught me . . . no, God has taught me through all of life's changes—from the years of evil before the flood to the year of difficulty on the ark to the years that have grown

323

chaotic again—that there is no one who can or will remain with us forever. Only the Creator is with us always. I've done my best to teach this to all our children and those who came from them. Noah has too.

Despite our faults, I have hope that the truth God taught us and we passed on to our children will be carried to every tribe and tongue and people and nation that come from our lineage. One day we will know.

Note to the Reader

The year I knew I would be writing this book, my husband and I toured the Ark Encounter in Kentucky to give me a feel for what living on the ark might have been like. The ark was *huge*! Just the thought of walking those floors day after day after day is exhausting. And Noah's wife was a lot older than I am!

Still, when it came to writing her story, just visiting the ark wasn't enough. One can't write a story about how the ark was put together without getting to know the people who lived through that adventure. And like so many Bible stories, the Scriptures give us very little to go on. We don't even know the name of Noah's wife. Emzara was the name given by the Book of Jubilees and used at the Ark Encounter, so I chose to keep it. The same goes for Keziah (though it was spelled Kezia), but I changed the names of Shem's and Japheth's wives to fit with what I read in a different source.

In my research toward the end of this book, I came across some fascinating information. When I did the math from Noah and Shem down through the genealogy of their descendants, I was astounded to discover that Shem lived through the births of Jacob and Esau! It sounds incredible, but if Shem lived six hundred years as the Bible says, then he was five hundred and fifty years old when those twins were born. Of course, that doesn't mean he knew them. Shem could have been living in a different area than Abraham, Isaac, and Jacob. It's interesting that God later told Abraham that He would give him the land of the Canaanites, the very people Noah cursed.

If you get the chance to study the genealogies of the people of Scripture and read Genesis 10, where the table of nations is given, you can better understand the names of the people groups mentioned during the time of Israel's kings. It's fascinating reading. Particularly because we discover that Canaan was the father of one of those groups, the Hittites, whose civilization was lost to history until recent archaeological discoveries indicated that they had an extensive kingdom *with its own language* that had been buried in the sands for centuries. Their discovery was one more testament to the truth of the Bible, which is the only place they were mentioned until that discovery.

I don't know if humans will discover the ark someday, as so many have tried to do. Then again, no one ever expected to discover the Hittites. And all these people tie back to Noah, his wife, and their three sons and wives, whom God spared during the worldwide flood.

You may think the flood story is just that—a story. But I don't see it that way. God preserved this story in Scripture, just like He did so many others, for a reason. And Jesus made the point of telling His disciples, "As it was in the days of Noah, so it will be at the coming of the Son of Man" (Matt. 24:37 NIV).

Are we coming to that day when our world is so infiltrated by evil that God is ready to say, "Enough is enough"? He warned Noah, and I believe He is still warning us today. His Spirit will not always strive with humanity.

Next time the judgment won't be a flood. But it will come.

Judgment is not a popular subject, but it's one we need to hear. Let us be a people who find favor with God because of our faith in Him. And pray that before that day comes, the whole world hears and believes.

In His Grace,
Jill Eileen Smith

Acknowledgments

I began this book three times before I found a good starting point, and that meant scrapping about ninety thousand words—the length of a normal book. I am still not a fan of first drafts!

But as always, I am grateful for the opportunity Revell offers me to write these stories. Their trust in my ability exceeds my own confidence, and I thank them for believing in me.

Thanks also to my agent, Wendy Lawton, for working with me on other projects during the writing of this one. She's become a dear friend, for which I'm also grateful.

To my fellow authors and pre-readers Jill Stengl and Hannah Alexander—thank you for your suggestions. I always treasure your insight.

As I wrote this book, we were still getting settled into our new home and dealing with an increasingly sick kitty. My muse, my Tiger, was not there during the end of the writing of the book. We said goodbye to him in August 2022, thus the book's dedication to him. Two kittens, Kody and Kaelee, will never replace Tiger, but they have made life more interesting and lovable.

We also welcomed a new grandson into our lives in November 2022 and had the joy of spending time with him and his big sister in Oregon. Family can bring such joy to our lives, and I treasure those joys.

Thanks always goes to Randy, whom I get to do life with. There is no one better except the Creator, to whom we belong. If not for the grace and unfailing love of our Lord Jesus Messiah, where would we be? There would be no rescue to an ark of safety and no hope of the redemption He provides. I am forever grateful to be among His family. I take refuge in Him.

Jill Eileen Smith is the bestselling and award-winning author of the biblical fiction series The Wives of King David, Wives of the Patriarchs, and Daughters of the Promised Land, as well as *The Heart of a King, Star of Persia: Esther's Story, Miriam's Song, The Prince and the Prodigal,* and *Daughter of Eden*. She is also the author of the nonfiction books *When Life Doesn't Match Your Dreams* and *She Walked Before Us*. Jill lives with her family in southeast Michigan. Learn more at JillEileenSmith.com.

Meet

JILL EILEEN SMITH

at **www.JillEileenSmith.com** to learn interesting facts and read her blog!

Connect with her on

Jill Eileen Smith
JillEileenSmith
JillEileenSmith

When the greatest joys she has ever known
are stripped away, the first woman must find
the courage to face an unknown future.

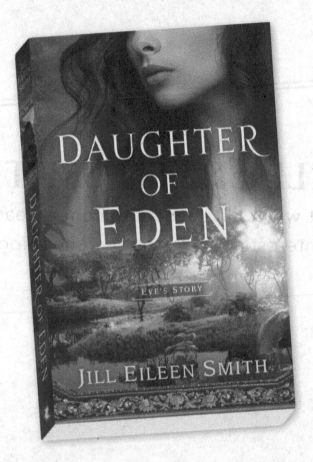

Eve has spent all her days in the garden of Eden, exploring with Adam and
walking with their Creator—until the day everything changes. Suddenly she
faces darkness she has never before experienced. How will she find the courage
to face the unknown future and trust in the promises God has given?

Revell
a division of Baker Publishing Group
www.RevellBooks.com

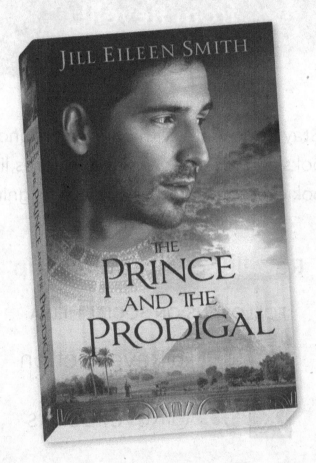